If Rome Hadn't Fallen

If Rome
Hadn't Fallen

What Might Have Happened if the
Western Empire Had Survived

Timothy Venning

Pen & Sword
MILITARY

First published in Great Britain in 2011
and reprinted in this format in 2020 by
Pen & Sword Military
an imprint of
Pen & Sword Books Ltd
47 Church Street
Barnsley
South Yorkshire
S70 2AS

Copyright © Timothy Venning 2011, 2020

ISBN 978 1 52679 194 8

Typeset in 11pt Ehrhardt by
Mac Style

Printed and bound in England by
CPI Group (UK) Ltd, Croydon, CR0 4YY

Pen & Sword Books Ltd incorporates the Imprints of Pen & Sword Aviation,
Pen & Sword Family History, Pen & Sword Maritime, Pen & Sword Military,
Pen & Sword Discovery, Wharncliffe Local History, Wharncliffe True Crime,
Wharncliffe Transport, Pen & Sword Select, Pen & Sword Military Classics,
Leo Cooper, The Praetorian Press, Remember When, Seaforth Publishing
and Frontline Publishing.

For a complete list of Pen & Sword titles please contact
PEN & SWORD BOOKS LIMITED
47 Church Street, Barnsley, South Yorkshire, S70 2AS, England
E-mail: enquiries@pen-and-sword.co.uk
Website: www.pen-and-sword.co.uk

Contents

with summary of nine turning points and nineteen speculated consequences

(a) Military 'What Ifs' from AD 9
(b) Instability from AD 180

Overview of real-life history. Decline and fall, how much has it been exaggerated, and was it inevitable? Problems of state structure and control. Religion, governance, and failings in the structure of the bureaucracy. Division of the Empire, militarily necessary, or extra problems? The state and the army: too heavy a burden, or irrelevant to the question of survival? Germans and Romans. 476, a convenient but misleading date? A vicious circle of gradual collapse? Potential alternatives and the crucial moments of Roman collapse.

1. The Romans win the Battle of Adrianople
2. Strong Roman leadership could have seen off the Germanic challenges 395–455. It only needed Theodosius, Stilicho, Constantius, Aetius or a combination of them to have lived longer

Earlier 'What Ifs': the crises that led to the creation of the later Empire.

3. Strong Roman leadership through crises in the Roman Empire of 235–284 after Septimius Severus

The Empire's problems in the third and fourth centuries. How might they have been reduced by earlier military successes?

4. Varus or Germanicus secure the Elbe frontier in AD 9 or thereafter

State structures and the succession: from 'First Citizen' to hereditary autocrat.

5. Better succession management overcomes the crises of the 250s

The 250s and after: dynastic mischance and its exploitation. The survival of the Western Empire: feasible with better luck?

(a) As a larger state: a match for the Germans and the East?

6. Theodosius the Great lives longer
7. Aetius avoids murder and overthrows Valentinian III
8. Justinian never becomes Eastern Emperor

(b) As smaller state, similar to reality.

9. The West regains North Africa in 462–3 (Marjorian) or 468 (Basiliscus)

What would have been the likely developments in the Western Empire had one of the foregoing scenarios occurred?

1. A kingdom of Britain. Roman Britain survives – no successful Anglo-Saxon invasion?
2. Continental developments. The Roman Empire annexes Jutland
3. Ireland. Pro-Roman client High King established in Ireland
4. Dalriada and the Irish overseas. Irish missionaries convert pagan central Europe?
5. Western Christianity – Emperor and Pope. Papacy remains subordinate to Imperial interests
6. Military matters. Western Empire able to hold off and subordinate Germanic tribes
7. The Viking threat. Viking invasions of Britain and France repulsed

Acknowledgements

Thanks are due to the staff who created the 'Trigan Empire' comic strip for *Ranger* and subsequently *Look and Learn* magazine, which first gave me the concept of 'what if' fantasy when I was at primary school in the late 1960s. This innovative science-fiction series showed what a Roman-type civilization might have looked like if it had survived to the Space Age, particularly due to the artwork of Don Lawrence. My exploration of the scenarios took off from there.

Introduction

The question of how much the course of history is dependent on personality and chance has always been a pertinent one. Historians have disagreed to what extent the outcome of events in shaped by broad social and economic developments as opposed to the quirks and decisions of strong individuals, and some have held it fashionable to downplay the effects on the mass of people of political and military struggles among those in authority. Dates and lists of rulers, once the staple of learning history in schools, were replaced in the 1960s and 1970s by studies of the lives of the ordinary people and the social, economic, and cultural factors that shaped their existences rather than the intricate and remote political events in their countries' capitals. But in recent years there has been a degree of reaction to that, with more recognition that individuals are not always powerless to shape the outcome of major events. One person's actions can alter the course of history, and a political or military mischance can touch off a catastrophic reaction that has repercussions over centuries. The geo-physical theory that a butterfly beating its wings in one continent can ultimately cause a hurricane in another one can have its counterpart in history. Whatever the importance of broad social or economic trends on the development of society, ultimately the safe existence and prosperity, and in many turbulent periods the lives, of the ordinary citizens depend on the nature and stability of the political structure of their states.

It is political and military leadership that determines the outcome of political struggles and military campaigns which decide whether a state survives and prospers or falls victim to its own feuding or its enemies' conquest. The nature of personal leadership is as crucial as the social and economic circumstances that give a state its strength or its weakness and enable these people to fulfill or fail in their struggles. This was particularly the case in constantly competing and threatened states, where warfare and conquest were the norm before the rise of a relatively stable international system of determining relations. Again, before the rise of a complex system of bureaucracy much depended on the personal leadership (or not) of the rulers, and one wrong decision on the battlefield or the untimely death of a charismatic leader could plunge a nation or an empire into decades of crisis.

Still important over much of the world today, these factors were particularly apparent in the Ancient World with its constant political flux between a multiplicity of dynastic kingdoms, city-states, and nomadic peoples. Both internal and external factors could easily bring a fragile state to chaos, and undermine the most extensive and politically cohesive one. Despite the powerlessness of any ruler and the limitations of his ambitions in the face of a natural disaster such as drought or an epidemic, a human mistake could be just as catastrophic – particularly in the event of invasion or a potential civil war.

The career of Alexander the Great provides the most notable example of the effect of one personality on the fortunes of peoples from the Balkans to the Punjab. The uncertain outcome of the titanic battles he was engaged in also invites the natural response. What if things had gone another way in one of them and a chance arrow or sword-thrust had cut his career short? It nearly did on two particular occasions, when Cleitus saved him at the battle of the Granicus at the start of his Asian campaigns in 334 BC and when he was shot down in an Indus valley town in 326. The premature death of Alexander at the height of his triumphs has also long begged the question of what would have happened if he had continued his career and not died at 32, with the nature of his future plans from June 323 only known in uncertain detail. This led to the first serious 'What if?' scenario of classical history on the subject of what might have happened if Alexander had lived longer, by Arnold Toynbee, based on a question first posed by Livy. His optimistic scenario had Alexander living to the approximate age of his grandfather Amyntas III and various of his own generals who died in their beds (i.e. dying in 287 at the age of 69) rather than his father Philip, assassinated at 46/7. Alexander would supposedly have gone on to conquer Carthage, India, and China and create a worldwide empire of provinces linked by trading and military co-ordination, ripe for conversion to the new religion of Buddhism in the third century. This is perhaps a little implausible, but the basic point is sound, that a long reign for the creator of a new order could have created a long-standing new empire in the same manner as Cyrus and Darius did in Persia in the sixth century BC.

What is true of Alexander, whose new Greco-Persian realm broke up into competing states led by his generals after the collapse of his posthumous son's regency, is no less true of Rome. Here the possibilities of alternative scenarios are as endless as for Greece, although the Roman Republican polity started out as a more stable long-term political structure than the divided, faction-ridden Greek states. Indeed, it was designed to minimize the effect of one person's ambitions on the state, supposedly due to a fear of a return to monarchy. The long-term international results of a few crucial events perhaps starts with the narrow margin by which Rome survived the threat of Hannibal in the 210s BC. What if Hannibal had achieved his aim of breaking up the Roman leadership of the Italian peoples? Seemingly unstoppable after the battle of Cannae, he could have returned Italy to the mass of competing peoples and states of the fifth and fourth centuries BC, restoring local independence to the once-powerful peoples of the South such as the Samnites and Marsi, or even physically have conquered Rome, expelled its people, made its Latin clients independent, and prevented it from restoring its fortunes after the Carthaginians had gone home.

Ironically, the results of the early death of Alexander had their impact on Roman history, as the alleged list of his future plans released by his generals after his death included conquering the Greeks' Carthaginian enemies. If Alexander had turned his vast armies onto Carthage after consolidating his Eastern conquests, at a date around 320 to 315 BC as surmised by Toynbee, the Punic state would probably have fallen and Rome had no rival in the Western Mediterranean in the third century BC. Given Roman leaders' appetite for intervention in neighbouring states that seemed to pose a threat, as Philip V's Macedon did to their Adriatic role in the 210s, Rome could thus have intervened in Greek affairs earlier and more strongly.

The permutations of the political conflicts of the declining republic saw a supposedly monolithic balanced constitution, designed to keep a long-term political order stable by preventing one man gaining undue power, collapse into vicious faction and ultimately revolution. The complexities of conquering and administering a spreading dominion around the Mediterranean, and the temptations of the wealth and mass of clients that went with that for the successful generals and politicians (the two were often the same) saw the emergence first of dominant politicians, some leaders of oligarchic factions and others demagogic 'populares' exploiting the troubles of the lower classes, and later of generals whose armies were more loyal to them than to the state and could be turned on the latter. In this scenario personal qualities of leadership were crucial and one lucky gamble or minor miscalculation could not only end a career but also affect the future of an empire. The conflicts that consumed and eventually destroyed the Republic in the first century BC may have been a probability, given the weaknesses of the outdated Roman constitution in coping with being a world power. The nature of Roman politico-military leadership and the problems of the social classes in the capital and Italy gave a broad outline of what sort of men would rise to power to exploit the situation, what they would do, and how Rome would alter. But the outcome of the struggles owed most to the individual qualities of the men that fought over and achieved power, both as political leaders and increasingly as generals whose success brought them wealth, popularity, a body of clients, and armies to use against their enemies. The careers of Marius, Sulla, Pompey, Caesar, Antonius, Cassius, and Octavian/Augustus depended as much on military as political skills, although there could still be political leaders who operated within more traditional civilian parameters while still commanding armies at times (such as Cicero, Cato, or Brutus). Octavian showed that a shrewd Roman leader with political skills could triumph without being a good general, provided that he understood and could play the role of a military commander as well as civilian faction-leader, knew how to manipulate propaganda and win popular acclaim, employed terror and patronage with equal effect on the political class, and had effective subordinates like Agrippa to do the fighting.

The chaos of the last Republican decades argued in favour of the emergence of rule by one man as head of all the potentially disruptive armies and suppresser of political faction. But the form that the new Empire took, as a superficial restoration of the existing republican constitution, but in fact a disguised autocracy, depended on Octavian's concept of what would secure stability and his own position. The fate of Rome would have been different if Pompey had prevailed against Caesar in 49–8 or the assassins of Caesar had prevailed in the struggles of 44–2 and restored the old constitution with idealistic determination, though an eventual renewal of faction and military challenge was inevitable. Similarly, if Antonius not Octavian had prevailed in 31 it is unlikely that he would have been any better than Caesar at making provision for long-term stability after his death, with or without a partnership with Hellenistic Egypt to rule the Eastern Mediterranean.

Once the Empire was established, the personal fates and politico-military choices of Emperors had substantial results even if the structure of the largely decentralized Empire before the reforms of Diocletian was such that chaos or misrule at the centre had limited effects on the provinces (apart from causing damage by civil war, as in AD 69–70). The quirks and psychological instability of Caligula, Nero, or Commodus may have been of little immediate importance outside political circles in Rome, but the personal nature of rule meant that the accumulative effects of prolonged misgovernment, or a frequent change of regime as in the third century AD, could seriously undermine the entire Roman polity. The repeated political crises after 180 and 235 may have developed independently of the rising pressure of external enemies (the Germans and Persia) on the frontiers, but they provided enemies with a chance to attack, limited the effectiveness of the Imperial response, and undermined the Empire's ability to ride out such challenges.

The system established for a smooth succession by Diocletian, a careful ruler who had created two senior Emperors, one for the East and one for the West, to guard each half of the huge Empire, arranged for pre-selection and training of two heirs, 'Caesars', to their seniors, the 'Augusti'. Galerius succeeded Diocletian in the East, and Constantius succeeded the other 'Augustus', Maximian. In the West it was meant to ensure that when the senior rulers died or resigned their successors would be ready to step in, though it is arguable how much it owed to the circumstance that Diocletian had no son, forcing him to improvise for the succession. It was at least partly intended to choose the best man rather than the closest genealogical heir (the normal procedure) to succeed, as it explicitly left out Maximian's young and inexperienced son Maxentius. Human nature being what it is, the latter then staged a revolt to regain his 'rightful' position, as did Constantius' son Constantine when the latter was denied the right to succeed his father too, and both, significantly, had military support against Diocletian's choices. The system collapsed within Diocletian's own lifetime; and Constantine duly reunited the Empire and took the epoch-changing decision to make Christianity the State religion.

Again, after the temporary restoration of stable government under Constantine's dynasty in 324–61 (interrupted by inter-family conflict and one external coup) the last of the family, Julian, was unexpectedly killed by an arrow while invading Persia in 363. Having endeavoured to reverse Constantine's imposition of Christianity, his timely death was greeted enthusiastically by the Church, and some said it was no accident. Another round of unexpected transfers of power saw first the accession of the capable general Valentinian I, then his choice of his brother Valens to rule the East against advisers' warnings to choose someone more experienced. Then came Valentinian's death on the eve of the East's greatest invasion by asylum-seeking Goths, in flight from the Huns. If the late Emperor had been available in 378, or Valens had waited for troops to arrive from the West to reinforce him, would the Eastern army have been destroyed by the Goths at Adrianople? After that catastrophe the first 'federate' Germanic kingdom was set up within Roman territory, an ominous show of Roman weakness for predatory neighbours.

When the new Eastern Emperor Theodosius the Great died aged 47 in January 395, only just having reunited the Empire, the thrones of the East and West were permanently separated. Each was occupied by a young and incapable ruler, and the West's military regent Stilicho was at odds with the Eastern government. The result saw Alaric the Goth able to revolt and play off each half of the Empire against the other. In due course the West suffered the sack of Rome in 410 (a temporary blow largely due to military paralysis when Stilicho was murdered) and province after province fell away from the control of the government, some to new Germanic kingdoms. A chain effect of disaster set in as each local loss encouraged the Empire's ambitious challengers to further depredations, while the Empire's ability to resist them was weakened. Even so, the crucial early deaths of four strong military leaders, Theodosius in 395, Stilicho in 408, Constantius III in 421, and Aetius in 451, greatly accelerated the collapse of the West. This collapse, as will be argued in this study, was far from inevitable.

The dynastic problems of the Julio-Claudian dynasty had military as well as political implications during the first century AD even if they did not produce such immediate major results as the conflict among Caesar's heirs and opponents. Most notably, chances for renewing the military expansion of the Empire in Germany were missed. Despite the major psychological impact of Varus' destruction by the Germans in AD 9, other such military disasters at the hands of Rome's neighbours had not halted its expansion. Roman armies had been slaughtered in Gaul with equal psychological effect upon Rome in 106 BC, but Caesar still conquered the region. The disaster at Carrhae in 53 did not inhibit Antonius' or Trajan's Eastern wars. If the Empire had had ambitious and competent military leadership during the following decades a new attack on Germany was logical. This major source of hostile manpower remained outside Roman control, and ultimately was to turn into an uncontrollable military challenge to a beleaguered, over-taxed, under-manned, politically unstable society. It is too ambitious to conceive of the Empire as having any sort of grand strategy over decades or centuries, despite the thesis for such a policy put forward by Edward Luttwak – Imperial military policy tended to be in reaction to immediate problems. But it is certainly arguable that it was within the bounds of current military strategic possibilities that the Empire could have renewed a major German war at several points, and thus brought about the favourable long-term consequence of the German tribes fighting with, not against, Rome in the third and fourth centuries.

In addition, the advance of the Roman frontier from the less defendable Danube river frontier to the mountain ranges of the Carpathians occurred in Dacia under Trajan, and seems to have been underway in Bohemia to the West in the later 170s. Had the Empire persevered with this policy, which immediately depended on Marcus Aurelius not dying when he did, it would have faced less of a northern military threat in the mid-third century and afterwards when it was weakened by plague, civil war, and the new eastern military challenge from Persia. More easily defensible frontiers and less Germanic enemies would have been a bonus for the weakened Empire, and arguably made the third century crises less catastrophic. It should have placed the Empire in a far better position to meet the challenge of its first serious threat from the steppes, Attila the Hun, in the fifth century even if the endless rounds of internal civil war, dependant on political factors and dynastic bad luck in Rome, had occurred as they did in reality.

From that hypothesis comes the whole question of whether the Empire's 'decline and fall' was inevitable, and to what extent it could have been avoided by a variety of political and military decisions taken centuries earlier. It is of course arguable that the fifth century saw not so much a 'fall' from Roman civilization to barbarian Germanic kingdoms as a political and social transformation, and this debate is very much in vogue at present. In addition, the political and socio-economic structures of the Eastern Empire survived intact through these crises and were strong enough to regain much of the West in the sixth century, the crises overwhelming the late antique world in the East not coming until the early seventh century.

But the facts of political turmoil, military defeat, ravaging of peaceful provinces, decline of urban life, collapse of a literate centralized power with a complex bureaucracy and one ruler into a multiplicity of tribally-based kingdoms, and impoverishment of material culture surely argue in favour of a major political as well as social and economic catastrophe for the Western Mediterranean world in the fifth century. Examination of the evidence for the nature of this process suggests that the ongoing crises that overwhelmed the West had a cumulative effect, as one crisis or disaster helped to bring about another. The political, military, and social turmoil of the third century brought about a decline in military and agricultural manpower at a time when the enlarged bureaucratic state and armies of the post-Diocletian Empire were putting new burdens on the citizenry, thus draining away resources from a state which was at war with itself and its neighbours far more in the fourth century than in the second. The loss of manpower and resultant socio-economic and military problems of the third century may have been due to plague, beyond human control, as much as to invasion or civil war. But without the latter the effects would have been less, and the Empire in a stronger position in the fourth century.

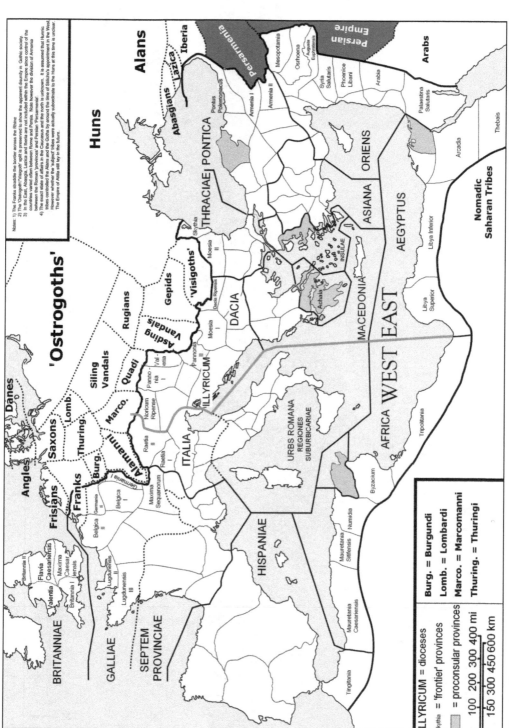

Map 1. The Roman Empire and Its Enemies, AD 395. (copyright: Ian Hughes)

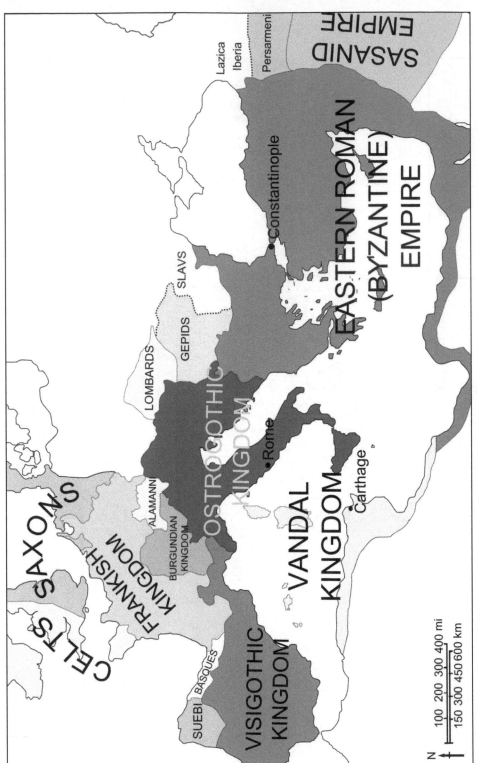

Map 2. The Dismembered Empire at the Accession of Justinian, AD 527. (copyright Ian Hughes)

Part I

Turning Points

Two Reasons for Rome's Problems – Did They Make Collapse More Likely? Were They Avoidable?

(a) Military 'What Ifs': Another German Campaign after AD 9 with a seasoned general as Emperor – a better position regarding the Germans?

The Parthian war of 114–117 and Britain apart, the only significant territorial situation that could have been different under the Early Empire was if Northern Germany had been annexed. Tiberius (ruled 14-37) avoided this; but what about his nephew and heir (who unexpectedly predeceased him)? Did Germanicus' sudden death in Syria in 19 (due to poison) damage the Empire in the long term?

Germanicus had fought a difficult war in Germania after 14 and would possibly have been too ready to remember the difficulties he had faced (not least from the troublesome North Sea tides) to launch an attack as Emperor to retake the would-be province that Varus had let slip in 9. But the memory of Northern hordes slavering for Roman blood was a potent one in the capital, having a long pedigree from the Gallic sack of 390/87 BC and the long wars with the Gauls in Northern Italy, and the sources make it clear that there was panic in Rome after the destruction of Varus' army. Destroying this threat would have been a major propaganda bonus for any Emperor, particularly a new ruler, though Germanicus or his eldest son Nero (a rash, easily-outmanoevured challenger to chief minister Sejanus in the late 20s) would have been more vulnerable to this temptation than Tiberius' cautious son Drusus. When Germanicus campaigned successfully east of the Rhine in 15–16, Tiberius (parsimonious, cautious or jealous?) reined him in. But as Emperor, Germanicus would have had no checks on his ambition. Had he lived to succeed Tiberius in 37, he would have been 52, little older than his brother Claudius was at his real-life accession and physically tougher. His son Nero would have been around 31.

The practicalities of the campaign were such that Rome could not spare the troops for an attack in overwhelming numbers – after the Pannonian revolt of 6–9 made concentration of troops on the Danube essential. The disaster to Varus' army in 9 in Germany – harassment and ultimately a trap in thick forests – was such that Rome could not overwhelm the enemy through force of numbers and better weaponry without risks, and the further the legions advanced from the Rhine the greater the risks of being cut off. A piecemeal occupation by a network of forts and the creation of a series of roads across the Rhine-Elbe area to speed reinforcements were essential, meaning a systematic campaign over years rather than a 'quick fix' of a speedy victory followed by the enemy obligingly surrendering. A long war like Caesar's in Gaul in the 50s BC or the British campaigns of the 40s and 50s AD would have been needed, though Germanicus had the experience of the Northern frontier that would have given him the ability to decide if this commitment was practicable.

Rome was notably desperately short of men after Varus lost his legions, with Augustus having to raise emergency forces of slaves and gladiators in the capital. The limit of troops available for any Northern war would have been similar to the three legions (plus temporary detachments from others) sent to Britain in 43. Conquered territory taken from the fierce tribes would need to be held down by force for years, with the mixture of forests, mountains, and marshes meaning that even the task of building Roman roads to connect forts would be slow and expensive. It is noticeable that, in a comparable situation, even 120 years after Caesar's conquest of Gaul parts of the North-Eastern tribes (nearest to potential allies across the Rhine as well as less urbanised) were willing to revolt and join rebel leader Civilis' tribal Batavians (Rhine mouth) in 69–70. The Germans would have been equally resistant and in need of long-term garrisons, with their tribal allies across the new frontier (the Elbe?) willing to aid them. The terrain of forests and swamps was conducive to a guerrilla war, though no more so than the Ardennes which Rome had held since Caesar's time.

If a glory-seeking Emperor had been willing to reverse the 'disgrace' of 9, he would have had to raise new legions for a long-term occupation, though the late Republic had been able to sustain a far larger army until Augustus demobilised it and five or so legions could have been sustainable. The political danger of putting such a large force in the hands of one general would have been a drawback, as he would have had to be carefully selected.

The new governor (of 'Germania Ulterior'?) would have had the potential to take advantage of weakness in Rome as rebel commander Vitellius did from the Rhine and Vespasian from the Jewish war in 69. Ideally, even if one general – preferably an Imperial male – was in charge of the annexation the subsequent province would need to be divided to reduce the number of legions available to a potential rebel. Alternatively, the troop-deployment East of the Rhine could be numerically matched by the force available to the governors of Lower and Upper Germany. That should dissuade the new governor from revolting in the event of a disputed succession in Rome.

The conquest of Germany: useful long-term consequences?

If Varus had defeated German leader Arminius' coalition in 9 problems would not have arisen to that extent, and the Empire would have avoided the shock of defeat. A better general than Varus would not have allowed himself to be led into a German trap far from the Rhine by supposedly loyal German 'scouts', or if he had done so he could have provided more inspiring leadership. A dogged defence of a strong position against wave after wave of Germans was capable of holding the lightly-armed tribesmen at bay until they became exhausted, even in heavy rain. The Romans had large shields, cuirasses, arm- and leg-guards, and a variety of swords and javelins plus some archers; they also had a tradition of discipline and fought in defensive squares. The Germans were lightly-armed and relied on the effect of a terrifying charge, plus individual combat. They were intimidating in the charge, but no good in a long pitched battle; the Romans would have had the advantage if they could hold out for several hours.

The prospect of a charge by thousands of savage Germanic warriors was not unusual to Roman soldiers, though it was always feared. Being outnumbered could be handled by a competent Roman general, as could unfamiliar territory. Marius, six times consul in succeeding years and Rome's greatest commander around 100 BC, had managed to win defensive battles against the equally intimidating Cimbri and Teutones when Roman legions had to tackle comparably daunting hordes. Once the enemy was forced to draw off, at worst the Roman general could have managed to withdraw slowly to the Rhine with his troops marching in fighting-formation and reducing the numbers of stragglers who could be isolated and killed. It would be more difficult to win through back to the Rhine if their scouts deserted, as Varus' did, but not impossible. The army would have been available for future punitive strikes – probably led by Germanicus around 12 – once they had received reinforcements and the temporary coalition of Germanic tribes had broke up, and would not have suffered the trauma of defeat.

But the forests, swamps, and mountains of North-West Germany were more difficult to penetrate and then hold down by a chain of forts than was equally truculent Gaul after Vercingetorix's defeat. The barren heathlands and thick forests did not give promise of a future of self-sustaining agricultural settlements and growing towns filled with ambitious Roman traders, at least for decades. The archaeological remains indicate a poorer culture of Germanic villages than in Gaul or 'Celtic' Britain – and even less wealth East of the Elbe. There would have been the danger of another trans-tribal leader arising, and the state of military morale in Augustus' later years and the ease with which mutinies commenced in 14 shows that the morale of the underpaid, overworked frontier troops was low at this crucial point.

The situation in 14 shows that Varus' victory would not have solved Rome's German problem – indeed, it could have posed a new threat by reassuring Augustus that the German tribes were not that great a threat. Augustus had been using as few troops as he could get away with ever since demobilising the Triumviral armies in the 30s BC, with around thirty not fifty legions, and sought a German victory on the cheap. Varus could have defeated the tribal coalition, ravaged their villages, destroyed stocks of food, and driven the surviving warriors into hiding in the forests – reassuring Augustus that the Germans were manageable. He could then have imposed a temporary submission in 9 or 10, Augustus installed a smaller garrison than was really needed, and an outbreak of mutiny in 14 inspired the Germans to revolt. The conditions for troops in frontier-forts in the German forests would have been as bad a they were on the lower Rhine, causing grumbling veterans who had had to serve longer than their promised time in service to decide that Augustus' death gave them an opportunity to insist that they were discharged. The mutiny of 14 would have occurred on the Elbe in that case, and probably led to evacuation of the new province.

The permanent acquisition of a new province up to the Elbe would have required a major effort over several decades before the danger of revolt abated, and still not have provided much in the way of local revenue. Timber for the fleet was the only obvious local resource. But if the frontier had been adequately defended and the local Germans not taken advantage of a change of Emperor to revolt, the impressment of tribesmen into the army would have added to Roman military manpower and denied it to potential opponents. The danger from the Rhine frontier became acute during the civil war of 69 due to the departure of many troops for Rome under Vitellius, the poor state of the remaining army, and inspiring and co-ordinating local rebel leadership under Civilis, but thereafter there was only one major war against the Rhineland tribes until the early third century: the campaigns under Domitian in the 80s. These tribes would have been part of the Empire and their menfolk enrolled in the legions so they would not have been a threat had Rome secured the Elbe frontier in 9 or the late 30s/40s AD, though the tribes beyond the Elbe could still have challenged the Empire at this point (e.g. if there had been a local Roman rebellion equivalent to that of Saturninus at Cologne in 88).

The concentration of legions in the new province would have provided a tempting force for ambitious generals to use against the Emperor, and in that case Vitellius could have been in charge of the troops – on the Elbe rather than the Lower Rhine – and have revolted in 69 as in reality on the Rhine. Would his departure have led to German revolt? But if Rome had come through 69–70 still holding the Elbe, it should have provided a hiatus of military activity until the 200s for Romanisation to develop and the German province to become as fully secure as Belgica and Civilis' rebel Batavian island in Holland were after 70. In that case, Rome would have had to face a smaller challenge from the local Germans in the third century and would have had many of the tribes facing the Rhine (including the Franks and Alemanni?) incorporated in the Empire and added to its legions. Indeed, if the conquest of the Marcomanni in Bohemia by Marcus Aurelius in the late 170s had been followed through (see below) Rome could have been defending a frontier from the Elbe to the Carpathians rather than from the Rhine to the Danube. The Empire would have had fewer opponents, though the tribes beyond the Elbe would still have been pressing against the frontier, and correspondingly less of a distraction from the wars on the lower Danube from the 230s.

Long-term results
The extra, Germanic, manpower available for these wars would have been invaluable besides enabling the Emperors and local generals to campaign more on the lower Danube and less on the Rhine. There would have been no need for Domitian's distracting Chatti wars in the 80s – though he could have attacked other Germans to gain much-needed (in his mind) glory. Holding 'Marcomannia' as far as the Northern mountains of Bohemia too

would have provided Rome with a more easily-defensible frontier in the North, with the enemy only able to use the gaps in the mountains – the Elbe valley, the Moravian Beskids, to either side of the Tatra, and Ruthenia – to invade the Empire. Thus there would not have been the need for huge garrisons on the upper Rhine or upper Danube, and more troops could have defended the Elbe and the gaps in the chain of Carpathian ranges. In this case, it is less likely that the Empire would have lost crucial battles such as Abrittus against the Goths in 251 – at least on account of troop-numbers, if not incompetence. The avoidance of the raids into the Empire and political 'break-up' of the Roman state in the 250s would have been momentous, though it should be remembered that Rome would still have lost manpower in the plague from 252. Incompetent leadership and/or the bad luck of a civil war were crucial factors that better frontiers would not have affected. There was also, of course, the perennial possibility of conquest in the Augustan/Julio-Claudian period followed by a 'pull-back' after 69 to save on men and money.

(b) Instability from AD 180: some of the 'What Ifs' of the period after 180 and how instability escalated. Bad luck or inevitable?

AD 180–93. The start of serious political problems in Rome
   As will be argued, the instability that afflicted Rome from the later second century onwards owed its beginnings to crucial events in 180. Firstly Marcus Aurelius died prematurely at the age of 58 during his Northern border campaigns against Marcomanni, leaving the throne to the weak-willed and inexperienced 18–year-old Commodus who proved a disaster as Emperor and opened his court to vicious in- fighting, favouritism and the most venal ministers seen since Nero's reign. Commodus' extravagance, divine pretensions, and fondness for performing as a gladiator had no serious political implications as far as government was concerned. However, his failure to listen to competent advice and his reliance from c.182 on men such as Saoterus, Cleander, and Perennis caused a mixture of heightened court intrigue, senior appointments of people who had openly bought office or were the personal nominees of the all-powerful favourite rather than experienced, a rash of executions that led to prolonged fear among the political classes in Rome, and a collapse in military discipline and morale (especially among the laxly-supervised Praetorians). The chaos in Rome in 193 was directly the responsibility of him and his ministers, and the

atmosphere of uncertainty and fear at the 'court' at the time of his murder was as apparent as under Domitian (a similar victim of alarmed intimates fearing that they were about to be executed).

The run of good luck for Imperial successions that ended in 180: how it could easily have ended earlier

Once the situation at the centre of government had been allowed to decline like this for over a decade, it was hard to restore order without repression that created its own problems. The end of the system of orderly succession – either within a dynasty or by nomination of an heir by the Emperor before he died – also caused the return of the chaos and insecurity seen at the end of the Julio-Claudian dynasty in 68. But it should be said that orderly succession was always a matter of luck in Rome, and there was no 'wise' and 'meritocratic' policy of adopting the best man as heir in the period from Nerva's adoption of Trajan (in 98) to 180. None of the emperors who adopted an heir had a son to succeed him, which the dynastically-orientated Guard seem to have preferred.

Galba, Nero's childless successor who took over in June 68, tried to adopt a well-respected young noble called Piso. He was thwarted by a Guard plot egged on by an ambitious ex-Neronian courtier, Otho, whose own hopes had been disappointed, and killed. Nerva, childless and over 60, needed to adopt a tough and competent general to ward off the threat from his undisciplined Guard who had just defied him in a rampage hunting down Domitian's killers in 97–8. Trajan adopted his nearest adult male relative, Hadrian, but the latter felt insecure enough to kill four ex-consuls on his accession in 117. Hadrian, third emperor in a row to have no children, initially adopted an unsuitable – and already ailing – candidate, Aelius Verus, who luckily died before him. He then selected his young protege and distant cousin, the teenage Marcus Aurelius (then 'Marcus Verus'), and Aelius' son Lucius as heirs for his new successor Antoninus 'Pius'. Antoninus had no sons either, and his daughter was married off to Marcus who was also his wife's nephew.[1]

The 'What Ifs' of 180 and of 31 December 192: no civil war in 193?

Had Marcus had no sons, he could have adopted an heir in this fashion and selected a better candidate than his surviving son Commodus. The latter could have fallen victim to one of the numerous plots against him and not spent twelve years misruling the Empire and allowing the Praetorians to become slack and arrogant. His first and probably most dangerous foe was his sister Lucilla, who was probably behind the attempt to stab him in a corridor at the amphitheatre in 182. The assassin, Quadratus, nephew of her husband Tiberius Pompeianus', stopped to declare 'The Senate sends you this!' as he waved his sword and was seized by bodyguards.[2] Either he or Prompeianus would have been the new ruler, as Lucilla's candidate, with her as power behind the throne like Agrippina 'the Younger'. Thereafter, the Emperor was on his guard and rounds of killings put off plotters until the Household and the current Praetorain Praefect turned on Commodus. Pompeianus, in exile but suspiciously back in Rome in time for the coup, was considered for the throne when Commodus was killed on 31 December 192. He turned down the offer of the throne from the assassins' choice: Pertinax, 66–year-old disciplinarian ex-governor of Britain. Had Pompeianus accepted, he might have avoided Pertinax's fate of being murdered by sulky and exasperated Guardsmen annoyed at the reimposition of strict military discipline on 28 March 193.

The coup may have been instigated by Praefect Laetus, who had fallen out with Pertinax, but the Emperor gave the troops enough reason to listen to such suggestions.[3] The civil war which followed took the form of refusal to recognise the next Emperor by three senior provincial governors – Septimius Severus on the upper Danube, Clodius Albinus in Britain and Pescennius Niger in Syria. All had recognised Pertinax, so, unless that had been a short-term expedient to cover intended later revolt, the civil war resulted from the second, not the first, coup. By that reasoning, had Laetus been exposed and removed or Pertinax been less personally abrupt to the troops, civil war would have been unlikely. Moroever, he had a son to succeed him if he could have stayed on the throne successfully.

What if Commodus' brothers had not died young?
From the events of 180–92 arose both the murder of the insecure new ruler, Pertinax, and the humiliating sale of the Imperial title that followed the murder. This led to civil war against the successful bidder, Didius Julianus. But it should be pointed out that Commodus happened to be the only survivor among Marcus' three sons, and if the other two (one his twin) had not died young in the 160s one of them would have been the beneficiary of Commodus' murder.[4] There would possibly have been two Emperors – brothers – ruling after Marcus, who had himself had a co–ruler, Lucius Verus, in 161–9. If both twins had survived, appointing both as Emperor was logical – not least if Commodus was already showing signs of poor

judgement and laziness. Given Commodus' fondness for gladiatorial combat and parties, he could well have left politics and adminstration to his brother – until his ambitious courtiers encouraged him to demand more power? Lucius Verus, reputedly lazy and spendthrift, had left government to Marcus in the 160s without any apparent tension. If the jealous Commodus had attempted to kill his brother(s), there is no guarantee that he would have succeeded and not been killed instead.

In the second place, the evacuation of troops from the territories of modern Bohemia and Moravia aborted the attempt to create a new province there and 'Romanise' the local tribes. If they had been at least partially tamed by occupation from c.180 to 250, and sending their menfolk into the Roman army, they would not have been in a position to raid the Empire when it was weakening. Their war-leaders, who launched the attacks, would have been Roman officers and possibly been moved from the region. The attacks of the Germanic tribes across the Rhine and the Danube – the centrepiece of the 'third-century crisis' – would have been easier to contain by the available troops. (This is dealt with later.)

The Severans, 193–235 – part of the solution or part of the problem? Did Septimius Severus make Rome's instability worse, and could he have avoided this?

Septimius Severus, the victor in the civil war of 193–7, proved to be a competent Emperor and in particular a much-needed success as a general, defeating both the Parthians and the Caledonians and restoring Rome's prestige after the civil war. He could not claim convincingly to have been the choice of Pertinax as his successor, though he did his best by arranging a retrospective 'adoption' and stressing his role as the late Emperor's 'son' and avenger in his propaganda,[5] and it is clear that a substantial part of the Senate hoped that his rival Clodius Albinus would win their confrontation in 197.[6] The repressive measures that he carried out in Rome were notably harsher after this, once he had faced the danger of revolt among people who had supposedly accepted him as their ruler in 193 but had proved to be potentially disloyal.

Severus' reliance on a small clique of his 'trusties' from his home province of Tripolitania, most notably the ruthless, venal, and arrogant Praefect Plautianus, was an inevitable result of his being a provincial outsider who faced potential disaffection in his capital and had no established networks of eminent friends to rely on there. (Albinus, by contrast, was an Italian.) He was not the only Emperor to impatiently flaunt traditional civilian mores in the capital, enter the Senate in armour (though more circumspect rulers had worn it under a toga), and treat Senators with open anger as potential enemies, carrying out mass executions without due care to see that only the obviously guilty suffered

It was said in mitigation that at least he did not kill people for their money.[7] Nor was he the only Emperor to rely on a ruthless and unhindered Praefect to keep order and terrorise his potential opponents into submission, Sejanus being the most obvious example (though Tiberius had more excuse in view of his age and his desire to retire at the time).

Severus had more excuse for running an effective 'reign of terror' against the civilian nobility than Tiberius or Domitian had, on account of the political situation. Augustus had been just as ruthless at purging the nobility, and both duly built up Senate inflitrated by their loyalists.[8] However, his attitude towards the centre of power and its traditions was markedly more contemptuous than any except the more eccentric of his predecessors, and sat ill with his claims to be restoring order and good government – Caligula, Nero, and Commodus had been openly determined to satisfy their whims. Apocryphal or not, there is a ring of truth to his supposed advice to his sons on his death-bed to keep the peace with each other, give the soldiers what they wanted, and ignore everybody else.[9] In his naked and cynical *realpolitik*, only Imperial Family unity and a loyal army counted as they alone could affect the holding of power.

Severus' reputation suffered on account of his lack of concern for preserving the appearance of traditional government. He was nicknamed the 'Punic Sulla', stressing both his foreign origins (and that he came from the same area as Hannibal) and his harshness.[10] It is probable that this sort of contemptuous remark about his origins made him even more suspicious of the Italian nobility. The excessively trusted minister Praefect Plautianus was an old crony from his home town, who was rationalised by one story as his ex-lover.[11] As with Sulla's ruthless re-establishment of the rule of the traditional oligarchy of senior patrician families by massacring all possible opposition, the façade of government was restored but the main lessons that future political and military leaders learnt was from the methods used to do it. Naked military power and the destruction of opposition rather than conciliation were effective in succeeding in restoring stability in the aftermath of 193 as they had been after 82 BC. But in both cases the regime established by the victor of a civil war was not long-lasting and it was challenged by men using the same methods that they had excelled at. From the point of long-term stability, it is possible that the Empire may have been better off if Albinus had defeated Severus in their final battle outside Lyons in February 197. This was a very real possibility as Severus' army blundered into a series of hidden pits and their Emperor was thrown off his horse.[12]

Severus' weak position as an outsider and the extent of instability and real or potential plotting and military mutiny seen since 180 partially explain his ruthless – and effective – reaction to the situation that faced him. He was in a weaker position than Vespasian, a similar victor of civil war but an insider from the capital's political classes (if only a marginal member of the elite), and unlike Vespasian he lacked an adult and competent son to act as his effective deputy. Titus was 29, a battle-hardened general, and the respected conqueror of Jeruslaem in 70; Severus' eldest son Caracalla was only 5 in 193 (and 9 in 197) and half-Syrian as well.

It is unthinkable that Vespasian could have tolerated the sort of arrogance and presumption that Plautianus displayed, for example, in erecting statues of himself in company with those of the Imperial Family, whether or not the story is true that when Plautianus was ill he would not let even Severus into his bedroom without the customary body-scarch. [13] Whether or not Plautianus coveted the throne, and however justified his son-in-law Caracalla was in killing him, it is clear that Severus allowed him incredible license and was reluctant to act against this supposedly loyal lieutenant despite evident abuse of his position. Plautianus' behaviour was diminishing the Emperor's own position (and majesty if the story about his security-arrangements is true), however useful he was in terrorising potential opponents. The supposed heir of Marcus Aurelius and Pertinax as a good ruler was putting himself in the same league of Emperors who let a favourite get out of control as Tiberius, Caligula (with Praefect Macro), Nero (with his freedmen and Praefect Tigellinus), or Commodus. But even today statesmen can find it useful to allow remarkable license to over-powerful 'hard men' in terrorising domestic opposition. Plautianus was the Beria or the Himmler of his day, or in modern British terms a sort of Prime Minsterial 'enforcer' (New Labour 'Director of Communications'?). It was Caracalla who eventually had to act to deal with the problem, unlike Tiberius had done in facing up to scheming Praefect Sejanus, even if his father evidently allowed him to do so. [14]

Severus showed a similar personal indulgence in refusing to do anything about the signs that Caracalla could turn into a poor and/or tyrannical ruler after his death, ignore his arrangments for the succession by killing his brother Geta, and endangering the dynasty's continuance and the stability of the Empire. The sources should be treated with some caution as they may suffer from hindsight in projecting clear signs of Caracalla's later character back into his father's reign and relating apocryphal stories, such as that he was suspected (including by Severus) of plotting to use his favour with the army during the Caledonian campaign to carry out a coup against his ailing father.[15] But it is apparent that the chosen senior heir, already a grown man of nearly 23 by the time of his accession in 211, had shown signs of his violent and impulsive nature and in particular that he and Geta loathed each other and could barely be restrained from personal violence.

Severus supposedly chose to take them on campaign to Britain to teach them some discipline after they had shown signs of getting out of hand in peacetime in Rome, and was aware that his death could well lead to fratricide.[16] It is apparent that, unlike the case of Marcus and Commodus who was younger (18) at the time of his accession, the Emperor had had adequate warning of what his son was capable of doing but had chosen to evade the issue. The solution he chose, of making both his sons joint heirs, was unlikely to do anything but postpone a violent resolution to the conflict. If he had been properly concerned for the State's welfare rather than that of his family, he had every excuse at least by 210 to have Caracalla executed (especially if he had been heard contemplating a coup during the Caledonian campaign) and to secure the succession of the more amenable (though still apparently headstrong) Geta.

The results of Severan repression, naked reliance on military power, and indulgence for the likes of Caracalla and Plautianus were such as to negate the Emperor's good work in restoring political and military stability. The worst threat facing Rome from 193 was political instability at the summit of power rather than any foreign enemy, together with that of the success of provincial governors in seizing power in Rome proving infectious and tempting one general after another to try his chances. But the danger of this occurring from 69 had been averted, and there is no reason why wise policies (and luck) could not have restored stability in a similar manner after 193. The essential lesson of both 68–9 and 193 had been to avoid a power-vacuum or disputed succession in the capital. The arrogant and mutinous Praetorian Guard of 193 that had been indulged by Commodus, murdered his disciplinarian successor and sold its services to the highest bidder, had been broken up and replaced with a new Guard of loyal Severan provincial troops.[17] If a succession of able and firm Emperors had continued to inspire confidence and obedience among their soldiers there is no reason that the crisis of 193 should have been resumed – until the next disputed succession

Military rule and instability: would it have been better for Rome if Caracalla had been killed or exiled by his father and Geta had succeeded alone?

The appearance that Severus created of a military despot relying on brute force was unfortunate for his reputation and for his relations with the Senate. But it mattered far less than allowing his unstable elder son to succeed him. Geta had shown no signs of being a better statesman or particularly mature, but at least he had a competent and trustworthy father-in-law and probable chief minister in Praefect Papinianus; his reign should have posed less danger of bloodshed and eventual regicide than his brother's.[18] The lesson of Commodus' reign should have been clear: any unstable ruler did not only cause alienation within the political classes (which Severus clearly discounted) but raised the risk of violent overthrow, another civil war, and a succession of copycat revolts by ambitious provincial generals. Severus dismissed the risks of the alienation of an erratic Emperor from the civil establishment as posing no risk to the throne, unlike military discontent. But it did not take a military revolt to have an Emperor murdered and a power-vacuum at the centre causing civil war. Pertinax was killed by his Guard but Domitian and Commodus were killed by potential victims of their paranoia within the Imperial Household and Caracalla was to be killed in a roadside attack during his Parthian campaign in 217 by a lone assassin (probably incited by the worried Praetorian Praefect).[19]

Severus drew inadequate conclusions of the measures needed to secure stability, though his reasoning about the Army and the Imperial Family disunity being most crucial was true as far as it went. Similarly, his failings as a conciliator increased the alienation of his family-based regime from the civilian leadership in Rome and decreased the chances of general reconciliation (though the necessary rise in military pay would have entailed higher taxes and some confiscation of suspects' property to pay for it in any case). All this helped to make the chances of Caracalla's overthrow and a new round of civil war more likely – and with each successful revolt the chances that long-term stability could be achieved diminished. As it happened, the brief non-dynastic interlude under Macrinus, in 217–18 after Caracalla's murder, was followed by the swift return of the Severan dynasty.

The latter drew a flimsy 'legitimacy' from the pretence that Elagabalus, the great nephew of Severus' Syrian wife, was really Caracalla's son and then by Elagabalus' adoption of his cousin Alexianus (only four years his junior) as his son. If Severus had seemed to be a 'Punic' alien in Rome, the Syrian bisexual transvestite High Priest Elagabalus, a bizarre and feckless spendthrift, was ten times worse. More importantly, the relaxation of strict discipline over the Praetorians after 211 by weak or indulgent regimes led to a recurrence of that arrogance and indiscipline that they had showed in 193.

'Out-of-control' Praetorians: the most dangerous legacy of Severus' reign?

Severus' open reliance on military power encouraged the Guards' self-confidence and made a return to the fatal indiscipline that they had shown in 193 more likely. A cynically pragmatic policy of favouring the soldiers may have helped to preserve the Severan dynasty in the short term but was no good for long-term stability. Vespasian, in a comparable position and equally ruthless with dissent, had emphasised his traditional methods of government and use reliable elements of the capital's elite. Severus did not use 'acceptable' figures in positions of real power and chose to rely on an overbearing and over-indulged Praefect from among his own small clique of fellow-Africans. This was a reflection of reality, but arguably made the Guards too arrogant and contemptuous of civilian control. By Alexander Severus' reign, in 227, they could murder a disciplinarian Praetorian Praefect (Ulpianus) and get away with it.

As with the Janissaries of Ottoman Constantinople, the Mameluke regiments of pre-Ottoman and Ottoman Cairo, and the Guards-regiments of eighteenth-century St Petersburg (or London under the 'New Model Army' in 1659), an arrogant and mutinous military force in the capital could be the Achilles heel of a great military power even if there was no revolt in the provinces. The Guards, having according to the (later) biographical evidence despised the insecure Macrinus, intimidated Elagabalus into removing his worst cronies in 221 and then murdered him in 222.[20] They seem to have been beyond the control of the weak government of Mammea, mother of Alexianus/Alexander, rejecting or murdering Praefects and fighting with the populace. After the interlude of military rule by Maximin in 235–8 they lynched the new civilian rulers, Balbinus and Pupienus, though from this point provincial military revolt returned to being the main challenge to stability. The Guards may not have been the only cause of returning instability after 211, but they played a crucial role in creating a wave of revolts each of which made it less likely that the Empire could return to the political stability of the second century,as any ruler – even an able one – who attempted to secure stability would cause resentment among the military and touch off new revolts.

The caveat in this argument is the fact that the Guards' power was helped immensely by the uncertainty in Rome after 217, no Emperor being adult, experienced, secure, or dynastically legitimate. Macrinus was a Mauretanian outsider suspected of involvement in Caracalla's killing; Elagabalus and his 'brother' Alexianus/Alexander were under-age Syrians; Maximin was a low-ranking soldier without civilian backing; Balbinus and Pupienus were Senatorial candidates without recent military experience or connections; and Gordianus III was a teenager chosen for the connection to his late relatives. The frequency of coups had given both Guards and provincial troops (and commanders) hope for the success of revolts, and made the latter endemic. By the time of the rule of the competent and experienced adults Praefect Timisetheus (for Gordian III) and Philip in the 240s, revolt had become a habit and did not need an Imperial defeat to touch it off; Philip resorted to giving his principal military command to his loyal brother, Priscus, but could not prevent another army revolting in 249. If Septimius had been succeeded by a ruthless but less tyrannical son – hopefully, Geta –and a line of adult Severan dynasts been established into the 230s and 240s, Septimius' reliance on the soldiers would have been less likely to result in a series of revolts that could be blamed on his 'Sullan' tendencies.

'Knock-on' effects of military coups on the Empire's frontiers
This round of continuous crises made the Empire less likely to be able to deal with external threats, and more likely to break up if facing disaster on the frontiers as a struggling Emperor faced revolt in his rear and could not concentrate on the foreign enemy. The ability of Emperors to deal with serious external threats was seriously reduced if they were liable to face opportunistic military revolt the moment their military power faltered, and the potential of the invaders to do serious damage accordingly increased. The Empire's brief success on the threatened Danube frontier in the later 240s only led to the victorious troops (allegedly) forcing their triumphant commander Decius to revolt against the unpopular 'Arab' Emperor Philip.

Decius, a stern moralist and energetic ruler and accepted by the Senate as an aristocrat, called himself 'Trajan' to echo past glory and was probably the most capable Emperor since Severus. He undertook an energetic programme of reform and also had two sons who lacked the fratricidal tendencies of Severus's sons. But by now any military setback could lead to an ambitious provincial general revolting, and the German attacks across Rhine and Danube began to escalate. He was thus in a more dangerous position than Severus, and needed to win his campaign against a massive Gothic crossing of the lower Danube into Thrace in 250–1. Unfortunately, he was killed in battle in the Danube delta.[22] This damaged Rome's military reputation and led to copy-cat attacks by emboldened Germanic neighbours, including seaborne attacks across the Black Sea.

After Decius' death in battle in 251, two crucial years of Germanic incursions across the Balkans saw Gallus, Aemilianus, and Valerian fighting over the throne instead of a concerted Roman counter-attack. In 260, Valerian's capture by the Persians touched off a series of revolts by provincial military commanders that temporarily broke the Empire into pieces, resulting in loss of both manpower and treasure on fighting civil wars and economic damage from roaming armies of Germanic and Persian invaders. (The exact numbers of invaders and extent of damage is unclear from the fragmentary sources, but it is clear that the overall results on Roman resources were catastrophic; the decline in size of the towns and numbers of walls erected around them are good indications.[23])

What if Geta had been sole Emperor from 211?

It would be excessive to blame Severus' priorities as the main reason why this chain of disasters was touched off. Had either Caracalla or Geta proved an adequate and long-lasting ruler, the disruption of the period of 180–97 would not have resumed until the next crisis of succession, particularly if they had ruled in a more self-disciplined manner. Geta, if his government had been stabilised by Papinian to make up for his youth and apparent lack of interest in business before 211, would have retained the loyalty of the troops to a greater extent than the non-dynastic disciplinarian and poor general Macrinus, the eccentric Elagabalus, or the ineffective Alexander did. He was less likely to be murdered than his brother unless he had developed similar paranoid tendencies and so invited a pre-emptive 'strike' by a potential victim (the fate of Caracalla, Commodus, and Domitian).

Given his military training by his father, he could have handled a Parthian war in Mesopotamia better than Macrinus did in 217, though the collapse of Parthia into decentralised anarchy and the takeover by the Sassanids in the mid-220s would have invited a risky large-scale Roman attack by an over-confident ruler. Roman conquest as far as the Persian Gulf might have been possible given the resources available to a contemporary Roman ruler, the ease with which Septimius had recently reached Ctesiphon, and the disorder in Parthia, encouraging the (half- Syrian) Geta to think of himself in terms of a Hellenistic conqueror. He as well as Caracalla could have been tempted by Parthian collapse to play Alexander the Great. The 220s could have seen Rome ruling Mesopotamia as in 115–17. But once the Sassanids had unified Parthia again Rome would have faced a strong attack from the Persian heartland c.232, requiring a determined effort to hold the new acquisitions. (Unlike Trajan, however, Geta would not have had to face a Jewish revolt to his rear.) If Geta had matured into a capable ruler, relying on able ministers, his regime could have lasted for decades and restored Roman stability until the major Danube attacks of the 240s.

Did any Emperor after 217 stand a chance of stabilising the Empire? The 'what ifs' of their surviving longer in power

Given the evident attachment of the Praetorians to the reigning Imperial family and a principle of dynastic rule where possible (as shown by the attempts of Elagabalus' and Alexander's ministers to declare their links to Caracalla), it is possible that Alexander as an adult, if not his eccentric and self-indulgent cousin, had a chance to stabilise the situation. Elagabalus never showed any interest in military matters or government, leaving the latter to his grandmother, Julia Maesa, and her minister, Eutychianus. Having alienated Rome by his bizarre behaviour (and probably caused fears of bad luck arising from his marrying a Vestal Virgin), he was induced to name his cousin Alexander as his heir – probably by his nervous advisers so they had a replacement handy. He tried to have Alexander killed to safeguard himself but the Guards refused to do it and turned on him; he saved himself on that occasion but was soon killed in a second mutiny (March 222).[24] The hand of Maesa, anxious to save the dynasty, was probably behind the act; and Alexander proved a more biddable and respectable ruler. Both youths had been passed off as Caracalla's illegitimate sons to improve their dynastic claims, though Alexander and his mother Mammea (effective chief minister after Maesa died) could not stop sporadic military mutinies. Had he proved an adequate general in Mesopotamia in the early 230s and subsequently on the Rhine and shown less attachment to having his domineering Syrian mother at his headquarters, he ran less risk of being despised by the troops as her puppet. A coup to depose him would have been less likely.

Given the creation of new senatorial dynasties and appointment to provincial governorships of Severan 'trusties' after 193, he did have alternative advisers to rely on. The execution of his first wife's father Seius Sallustius, Praetorian Praefect and 'Caesar' so effectively his deputy, around 228 seems to have been a power-struggle with Mammea whether or not the charge of attempted revolt was justified. He could have been a viable senior civilian minister, a 'strong man' able to preserve the government, and averted the military rebels' charge in 235 that Alexander was an incompetent dominated by female control – provided he did not annoy the restless Guard. Another, demonstrably competent, senior minister, Praefect Ulpianus (a distinguished lawyer), was murdered by the Guard (c. 224) for excessive strictness – a return to the defiance their predecessors had shown in killing Pertinax. With a vague story in the (inadequate) sources about the Guard fighting the Roman populace for three days circa 223, it is clear that skill, charisma, or bringing in provincial troops to disband the mutineers (Severus' solution) was needed. Alexander lacked this ability, and his long survival would have been problematic even if he had not had to campaign – possibly not as feebly as subsequently believed – against the new Sassanid dynasty that had seized power in Persia. He ended up despised by his troops as his mother's puppet and an ineffective commander, and was killed in a mutiny at Mainz.[25]

Maximin, a popular choice to lead the uprising of 235 and a capable general on the Northern frontier, had more of a problem as an ex-'ranker' and a Thracian soldier who had no civilian connections in Rome. Relying on his trusted military associates to control the turbulent capital, he was bound to spark off resentment as a 'tyrant' relying on non-senators. Even the equally non-aristocratic 'outsider' Macrinus, a Mauretanian, had come up through the Imperial bureaucracy to be Praetorian Praefect. Maximin was vulnerable to a revolt within the Severan Imperial 'clientele', as seen by the plots on behalf of Alexander's friends, in the capital, or by senior governors and generals, and the unpopular rule in the capital by his trusted military associates was inevitable, as was Senatorial disdain. He could have saved his throne by prompter action in 238 or a wiser choice of deputy in Rome; his choice was a harsh general who sparked off the revolt in favour of the Gordians in 238.[26]

The elderly Gordian I was clearly not going to reign long even if his army had defeated Maximin's troops in Africa and enabled him to reach Rome in safety to benefit from the Senatorial rebels' defeat of the 'despot'. But he had a son to succeed him, though the sources are too muddled to make it clear how competent the latter was. The capable Praefect Timisetheus could have preserved the young and inexperienced Gordian III's regime beyond 244 had he lived, or the competent and ruthless Decius defeated the Goths in 251 and led his armies against the next waves of invaders. Decius was a harsh but capable ruler, promoting himself as a second Trajan and 'restorer' of ancient values, and had the energy to be a second Vespasian or a luckier Pertinax – and his military capabilities would have given potential rebels pause for thought before revolting against him. He had one adult son, Herennius Etruscus, so he could have safely left the latter in Rome to govern while he fought the attackers on the Danube. Herennius was killed with him in battle against the Goths; a younger son, Hostilianus, was titular ruler in 251–2 but only a teenager and so at risk of overthrow by his senior general, Gallus. As it was, Hostilianus died in the plague of 251–2 and the throne was up for grabs to any well-supported general; chaos duly followed.

The violent overthrow of none of these men – except arguably Alexander – was inevitable, and a successful reign of one or two decades by one of them would have discouraged would-be rebels. It would have aided stability despite the events of 193 encouraging potential provincial army rebels to take a chance. Maximin, Gordian I and Decius had heirs to hand – adult heirs for the latter two – as had the less successful Philip, meaning the potential for a dynasty lasting several decades, although the young and childless Alexander and Gordian III would have had to rule for decades to leave an adult heir. It was the endless round of successful revolts from 235 that prompted further military disobedience and opportunistic rebellions, leaving the Roman government critically unstable when the first major Germanic challenge since the 160s and the first Eastern threat since the 40s BC combined in the 240s and 250s; this vulnerability, no doubt, emboldened Rome's enemies to attack. Had a stronger ruler, in power for decades without a successful challenge, and a long-lasting dynasty faced this challenge instead of a succession of ephemeral sovereigns facing imminent revolt, the threat of the crisis breaking up the Empire and undermining its economy would have been far less.

Disaster and recovery from 253. The added burden imposed by Persian attack: the inability of the Empire to fight on two fronts
Even in the 250s, when the Empire faced multiple attacks and the effects of plague on the available manpower to fight them, it could have survived intact

with mutually trustworthy commanders fighting in each area. This is what Valerian, the victor of the civil wars of 252–3, attempted to do after 253. He used his adult son Gallienus as co-ruler to campaign on one frontier (the Rhine) while he was occupied elsewhere. Furthermore, Gallienus was lucky enough to have a teenage son available to rally loyalty too. The first geographical division of the Empire probably followed . But by that point revolt had become a habit as soon as the current ruler faced a setback. Crucially, Valerian could not concentrate on both the Germanic attacks over the lower Danube and the seaborne raids across the Black Sea into the Aegean, leaving the latter to spread unchecked and humiliate the Empire. It was at this point that Athens appears to have been sacked, as well as one of the 'Seven Wonders of the World' (the temple of Artemis at Ephesus) burnt.

Imperial failure – probably helped by loss of manpower to the plague – then encouraged Persia to attack on the Euphrates. Without this, the Empire could still have held out; by this reckoning the replacement of the decentralised and coup-prone Parthian monarchy by the aggressive Sassanid dynasty in 224/7 provided one foe too many for Rome. The Sassanid monarchs constantly harped back to the glorious days of the Achaemenid empire in their propaganda, which meant reclaiming all its old territories – as far as the Bosphorus. The biggest 'What If?' of the disasters which hit the Empire in the 250s is probably the question of the Sassanids' overthrow of Parthia. Plague-weakened Rome had faced massive Germanic incursions over the upper Danube in the late 160s, though not on so wide a front, and survived. This time there was a major Persian invasion on the Euphrates as well. Valerian had to take an army to Syria and leave the Balkans alone. Had he not had to march East, the presence of both him and Gallienus on the Northern frontier would have deterred too many local rebellions as long as they were winning against the Germans.

The capture of Valerian by the Persians near Edessa in 260 duly opened the floodgates to a mass of rebellions, not to mention the humiliation. ('Great King' Shapur is said to have used Valerian as his footstool when he wanted to mount a horse, and when Valerian died he stuffed his skin as a trophy.)[27] As Gallienus had to leave the Rhine to return to Italy the troops there revolted and murdered his son. The North-West of the Empire broke away under a usurper, Postumus, in 260 and was not regained until 273, with Gallienus unable to spare the time to reconquer it as he had to save Italy and the Balkans.

An escalating cycle of Roman civil war and external defeats thus led to catastrophe in the 260s, with a multitude of Emperors who all lacked the military resources to overwhelm their rivals. With the surviving Roman army in the East too busy driving raiders out of Asia Minor and backing its own Emperors (the two Macriani), the Persian invasion of Syria had to be halted by the local Greco-Arab ruler of the desert trading-post of Palmyra, Odenathus. His widow Zenobia then became unofficial ruler of the East around 267, and had to be deposed before the Empire could reassert its authority there.

Luckily, the leadership and resources available to the 'central region' of the Empire, based on Italy, enabled its rulers – Gallienus to 268, then Claudius II to 270, and finally Aurelian – to hold out and defeat all their rivals, Roman and invaders. The Empire was reunited by Aurelian in 270–4, defeating Postumus' heirs and Zenobia. His surprise assassination late in 275 did not halt the recovery, which continued under his equally competent successors, Probus (276–82) and Carus (283–4). The civilian Greek outsider, Diocletian (284/5–305), then created a whole new bureaucratic and military apparatus to run a stabilised Empire as an efficient – but hugely costly – hierarchy. His attempt to stabilise the succession by introducing a regular system of deputies was however a disaster. He divided the Empire into two geographical halves, with himself in the East and his friend Maximian in the West, and from 293 they had deputy rulers ('Caesars'), Galerius in the East and Constantius I in the West. The plan was that they would then retire together (305) and let these men take over, with two new 'Caesars' then being appointed. Inevitably, personal ambition overturned the neat system, as Diocletian's plans to nominate the most competent (or loyal) officers to Imperial office was wrecked by men who had their own relatives to promote. Prolonged civil wars from 306 ended in the triumph of Constantius's son, Constantine 'the Great', the first to challenge the system, in 324 as sole Emperor.

The crisis is unlikely to have commenced had Decius not been defeated by the Goths at Abrittus in 251, as it was that which emboldened the Germans to invade across both Rhine and Danube at a time of Roman civil war. Decius was a vigorous and competent general, with two sons who would have been adult and available for command in the 250s. A crushing Roman victory in 251 would have discouraged some of the tribal attackers beyond the Rhine and Danube from invading at all, though the plague of 251–2 would still have reduced Roman manpower.

Chapter 2

The Roman World – The Western Empire in the Fifth Century

Overview. Decline and fall? How much has it been exaggerated, and was it inevitable?

The basic argument is that the fall of the Western Empire was not inevitable, despite its comparative structural weaknesses that made it more vulnerable than the Eastern Empire. The latter survived in various, increasingly Graecicised forms until 1453 under a continuous line of Emperors: so why did the West collapse? Was it the long Western Empire frontier with the Germanic tribes to the north, open to penetration as soon as the Rhine and upper Danube were crossed? The East only had a shorter frontier on the lower Danube, and marauding tribes could be stopped at the Bosphorus and Hellespont. The East's Gothic invasions from 376 saw the East's army severely damaged at the Battle of Adrianople, yet the enemy were contained in the Balkans. The massive raids by Attila and his Hunnic-led empire in the 440s were similarly confined to the Balkans, as were the rampant Ostro[East]goths in the 470s and 480s. The mid-sixth century raids by the Kutrigur and Utrigur Bulgars reached the walls of Constantinople at a time when Justinian had secured control of Italy and part of Spain; this Balkan-born Emperor could not preserve his homeland from widespread ravaging despite an exhaustive programme of fortification testified to by Procopius.[1] New arrivals in the Hungarian basin, the Avars, engaged in semi-permanent warfare with the Empire over the Danube valley and then Thrace from 568. We know little of how this endemic insecurity damaged agriculture and reduced the availability of peasant soldiers for the army, but it must have been a serious problem, and by the 580s the ravaged Balkans were being settled permanently by the Slavs. None of these attacks by a locally powerful foe ranged right across the East to its permanent disruption; and Asia Minor remained secure apart from one bout of Hunnic raiding south from the Caucasus, which even reached Syria, around 400.

But in the West three major Germanic tribes' crossing of the Rhine in 406 led to permanent barbarian settlement in Gaul and Spain and in due course North Africa. This was not the case in the East, despite the mass movement of the Tervingi and Geuthungi Gothic peoples into the empire in 376–8 that was similarly militarily successful. The initial Gothic autonomous 'federate' tribal state in the Balkans, conceded to them by the East in 382 as they were too powerful to be evicted, was not a permanent solution, as seen on both sides. A Roman revival was hoped for by the Eastern orator Themistius in his up-beat propagandist account of the treaty to their Senate, where the Goths were portrayed as defeated and as turning into peaceful farmers; and a desire within the Gothic leadership for further pressure on the Empire was shown by the next Gothic leader, Alaric, in his aggressive behaviour in 395.

But had the Goths' joint leadership of the 370s or a friendly Gothic ruler like Fritigern been in place, would this attack have occurred at all? After the mid-390s Alaric shifted his activities West, and Gainas, an over-powerful Gothic general who did secure supreme military command in Constantinople, was soon killed. The same Eastern ability at containment applies to the next two Gothic tribal states, both ruled by a Theodoric, in the Balkans in the 470s and 480s, as Emperor Zeno induced their unifier Theodoric the Amal to invade Italy in 490. But in the West, the Goths followed their wanderings across Italy, southern Gaul, and Spain by securing a 'federate' state in Aquitaine in 418, and other parts of Gaul and Spain fell away too. Britain was abandoned to its own devices in 410, and the Vandals (part of the 406 Rhine coalition) moved on from Spain into North Africa in 428 and secured its capital, Carthage, in 439.

Losses in the West were thus permanent, and each one weakened the state's revenues, and ability to field an army, further. In turn, this encouraged further attacks. It was true, however, that the decline of Western power was not a smooth downward curve but came in sharp bursts. Each was precipitated by a specific political crisis. Due to personal charisma and military power, the Western supreme commander Aetius (in power 433–54) was able to call on the semi-independent Germans of Gaul to aid him against the invading Attila in 451, and central and northern Gaul were ruled by a mixture of Roman and German authorities until his murder in 454 saw the Goths turning on the fatally weakened Empire and extending their domains. Arguably, Aetius' influence over his allies in Gaul was personal, not institutional, and he had a valuable past knowledge of Germans and Huns alike that aided his success. He had been an exile in the Hunnic state in the early 430s and used them as allies to regain power in the Empire. His vigorous campaigns against Germans and peasant brigand rebels ('bacaudae') gave him the respect of individual leaders, in an era when personal ties were crucial to such warlords.

Independence or autonomy for German polities in the Western Empire thus did not mean an end to Roman power or influence, with successive generations of Gothic leaders hankering after adopting Roman lifestyles or gaining Roman political influence. The Romanised social behaviour of Gothic king Theodoric II (reign 453–66) was praised by his Roman client-emperor Avitus' son-in-law Sidonius Apollinaris, a contemporary Gallic poet-aristocrat who scrupulously aped classical literary culture. Indeed, the piratical Vandals in North Africa after Gaiseric's time (post-477) adopted a sybaritic Roman lifestyle, to which their military decline after the 460s was to be attributed. In central and southern Gaul the Goths seem to have lived separately from the Romans, shunning the towns, and to have preserved their own culture and traditions, as described by Sidonius Apollinaris. The Franks mainly settled in less urbanised northern Gaul, and the only semi-Romanised sybarite ruler with cultural pretensions (as seen by Gregory of Tours) was Chilperic of Soissons, who died in 584. Landed estates in at least two ceded Roman areas, Gothic Aquitaine in 418 and Italy in 476, were formally divided between the two peoples.

In 408 the rebellious Alaric the Goth initially sought his late foe Stilicho's supreme Roman commandership-in-chief from the supine Western Empire, and set up Attalus as his own puppet Emperor; the sack of Rome only followed the failure of his plans. He was seeking blackmail money to pay off his armies, not the destruction of the Empire, and made huge but manageable demands for gold and silver from the weak government of Emperor Honorius, then sought to replace it. His brother-in-law Athaulf spoke of wanting to fuse Roman and Gothic peoples into one state according to a story which reached the historian Orosius, and married Honorius' kidnapped half-sister Galla Placidia.[2] His murder in a private feud ended this attempt to set up a German-Roman state based at Narbonne, and his successors were driven west into Aquitaine in 418.

After the disasters of 454–5, the Goths of Toulouse used their military supremacy in Gaul to impose their own nominee, Avitus, as the new Emperor in leaderless Rome, thus seeking to influence the state rather than revolt against it. Avitus was a former supreme civilian official in Gaul so he knew the Gothic leadership, and had been sent to seek their alliance by the new Emperor Petronius Maximus after the latter had his predecessor Valentinian III murdered. This plan was forestalled by the Vandal attack on Rome. With Petronius in flight and killed, and Rome sacked by their rivals, the Goths then installed Avitus in his place. But the point is that now (455) it was the weakening Empire seeking Gothic military help, which it had firmly resisted when it was Alaric attempting to force his military assistance on the Empire in 408–10. In 416–18 Constantius III had been insistent on containing the Goths in far-away Aquitaine and recovering Princess Galla Placidia for himself, but after 454–5 the Goths, and then German generals in the Western army, were the senior partner in any Romano-German alliance.

Attila also sought to blackmail the Eastern Empire into sending him huge subsidies and gifts rather than conquering it in the 440s, though he did annex the middle and lower Danube valley from it too. He was aided prodigiously by sheer luck. His attacks and advantageous treaty with the East in 441–2 followed the departure of part of their army to fight Gaiseric in North Africa, and in 447 the walls of Constantinople and other cities were damaged by a massive earthquake. His open aggression towards the West in 451 followed an appeal from the disgruntled Princess Honoria for his hand in marriage which the government disowned, an excuse for a politically logical attack, but still useful to him. The flattering servility and massive bribes offered by the latest Eastern embassy to him, led by the supreme civilian official, 'Master of Offices' Nomus, had bought the East a temporary reprieve. Allegedly he had grudges against a Western banker for keeping plate promised to him or maybe was also bribed by Gaiseric the Vandal. He had already considered attacking Persia instead, according to Eastern envoy Priscus, but the geography was prohibitive as he would have to cross the Caucasus.[3] His choice of Gaul, not Italy where Honoria could be found, shows practicality; it was easier to cross the Rhine than the Alps. The nature of this steppe-based state was clearly based on warfare by restless nomads, unlike the relatively settled German lands bordering on the Danube and Rhine frontiers, where farming not pastoral herding predominated and the Germans had long been semi-integrated into the Roman world as mercenary-supplying vassals.

A leader like Attila needed constant success and loot to keep his followers contented, and the Empire was the richest source of both. Indeed, as of the

Romano-Hun negotiations of 411 there had been several Hunnic kings; the sole rule of Attila was a novelty. This meant that Attila's power depended partly on his success in imposing unity as a war-leader, and partly in his role as the sole conduit of loot (or Roman bribes) to his warriors. War was more useful to him than peace and the Empire had far more gold than his German neighbours, though if they extorted huge Roman subsidies he could channel these as sole negotiator with the Empire. Buying him off permanently was an unlikely result of Roman appeasement diplomacy, given the way he shamelessly raised his demands year by year. Possibly the East paid, rather than fighting, in 442 and 447 due to temporary strategic weakness, not out of fear or military incompetence. Its army was occupied elsewhere on the first occasion, and the earthquake had struck on the second. Had Attila been satisfied with the results of blackmail on East and West alike he would still have needed targets to conquer, and we have seen that he considered Persia.

Botched plans by Eastern chief minister Chrysaphius to assassinate him in 449 and the apparent appeal to him by Honoria exacerbated tensions, but any wiser Western submission would have left Attila with a problem of keeping his warriors occupied. He would probably have sought other excuses for aggression and the East could hardly afford to pay him any more; his demands had already risen ten-fold in a decade. But his court included Romans as well as Germans and Huns, with his secretary being the Roman Count Orestes who was later to become father of the West's last Emperor. It is too simplistic to present a notion of an irrevocable 'Romans vs. Germans and Huns' estrangement leading to the latter all pursuing a settled policy of seizing Roman territory. Rather, the more aggressive Germanic and Hunnic leaders made use of the opportunities that presented themselves in the decades after the first Danubian crossing in 376. The nature of newly established dynastic sole rulers, first Alaric, then Attila, in peoples used to no or multiple kingship encouraged the successful warlords to wage war and secure success and loot which benefited them personally.

It should be remarked here that the allegedly irrevocable, hostile Gothic crossing of the Danube by the Tervingi and Gaethungi in 376 was a refugee problem, a response to the loss of their steppe lands to the Huns, not anti-Roman aggression. The contemporary historian Ammianus claimed that Emperor Valens was pleased with their arrival as providing thousands of useful Gothic military recruits, at a time of rising tension with Persia (he was at Antioch in Syria preparing for war). He had previously negotiated successfully with these peoples as dependant allies at the end of a three-year war in 369, albeit probably forced to moderate his terms by the need to relocate east to a Persian war over Armenia. The Romans had been using their Danube neighbours for this purpose, and admitting thousands of agriculturalists to boost their denuded farming communities, for centuries. Constantine secured large numbers of recruits from the Goths in 331, and his son Constantius II did the same with the Sarmatians in 358–9. In recent years, one leading Gothic king (Athanaric of the Tervingi) had tried to limit, not extend, Gothic dependency on and supplies of troops to the Empire in the 369 treaty; the Hunnic attack forced a re-think as the Goths now needed sanctuary. The mass immigration in 376 was not a new phenomenon, either; the Empire had admitted thousands of Carpi from the Danube in 300. The main difference with the 376 phenomenon was that on the latter occasion the Goths obstinately stayed under the direct control of their own war-leaders; the Romans usually hastened to split bodies of armed immigrants up into manageable numbers under Roman command. Presumably this normal practice was Valens' intention for 376–7 too, but was hampered by circumstances such as the sheer number of the Goths and probably the lack of Roman troops to supervise them at a time of war with Persia.

As of 376–7 the Goths were interested in land and food, not attack; the situation only turned ugly after they were moved on South to local Roman commander Lupicinus' base at Marcianopolis and the Gaethungi crossed the Danube unilaterally to join the Tervingi. Lupicinus and other officials seem to have been operating a 'black market' in food-supplies and their extortion bred resentment. Valens should have sent reliable officials to avoid this in such a delicate situation. Lupicinus then panicked and tried to murder the Gothic leaders at a banquet, a logical move to decapitate the threat and hopefully force the leaderless Goths to obey Roman orders. Instead the targets escaped and war resulted, with Valens hundreds of miles away and unable to react quickly. The attempted strike at the enemy leadership was to be repeated, equally unsuccessfully, by chief minister Chrysaphius attempting to murder Attila in 449.

When Valens did arrive and march into Thrace in July 378, he seems to have expected to meet only around 10,000 Goths who he outnumbered, but faced at least twice or thrice that; possibly he had not heard that the Geuthungi had now linked up with his initial foes, the Tervingi. The size of the Gothic cavalry charge onto his army as it attacked the Gothic camp near Adrianople on 9 August then precipitated disaster.[4] Was his defeat therefore due to over-confidence or faulty scouting? It is arguable that what distinguished the disaster of 376–8 from successful Roman management of mass-immigration in 331 and 358–9 was that on the first two occasions the Emperor had been on the Danube with an army to supervise the process; in 376–8 Valens was in Syria and left it to under-resourced and corrupt military officials. The resulting damage to the Empire was permanent, but it was not an unavoidable invasion of the Empire by hostile barbarians.

The overall amount of Germanic looting and pillaging has also probably been played up by rumour and apocalyptic exaggeration by Christian writers, to whom the catastrophic collapse of the Christian Empire was a sign of God's disfavour and portended the Last Days foretold in Revelation. In 395–6 the Goths ranged at will across the major sites of ancient Greece, sacking Eleusis, Sparta, and Olympia and blackmailing Athens into paying ransom, a major psychological blow to the Empire.[5]

In 402 Alaric attacked the Western capital at Milan by surprise, forcing the court to take refuge permanently in the inaccessible marshes of Ravenna, hardly the situation of a militarily confident government.[6] Thereafter Alaric returned to an uneasy role as a 'federate' ally based on the Illyrian border of East and West, playing them off against each other. An independent leader, Radagaisus, invaded Italy on his own in 405 and was defeated. Although our account of the attack (by Zosimus) is garbled it seems that he had nothing to do with Alaric's Goths but crossed the upper Danube from Bohemia. The West was thus starting to attract copycat opportunistic invasions, and on 31 December 406 a multi-ethnic German coalition crossed the Rhine. Led by the Vandals and also including the Alans and Suevi, they rampaged at will across Gaul and produced apocalyptic comments about the end of civilization from local writers (e.g. Prosper); the lack of Roman Imperial military re-action led to the commander in Britain, Constantine (III), taking action unilaterally and claiming the throne. A revolt against his authority by his general Gerontius then enabled the Germans to move on into Spain, which was divided between them without any need to consult the Empire.

In 408 the murder of Stilicho left the West open to another invasion of Italy and threats to pillage Rome. Alaric shamelessly raised the stakes of protection money for leaving, and eventually lost patience. The Goths' sack of Rome in August 410 was a relatively disciplined and organised affair, with the Christian, albeit heretic Arian, Goths treating the churches and the Papacy with some respect. Indeed it was a result of Alaric's blackmail of the government in Ravenna failing to extort the pay-off he expected, not a long-term plan.[7] If the Western military high command had not been decimated by the anti-Stilicho purge in 408 he would have been unlikely to reach Rome at all. He had after all simply been attempting to secure power within the Roman 'system' as commander-in-chief to his own new puppet-emperor, Attalus. But the psychological effect was immense, with St. Jerome in distant Bethlehem summing it up as symbolising the destruction of the world.

In reply to the pagan reaction that it was the gods' revenge on the Empire for abandoning them, St. Augustine of Hippo wrote 'De Civitate Dei' arguing that the real 'City of God' was the new, spiritual Christian world not an earthly city. This was not a new reaction to the difficulty of fitting in the spiritual world of Christianity to a state that had initially persecuted it, and abandonment of the ungodly secular society was a desirable course for the virtuous Christian long before 410. But the sack of Rome gave Augustine an opportunity to establish a theological basis for the separation of the aims of Christianity and of the state, and to place the former as infinitely preferable. This fed into the claims of the Papacy to religious authority and prestige in place of the Emperor as lord of Rome, although Constantine had already given the Popes supreme jurisdiction over their ecclesiastical subordinates in the Western part of the Empire, effectively as 'Patriarchs of the West'.

The Vandals' sack in 455 was more brutal and secured a far greater haul of loot, but also opportunistic, and unlike Alaric, Gaiseric was not likely to be bought off before his forces attacked the city.[8] Like Attila in 451, he used the excuse of wanting the implementation of a promise (this time in a formal treaty) of an Imperial heiress, Valentinian III's daughter Eudocia, destined for his son Hunneric but unlikely to be delivered willingly to a barbarian. In political terms, it was extremely implausible that Gaiseric would have secured the Imperial succession for Hunneric. Even if the son-less Emperor had been forced to marry his elder daughter to Hunneric to avoid war, or after the murder of Valentinian his successor Petronius Maximus had done so, the succession would not have passed to Hunneric. The main political aim of Gaiseric in 455 was probably to forestall Petronius' planned alliance with the Goths (via Avitus' embassy), which could lead to a Romano-Gothic attack on the Vandals in North Africa. Had the alliance been implemented and Gaiseric not reacted, the Vandals would probably have faced the same dangerous level of attack from north, east, and west as they had in 441–2 with the Eastern Empire able to join in with greater German participation than earlier thanks to Attila's death.

The written evidence suggests that what came to be known to much later centuries as the eponymous 'vandalism' by the Vandals in Rome and elsewhere, systematic and deliberate destruction, was an occasional rather than a commonplace occurrence. At most, Gaiseric collected all the valuable moveables he could and stripped the roofs from temples in Rome to carry off the precious metals. Most damage to the fabric of the Empire's cities and towns was done gradually, not by concentrated barbarian assault. Across the West, buildings collapsed over decades for lack of maintenance rather than being pulled down by German attackers, and it is now suggested that the evidence of fires in excavated villas (e.g. in Britain) is not necessarily due to arson by passing Germans. Nor did hordes of Goths storm the walls of Rome in 410; the gates were opened for them by runaway slaves. In 455 Petronius Maximus fled the city and Pope Leo surrendered sooner than face a massacre.

There was widespread insecurity and anarchy, at least in some areas where governmental authority had collapsed, e.g. the mid-fifth century middle Danube written about by the local St. Severinus[9]. The decline in building standards of what little new works were undertaken, and the use of wood not stone, in the fifth and sixth centuries West suggests an inability to find adequate craftsmen or materials[10]. If this is not physical 'decline' into an atomised society, what is? But it should be remembered that in less affected areas such as mid- and southern Gaul, the local Romanised aristocracy were still in existence as a cultured, Latin-speaking elite and running the Church throughout the sixth century. The world of the 590s historian Bishop Gregory of Tours was post-Roman politically, but not culturally, and the Church remained a strong bond with the city of Rome. Even in seventh century Anglo-Saxon England the international links of the Catholic Church, restored to the Germanic kingdoms there from the time of St. Augustine's mission in 597, could allow for the imposition of Theodore, a Greek, as Archbishop of Canterbury, who came from distant Tarsus in Cilicia in 669.[11]

The fall of the Western Empire was not the end of the international world of a Mediterranean-centred Church. Indeed, the concept of 'Roma Aeterna' as the centre of the civilised world now applied to spiritual rather than political leadership, and was played up by Pope Gregory the Great, who was from an old Senatorial family but with a monastery established in his ancestral mansion. The collapse of the central institution of the Senate did not occur in 476, as it was still functioning and given practical autonomy in Rome by the Romanophile Gothic king Theodoric from 493. It only went into eclipse after the disruption of the wars between Eastern Empire and

Goths over Italy in 537–54, when Rome was captured several times and Gothic leader Totila once evicted its declining population.[12]

The thesis of a weaker Western army open to greater recruitment from unreliable German troops and Germanic supreme commanders has also been suggested as damaging to the West; the West had a Germanic supreme infantry and cavalry commander ('magister utiusque militiae') and effective regent, Stilicho, in 395–408 and eventually fell victim to more German generals after 455. But the East's army also relied on extensive Germanic recruitment, as in 331 (Goths) and 359 (Sarmatians). The East's senior German officers included one man who briefly held supreme military power in the capital (Gainas in 399–400) and one who served as military commander and chief minister (Aspar, 450–467). Both were murdered and their partisans massacred, as was Stilicho; but after Stilicho's fall the powerless Western court was at the Germans' mercy in 408–10. The East, however, fought off its Germanic challengers after their similar coups in 400 and 467. After Gainas and Aspar were killed their surviving troops were left at large in Thrace but could only plunder the countryside. Did the West face a more concentrated and resource sapping Germanic challenge than the East? Did its geography make attack easier and its containment more difficult?

Problems of state structure and control. Religion, governance, and failings in the structure of the bureaucracy
Much has been written about the top-heavy bureaucracy and court, and the vast armies imposed on the Empire by Diocletian at the end of the third century[13]. A new governmental system was set up after he took power in 284 (East) and 285 (West). He ruled for twenty years in a rare period of stability, though it is unclear how much was entirely his work as opposed to further innovation in the early fourth century. This was a time when Roman taxpayers' ability to fund this had been weakened by decades of insecurity and disastrous losses of manpower to the plague in the early 250s. Greater centralization was a logical reply to the multiplicity of revolts by provincial military commanders in the 250s and 260s. The Empire also faced a much more organised and determined military threat in the East than before, from the time that the aggressive Sassanid regime and its armies replaced the decentralised Parthian government in Mesopotamia and Persia in the mid-220s.

A small household Imperial entourage in the early Roman Empire had become a large, Persianised staff with a strict hierarchy and protocol, reflecting the religious overtones of a semi-divine Emperor, living in a Sacred Palace surrounded by quasi-religious ritual, who came to be associated with the cults of 'saviour' gods. Initially the old Romano-Greek pantheon was preferred, with Diocletian identifying himself and his colleague Maximian with Jupiter and the monster-destroying hero Hercules. An alternative version linked the Emperor to the cult of the sun god, 'Sol Invictus', to whom Aurelian, restorer of unity and conqueror of autonomous regimes in Gaul and Syria in the 270s, built a massive temple in Rome[14]. This identification of the Emperor with the state's protective gods later transferred to Christianity under Constantine the Great, with the Emperor as the 'thirteenth Apostle' and his court as the reflection of Heaven.[15] As a result, the Church was co-opted into the State bureaucracy, with a hierarchy of bishops under district metropolitans and supreme Patriarchs reflecting the civil bureaucracy. The government also set the correct form of worship and the only legal form of Christian doctrine, as shown by Constantine at the Council of Nicaea in 325. The doctrine established there is still the basis of Catholic and Orthodox theology. Constantine enjoyed debating and pronouncing on theology, as approved by his Church panegyricist Bishop Eusebius. This was a new move for a Roman ruler, as the traditional Roman cults were rituals lacking in doctrine.

As a result, the mid and later fourth century and the fifth century saw Emperors changing the state Church's doctrine to fit in with their personal beliefs, and enforcing their subjects' adherence. Constantius II backed Arianism in the 340s and Valens did likewise in the East in the 360s. In the 440s Theodosius II backed Monophysitism. Success for one particular doctrine depended on its promoters having the Emperor's ear; the Arian Bishop Valens was a major influence on Constantius II and in the 420s Theodosius II had to be dissuaded from imposing the controversial Christology of his new Patriarch Nestorius. Defeated at the Church Synod of Ephesus thanks to the forcefulness of the ultra-Catholic Egyptian bishops, Nestorius was banished to Syria and his sect flourished only outside the Empire, especially in Sassanid Persia. (It later developed an offshoot in China.) In the later 440s, Theodosius became a convert to the mainly Syrian and Egyptian Monophysite doctrine and attempted to impose it on his capital. In the manner of Henry VIII (or later Stalin and Chairman Mao), if the ruler changed his doctrinal beliefs everyone was required to follow suit.

On all such occasions, the death of the Emperor responsible saw an orthodox Emperor restoring Catholicism, his bishops denouncing the defeated doctrine as heresy and banning it. The triumph of Christianity in attracting State backing under Constantine opened up opportunities for rival interpreters of doctrine to win over Imperial support and lobbying by clerics at Court, and those who lost out could be portrayed as traitors to their Emperor. Such treason was a matter of dates and luck. The long career of Catholic champion St. Athanasius, Patriarch of Alexandria 328–73, saw him alternately in favour under Catholic rulers like Constantine and exiled under the Arian Constantius II and the pagan Julian. Arianism (called after the Alexandrian theologian Arius) only triumphed with those German tribal polities that had adopted it outside Roman borders in the fourth century, when Bishop Ulfilas had been able to proselytize North of the Danube. Constantius II backed Ulfilas' mission, and re-settled him and some of his Gothic converts when they were driven out by the Tervingi leadership in 348. These tribes (principally Goths and Vandals) kept to this doctrine after they moved into the Empire, and this caused difficulty when they took over Catholic provinces.[16] Some persecuted the locals (most notably the Vandals in Africa), though this could be linked to fears of the Catholics' political intrigues with the Eastern Empire rather than heresy-hunting intolerance.

It is a plausible theory that the Arian beliefs of the Goths ruling south-western Gaul (and later Spain) helped to alienate them from the local Catholics and to keep them at arms' length from the latter's clergy and town-based bishoprics. Greater unity with the local population followed their conversion in the 580s. In contrast, historians have seen the choice of Catholic baptism by Frankish conqueror Clovis as inaugurating centuries of co-operation between Frankish rulers and their Church. The reconquest of Arian-ruled Vandal Africa by Justinian in 533 could be played up as a righteous liberation from heresy. But did the different faiths of Germanic conquerors and local ex-Roman subjects really exacerbate their mutual alienation to a dangerous extent? Or is this just a modern assumption based on the swift collapse of the Arian-led German states in Italy and Africa in the face of Eastern invasion?[17] Would the conversion of the Goths and Vandals to Catholicism by a different set of missionaries in the fourth century have produced stronger post-Roman German kingdoms? The Papacy in Rome had more autonomy under the Arian Theodoric, living in distant Ravenna, than when it was supervised after 537 by Justinian and Theodora.

The failure of the religion of peace and love to tolerate its own dissidents, about which St. Athanasius was unapologetic, was duly ridiculed by the apostate Emperor Julian.[18] 'Paganism' (a term from 'pagus' meaning 'countryside', i.e. the rural remnants of ancient Romano-Greek religious cults), was initially the persecutor of 'unpatriotic' Christians under Decius, Valerian, and Diocletian but from the 380s was exposed to legal bans on its public practice and seizure of temple property by Theodosius. This led to alienation between the aristocratic practicers of the ancient cults in Rome and the government in Milan and Ravenna. The Roman nobility, however, had been disconnected from court life and service since the Emperors moved out of the city in the mid-third century anyway. If there was any disastrous loss of competent manpower to governments from the end of allowing senators to serve as provincial governors, this was a mid-third century law by Valerian's son Gallienus not a result of pagan alienation from a Christian Empire. Constantine re-employed the aristocrats. The reason for Gallienus' measure seems to have been state fear of well-connected, rich aristocrats using their provincial armies to stage revolts. The Late Empire created a table of ranks with honorifics dependant on service, like Peter the Great in Russia.

Arguably the failure of the State to tolerate any dissident religious sects alienated many potential supporters and led to unnecessary diversion of time and resources to persecution, as well as to the flight into hiding or exile of the defeated. But was this only temporary and played up by the polemical partisans of the victims, such as the senior Catholic clergy under Constantius and Valens? Did most people quietly conform, as they had done during the Diocletianic persecutions? It has also been argued that the emergence of monasticism led to many religious people dropping out of state service (or paying taxes) to live a holy life in the wilderness and save their souls not the state. St. Martin of Tours, a soldier turned monk turned bishop, was one famous example; and the persecutions of Christians in the early 300s saw thousands of dissidents fleeing to live as monks in the Egyptian deserts.[19]

How much this factor mattered in the less monasticised West is uncertain. The peasant flight from the land due to oppressive taxes, demands for supplies to the army, and legal semi-serfdom as tied tenants ('coloni') was more of a long-term problem. The high profile wealthy who rejected their secular lifestyle to set up monasteries, live as hermits, or go on pilgrimage to the Holy Places, e.g. Paulinus of Nola, ex-Empress Laeta, and the heiress Melania, were played up by approving supporters like St. Jerome, but were numerically few. There were not many clerics, exempt from tax, and not contributing to civic society according to critics from Gibbon onwards, compared to the state bureaucracy. Did they really make a difference to the state?

In political terms, the new order did pose one major problem. The Emperor was now a much more remote and semi-divine figure than the first citizen of the early Empire or even the rough-and-ready military Emperors of the mid-third century, when a brutal survival of the fittest and frequent revolts meant that only the most competent (or luckiest) rulers survived long. The men who saved the Empire in the 260s, 270s, and 280s, such as Claudius II, Aurelian, Probus, Diocletian, Maximian, and Constantius I, were usually experienced soldiers of humble birth. But once order was restored, the Emperors were more often immobile in their capitals than fighting in the field, with limited knowledge of the world beyond their court, though this did not apply to the autocratic Constantine the Great, Valentinian I, or Theodosius. They had their own failings: Valentinian seems to have been over-suspicious and persecuted alleged plotters, and Constantine and Theodosius gave full support to brutal and corrupt ministers such as Ablabius and Rufinus. This was not new, as shown by the activities of Sejanus under Tiberius, Tigellinus under Nero, and Cleander and Perennis under Commodus, and in all cases the misrule of individual favourites at Court did not affect the lives of ordinary citizens. But now the State was under greater threat and needed competent officials to advise a Palace-bound ruler. The danger of all the ritual acclamations at public ceremonies (even the Games) and obsequious language from courtiers to the sacred Emperor was that the latter would confuse the image of harmony at Court with the reality of life in his Empire.

It is noticeable that the records we have of the most senior Palace-based ministers, and great provincial bureaucrats headed by the Praetorian Praefects, suggest a quick 'turnover' rather than a system of long-serving men who could grow in experience and competence. Late Roman bureaucratic office had to be bought, and applications for favours from these high officials had to be paid for. Official salaries were small – hence the predominance of officials from the landed 'gentry' class, like the mid-fourth centuryAntiochene orator Libanius, who could 'pay their way'. A case-study of the East's senior bureaucracy in the career (and complaints) of the sixth century John Lydus suggests that raising money was a major concern of officials, to pay off the debts from one's previous promotion and to afford the next one.

Did all this lead to what we would nowadays categorise as a lack of concern for competence or (in senior ranks at the Palace) policy-making? It may not have been vital to the Empire's survival, as were military mistakes, but it arguably led to such venal incompetents in high office as Rufinus. Rufinus did considerable damage to the Eastern leadership in the early 390s. His most eminent victims, ex-finance minister and current Praetorian Praefect Tatianus (exiled) and his son Proculus (executed), were the sort of capable and honest ministers who the Empire needed in the crises after 395. Zosimus' attack on Rufinus' intrigues, cruelty, and corruption, which Theodosius did nothing to halt, is hardly just political partisanship, and is an indictment of Theodosius' abilities in civilian rule[20]. Would East and West have co-operated better against Alaric at the crucial moment of military crisis in 395 but for Rufinus, or would Stilicho have undermined any independent-minded Eastern chief minister?

There is also a highly significant trail of evidence pointing to the unwise political advice offered to impressionable Emperors by their (eunuch) chief chamberlains, from Eutropius under Arcadius to Chrysaphius under Theododius II and Heraclius in the West in 454, who advised Valentinian III to murder Aetius. Such household intrigue was not new, but it was more dangerous at a time of severe crisis, particularly if it concerned foreign policy (murdering Attila) or the army (murdering Aetius). Court favourites destroyed both Stilicho and Aetius.

After 395 no Eastern Emperor commanded his troops in person and the only Western Emperor to do so in 395–457 was the short-lived Constantius III. This probably gave him a reduced insight into the problems facing his government, let alone the lives of its ordinary citizens, as bad news could be filtered by his courtiers and he had a slower reaction to crisis. The sons of Theodosius the Great, Arcadius and Honorius, and the latter's nephew Valentinian III seem to have been particularly politically inert and vulnerable to court factions. But this was a personal, not institutional failing; all three were weak characters. The charge that a remote and suspicious Emperor living in the closed world of the court was listening to bad advice, following the dictates of flatterers, punishing loyal and competent ministers at the behest of intriguers, and neglecting honesty for servility was made strongly against Constantius II in the 350s, and played up by his overthrower, Julian.[21] It was not a new phenomenon, but the nature of court life made this threat to capable leadership from the centre greater than before, though it did not weaken the Eastern Empire, perhaps more used to autocratic rule by pre-Roman dynasts, as it did the Western.

Division of the Empire – militarily necessary, or extra problems?
Diocletian divided the Empire into East and West, with two senior 'Augusti'
and two junior colleagues, 'Caesars' who would in due course succeed them.
This was meant to avoid struggles over the succession by pre-nominating
competent adult heirs but predictably collapsed into chaos. He and his
partner Maximian abdicated in 305 and their deputies Galerius and
Constantius I took over as the senior Emperors ('Augusti'); however the new
deputy Emperors never secured recognition and Maximian's and
Constantius' sons joined in the struggle. The succession reverted to the
ruler's immediate family, brothers or sons, if available, with each ruler
having his own court and mobile 'comitatus' field army. Constantine the
Great, who had first challenged Diocletian's system in 306 by claiming the
succession to his father Constantius I, defeated Maximian's son Maxentius
(usurping ruler of Italy and Africa) in 312; Maximian, who had staged a
come-back and then deserted his son for Constantine to betray him too, was
also eliminated. Constantine reunited the Empire in 324 but left it in 337 to
his three sons by Maximian's daughter Fausta: Constantine II, Constantius
II, and Constans. He intended to leave two sub-states to his nephews
Dalmatius and Hannibalianus, but they were murdered.

The eventual reunion of the Empire under Constantius II (353–61) and
his nephew Julian (361–3) was followed by the extinction of the dynasty in
363.This was avoidable: Julian was only thirty-two, had had two marriages
without children, and was killed by an arrow in a skirmish on the River
Tigris while invading Persia. Arguably, if the militarily competent Julian,
who had defeated the massive Alemannic attack on Gaul in 355 despite
minimal military experience and so was a natural general, had been able to
complete his Persian campaign in 363, withdrawing in good order, the
Empire would not have been weakened by the surrender of vital fortresses
West of the upper Tigris which his successor Jovian agreed to.

Evidently panicking with the Persian cavalry pursuing his demoralised
army, the Emperor Jovian abandoned this frontier region (the modern
south-east Turkey) in return for peace, and so opened the way for extra
Persian pressure on the Roman frontier, and Armenia, from a much more
secure position than formerly. Major fortresses that had protected Syria and
Armenia, such as Nisibis, were lost and the Empire forced to divert troops
and Imperial policy-making to planning a military recovery. Was it thus that
Valens was fatally distracted from the Danube in the 370s and the Empire
put at greater risk of a disaster like Adrianople? Would Persia's threat have

been more containable but for the long-term disaster of Jovian's treaty, or would an over-confident Emperor have neglected the Danube for the chance of glory in Mesopotamia anyway?

Jovian accidentally suffocated from paint fumes. His elected successor Valentinian, a capable Danubian general, took the West and handed the East to his brother Valens, against advice to empower an experienced minister or general. Valentinian died of an apparent fit of rage while shouting at some insolent German envoys during a Danube campaign in 375, aged fifty-four. If he had been alive in 378 he was experienced enough to have done better than his son in dealing with the Goths in Thrace, if not to destroy them.[22] Would Valens have waited for his more experienced brother to arrive to join him before he tackled the Goths in autumn 378, unlike he did for teenage Gratian?

Valentinian I was succeeded in the West by his sons Gratian (sixteen) and Valentinian II (four), and after the violent deaths of both (and their usurping successors) his empire fell to Valens' successor in the East, Theodosius the Great. The latter had been appointed by Gratian to clear up the Gothic war in 379, but Valentinian I, who executed Theodosius' father, would not have given him this chance. Theodosius died within months (January 395) and left the two halves of the Empire to his two sons; this time the division was permanent. But the division could have been as ephemeral as the previous multiple divisions of 337 and 375, or Theodosius never gained the West at all had Gratian or Valentinian II survived and left their thrones to sons. For that matter, the triple division of 337 could have lasted and three Empires, not two, emerged with their capitals at Trier (to face the Germanic threat on the Rhine), Milan (to guard the Danube), and Constantinople (the East). The notion of a careful, planned permanent division of the Empire in 395 owes much to hindsight.

The State and army: too heavy a burden? Or irrelevant to the question of survival?

The multiple courts of a number of Emperors, ruling as colleagues, and their ministers were followed down the administrative hierarchy by a large number of provinces, many more than in the early Empire, plus over-governors, 'vicars', ruling groups of provinces. All these men needed officials, and the armies of over 300,000 men now included both the field armies and local frontier garrison 'limitanei'. The precise size of the army is unclear, as it can only be estimated from the early fifth century administrative summary in the 'Notitia Dignitatum', which may have been out-of-date or reflecting an idealised picture. But it was clearly much larger than the twenty-nine legions (120–150,000 men?) of the early Empire. Now each province had its own military commander ('dux', leader or general, hence our 'duke'); the civilian governors ('praeses') had been stripped of troops to discourage revolt. The army apparently took up two-thirds of the Imperial budget.[23]

Service in many professions such as the army and farming was meant to be hereditary to ensure continuity of manpower in an Empire denuded of manpower by war and plague. The costs of the Imperial courts (there was usually more than one Emperor after 286), officialdom, and armies made the tax base shoulder more costs than it had in the second century, coinciding with difficulties in payment. The always fragile monetary economy was weak, as seen in the hyper-inflation of the later third century and the drastic regulatory measures taken to counter-act it. It is noticeable that there was both a reluctance to serve in urban civic offices, the middle-class social and economic basis of city life who could not escape the burden of tax, and a flight from the land by agricultural workers, defying the legal requirement for hereditary service in both cases. The dramatic decline in the commissioning of inscriptions commemorating public works by the provincial 'curial' middle class has been taken as a definitive sign of their impoverishment, flight from their responsibilities, and probably a lack of concern for the early Empire's pattern of civic improvement. There was certainly greater fourth-century spending on private than public life.

Indeed, the declining ability of the over-taxed urban middle classes to fund urban building projects and civic public life seems to have added to the shrinkage of towns and lack of new public works compared to the early Empire; the most impressive new building was carried out by the well-funded and staffed Church. All this testified to a much different state of society from the relatively under-governed and prosperous first and second centuries AD. The new government interference in private life, prescribing belief and hunting down dissidents, first Christians, then heretic Christian sects and pagans, added to the sense of permanent crisis. But case-studies of places such as fifth century Syria and fourth to fifth century North Africa have shown that these areas were certainly still prosperous, with flourishing agriculture and farms, and even in raid-hit Britain there were grander villas than ever before in the fourth century. Recent estimates of the late Roman population and prosperity have painted a far less gloomy picture than was once assumed. On this basis the populace and the tax-hit 'curial' classes were better able to sustain the burden of taxation. Possibly earlier reckonings relied too heavily on Gaul and the Rhine valley, badly hit by the third century invasions.

Germans and Romans

The Empire was restored as a viable structure by Diocletian and his successors, but was still vulnerable to insecure successions and civil wars. Then from the 370s a series of massive incursions by 'barbarian' Germanic tribes seeking new homes, commencing with the Goths, added to the constant pressure of frontier wars against smaller, usually disorganised Germanic attacks from the north and a 'cold war' that erupted into sporadic conflict with Rome's only major rival state, Sassanid Persia, to the east. The defeat and death of Eastern Emperor Valens at the hands of the Goths at Adrianople in 378 broke the myth of Roman military supremacy and encouraged further tribal attacks, besides leaving a permanent autonomous Gothic presence within the Roman borders that the Empire had to accept.

When the next chance for Germanic attack arose on the death of the strong Eastern Emperor Theodosius in January 395, revolt by the Goths followed; and incursions from north of the Rhine and Danube resumed. The Empire was permanently divided into the East, with its capital at Constantinople, and the West, with its official capital at Rome but the Emperor's court now at Milan or Ravenna, and help from one half of the Empire to the other was not guaranteed. In 406 a coalition of tribes crossed the Rhine into Gaul; they had done so before, most notably in the 270s and 350s, but this time they could not be driven back.[24]

But was this permanent irruption of Germans into Roman lands the inevitable precursor of the fall of the Western Empire? The apocalyptic notion of a 'Fall of Rome' has been debated, as Roman civilization, its social and economic structures, its Church, and use of its Latin language survived across much of the post-Roman West; the main break in social and economic continuity occurred in the seventh century with the Arab invasions and collapse of Mediterranean trade. But the end of formal Imperial authority and the administrative structure of the Late Empire is undeniable, commencing with the outer provinces like Britain and the Rhineland.

The notion of a massive 'volkwanderung' of hordes of hundreds (or at least scores) of thousands of Germans across the Empire from 376 was played up by romantic nationalists in the nineteenth century, but is now largely discredited.[25] For one thing, there had been substantial Germanic settlement within the Empire and recruitment to its army already in the fourth century, an era characterised by shortages of manpower in the Empire after the plagues and wars of the third century. As we have seen, there had been assimilation of bodies of thousands of Germanic warriors (and/or farmers) from across the Danube into the East after 331 and 358/9. There were Germans at Court and in high military command by the 360s, as shown by their names. Valentinian II as well as Honorius had a German commander-in-chief (Argobast).

Nor were the German peoples who invaded the Empire necessarily neatly divided into permanent and recognisable tribes, all strictly delineated by descent and recognising unchallenged war-leaders. What is attested by archaeology is that certain widespread Germanic agricultural settlements North of the Danube disappeared after the fourth century, e.g. the 'Cernjachov' culture in Wallachia and the Moldova-Ukraine region (largely peopled by Goths) and the 'Przeworsk' culture of Bohemia, Slovakia and southern Poland (the Vandal area). The abandonment of these settlements is obviously linked to large-scale immigration into the Empire, whether in the specific invasions testified to by the literary sources or more gradually. The culprits for the mass-movement were presumably the nomadic, horse based Huns.

Names that were later adopted by separate tribal kingdoms are used to define particular military groups who fought the Empire in the later fourth century and the fifth century, e.g. the Goths (East and West), Franks, and Vandals; but this is not to say that their armies consisted solely of men from that tribe. It is more likely that there was a fluid situation of assorted warriors (plus their families) from mixed Germanic backgrounds supporting the most promising leader available, with a successful leader attracting a growing coalition of warriors who might become a permanent, coherent grouping if they secured a geographical 'state' to settle in. Identity was as much 'cultural' as ethnic – by choice as well as descent successful warbands became the allied kingdoms that fought the Empire and were then sometimes recognised by treaty as occupying particular Roman territory. As described by the Roman historian Tacitus in the first century AD, Germanic kingship was divided between ephemeral military commands, created for particular wars by the election of the best or most forceful war-leader, and permanent judges and religious leaders. All came from hereditary noble or royal lineages; the former only emerged when needed.[26]

There is no continuous record of any dynasty ruling a stable kingdom of one particular Germanic people for centuries before the invasions of the

Empire from 378, even when the name of a people is continuous. The ancient lineage of the Goths' leaders was probably exaggerated by their sixth century propagandist Jordanes, back-dating its length to add to their descendants' prestige. But Rome preferred to deal with individual kings, who it could control with gifts or military pressure, than with anarchic bands of warriors, and so built up its allies beyond the Rhine and Danube as rulers from the first century. All the evidence suggests that these kingships, e.g. of Maroboduus in Bohemia in the early first century, were personal and temporary. Arguably, indeed, it was the need for permanent military leadership as the Germanic peoples invaded and settled in the Empire that led to permanent kingships; Alaric's relatives ruled the 'Visi[West]goths' from the 400s. But there were undeniably Germanic hereditary elites by the fourth century, with Athanaric the Goth (fl. 376) being the son of a former noble hostage in the Empire and 350s Alemmanic leader Serapio called after the god Serapis by his royal hostage father. The Alemannic-led invaders of the Rhine frontier in 355–6 had seven kings, and the Tervingi and Geuthungi Goths of 376–8 had multiple leadership too. Athanaric and others were linked to previous kings (i.e. war-leaders) or judges, but not to any long-lasting, permanent patrilineal rulership.

On an archaeological level beyond the Roman frontier, there is evidence of elite, maybe royal, residences in fourth century tribal territory lacking in earlier centuries, such as Urach, in Alemmanic territory. New wealth, and goods from the Empire, was clearly concentrated in a few hands, and status could be hereditary. Arguably, this posed an extra danger to the Empire that had been absent in the first or second centuries, as such leaders could look to war with Rome to boost their reputation and leadership. An agricultural revolution of greater arable yields has also been traced, as seen in the 1960s at the excavated fourth century settlements of Feddersen Wierde (Germany) and Wijster (Netherlands)[27]. Did this produce greater survival rates for the populace and a hunger for lands, leading to more pressure on the Empire?

All this is suggestive of a probability of extra problems for the Roman frontier and new aggression by an emerging royal elite of Germanic war-leaders. But their tribes' leadership in the fourth century was multiple, even when attacking the Empire (355–6 on the Rhine and 376–8 on the Danube). Individual kingship only emerges in the fifth century, among peoples traversing or settling in the Empire, and did not emerge among the fifth century Ripuarian Franks who were not in contact with Rome. Would these dynasties have emerged but for a permanent military confrontation with or settlement within the Empire?

Less successful warbands broke up and less successful tribes were amalgamated into their rivals' kingdoms; the fifth century is littered with the names of leaders without their own tribal following (e.g. Odovocar) and tribes who disappeared from history (e.g. the Heruls). In Gaul, the Merovingian dynasty originally only ruled a small section of the Frankish peoples, based around Tournai in Belgium in the mid-fifth century. Many other Frankish groups (e.g. the Ripuarians on the Rhine) and their kings fell victim to Clovis and his sons after 481.[28]

Indeed, it should be recognised that the empire of Attila the Hun, the supreme charismatic non-Roman leader and loot-plunderer whose state collapsed after his death, was not a coherent grouping of Huns alone. The latter were described by contemporaries as Mongolian in feature, attacked the Goths on the Ukrianian steppes in the 370s from the East, and were assumed to be unholy savages (the 'scourge of God') by fifth century writers from their appearance and ferocity. Ammianus in 376 already recognised them as a distinct, aggressive, non-Germanic people relying on cavalry archers not the usual foot-soldiers.[29] Attila himself seems to have turned on violence as a matter of policy, and received the East Roman embassy of Priscus in 449 coolly enough despite a recent Roman assassination-plot. But the state created by Attila from the Rhine to the steppes in the 430s and 440s consisted of Germanic tribes he had subdued as much as his own Mongolian steppe horsemen, and many of them revolted and resumed their tribal identity in 454. Other nomadic states generally referred to as Hunnic existed on the steppes and raided the Balkans through the later fifth century and into the sixth century, but ethnically are now known as proto-Bulgar. It is possible that their newly sedentary settlement on the Hungarian plain after 400 speeded up the Huns' centralization into a state, changing their manner of leadership.

476 – a convenient but misleading date?

The end of the Western Empire is conventionally dated at 476 when the final Emperor exercising authority in Italy, Romulus 'Augustulus', was deposed; but in fact there had been a vacancy in a resident Emperor in the region in the 460s after the death of the shadowy Libius Severus in 465; commander-in-chief Ricimer ruled alone, recognising the Eastern Emperor as his sovereign. The interregnum ended with the arrival of Anthemius with an army from the East in 467. After the deposition of Romulus in 476 the Germanic successor-state of Odovacer recognised the titular authority of the Eastern Emperor Zeno, a return to the situation of 465–7, not an innovation. It turned out to be permanent, with the regalia sent to Zeno in Constantinople, but he could have named a new Emperor as Leo I had done in 467.

Indeed, the real authority of a Roman Emperor, sitting in Constantinople, was restored to Italy, North Africa, and even part of Spain in the 530s–550s by Justinian's generals and did not end in Rome itself until the eighth century. Ravenna, seat of Eastern Roman power in Italy, did not fall to the Germans until 751. The last Eastern Emperor to visit Rome was Constans II in 663, and he was resident for some years in Sicily not Constantinople. The Eastern Emperors regarded themselves as fully Roman despite residing in a Greek city on the Bosphorus and from the early seventh century using Greek as the official language of State, the modern term 'Byzantine' for the Eastern Empire is a seventeenth century invention.[30] In parts of southern Italy, the Eastern government exercised authority until the Norman conquest in 1071.

The notion of a Western Empire falling and the creation of a medieval, post-Roman world in 476 would have seemed inaccurate to its contemporaries. As far as Justinian, ruling from the Cadiz area across the Mediterranean world to the Euphrates, and his heirs were concerned the Roman Empire was still functioning. It was indeed as a Roman Emperor of the 'Romaoi' that Constantine XI fell defending the ramparts of Constantinople against the Ottoman Turks on 29 May 1453; that date was the end of the Roman Empire. The term 'Rumelia' for the ex-Roman Balkans continued to be used by the Ottoman state, and the restored state of Greece provocatively numbered its first King Constantine (reigned 1913–17, 1920–2) as 'XII' not 'I'.

The timing of the end of Rome was thus seen as different in the East than in the West. And other questions need to be asked about the undoubted end of a separate Imperial-led governmental structure in the West in the 470s. How much did the contemporary chroniclers exaggerate the extent of disruption to ordinary life in the Western provinces caused by the invasions? Would the post-378 Germanic invasions, whose numerical scope has been revised downwards in recent decades, have occurred but for a lapse in strong, unified Roman leadership? And were they bound to lead to the collapse of Imperial authority across the entire Western empire?

For example, the shocking sack of Rome by Alaric's Goths in August 410 was traumatic but not politically decisive; it was followed by a revival in

Imperial power in the central lands of the West under strong leadership by Constantius III in the later 410s. He tackled the Germans within the frontier as well as assorted Roman pretenders systematically, and restored a measure of peace by 418, only to die within months of gaining the co-emperorship. Britain, the Rhine frontier, parts of Gaul and Spain, and from the later 420s North Africa were already or subsequently lost, but after a bout of civil war unity was restored by new Imperial commander-in-chief Aetius from 433–54. He preserved Rome's military predominance over its allies in Gaul and Spain, secured Eastern help to tackle Gaiseric, and fought off Attila the Hun (with Gothic help) in 451. Usefully, he had once lived among the Huns as an exile and understood 'barbarians' better than many haughty Roman aristocrats. The failure of Attila's invasion of Italy in 452, probably due to plague as he did not suffer military defeat, and his death in 453, which caused his empire (a tribal confederation owing personal allegiance to one war-leader) to collapse seemed to leave the Western Empire intact within its shrunken post-420s borders.

Apart from Gaiseric the Vandal and his large Mediterranean fleet the Western Empire faced no serious military challenge, and even after Gaiseric had sacked Rome in 455 his realm came close to defeat by a massive Eastern Roman naval attack in 468. As far as military collapse was concerned, was the irreversible destruction of the Empire only dateable to 455 or 468? Even after that, Odovacar could have named a new puppet-emperor in 476 and kept the 'kingdom of Italy' in being under a titular Emperor until he was overthrown by Theodoric in 491–3.

A vicious circle of gradual collapse?
The final collapse of Imperial power outside Italy, and the reduction of the tax-starved government to being the victim of its German-dominated armies, only followed the murders of Aetius in 454 and his killer, weak Emperor Valentinian III, in 455. Even after the sack of Rome by Gaiseric's Vandals later in 455 one competent military leader, Emperor Majorian, could revive Roman power to a limited extent in its central lands in 457–62. The East brought a new Emperor (Anthemius) and major military aid in 467–8, and its incompetent commander's defeat in North Africa was arguably the final blow to the Empire's security as a viable government controlling Italy and southern Gaul.[31] Even after that, the over-powerful German military commanders at the Western court (Ricimer and then Gundobad) controlled Italy and kept up a series of puppet-emperors, a regime that could have survived for decades.

The decline of the central government's control of its provinces was thus sporadic, and could be (temporarily) reversed by determined action by Constantius, Aetius, and Majorian; but each new crisis led to further aggression by its enemies against a state whose ability to fight back was weakening. It led to a vicious circle through the years 395–476; each loss of extra provinces and revenues weakened the Empire further, thus emboldening its ambitious neighbours to attack again. And on each occasion it was less likely to fight back successfully. It is no coincidence that the death of Theodosius in 395 was followed by Alaric revolting in the Balkans and playing off East against West. The murder of generalissimo Stilicho in 408 led to Alaric attacking Rome, the deaths of Constantius and Emperor Honorius, in 421 and 423, led to civil war, and the Vandal attack on Africa, and the murders of 454–5 led to Gaiseric's attack on Rome.

Potential alternatives and the crucial moments of Roman collapse
The proposal considered is that a crucial preservation of strong leadership in the later fourth and early-mid fifth centuries in particular should have seen off the challenges of the Germanic peoples to the unity of the state. Outlying provinces and their resources might have fallen away under the pressures from outside from around 395, but the core Empire would have remained intact if there had been domestic stability and an unbroken run of powerful military leaders from Theodosius the Great to Stilicho to Constantius III to Aetius to the latter's heirs (e.g. Majorian). The collapse of the Western Empire was brought about by a series of internal crises and invasions from the death of Theodosius, with the first establishment of an autonomous German 'federate' kingdom within Roman borders (382) by the Goths in Thrace being followed by its successful attacks on both East and West, crucially at odds with each other at the time, from 395 to 410.

It is of paramount importance to remember that in the crisis of 395–7, when Alaric roamed at will across Greece and the south-western Balkans, the Western commander-in-chief Stilicho (regent for Theodosius' younger son Honorius), a Vandal by birth, so looked down on by aristocratic Romans, brought aid to the East but was not trusted by their government. He was suspected of wanting to rule the East as well, Honorius' elder brother Arcadius being mentally feeble and a puppet of his ministers. His panegyricist Claudian referred to him as entrusted with the regency of both Empires by his late master Theodosius I, a claim evidently not accepted by Rufinus who Stilicho's German allies in the Eastern army then killed in late

395 after returning from service with Stilicho. He was also suspected of not destroying Alaric in Greece while he had the chance in order to use him as a military weapon against the East. Alaric's army was able to survive a half-hearted Roman blockade in Epirus and secure another grant of a 'federate' state on the Eastern-Western borders. From this vantage point Alaric was able to invade the West in 402, and despite defeating him at Pollentia near Milan Stilicho failed to destroy him again. But had Stilicho or a competent Eastern general cornered and destroyed Alaric's men, most obviously during the time they were trapped in Epirus, the Gothic survivors would have been reintegrated under direct Roman military command or driven into flight to the Danube. The Gothic troops of Gainas in the East met this fate in 400, after their leader and his closest officers were killed in a coup in Constantinople. Italy would then have been safe from the attacks that Alaric was to launch from Illyria in 402 and 408.

Alaric's survival as a major military threat to East and West through the period 395–408 was fortuitous and partly due to internal Roman politics, namely Stilicho's ambitions to rule the East; and when Arcadius died in 408 Stilicho apparently preferred to plan taking over the Eastern regency for Theodosius II to using the Western army against the invading Germans in Gaul. This gave the latter a breathing-space to spread further afield, whereas in the 270s and 350s the Empire had acted swiftly to contain them. In 407 Stilicho was planning some sort of move on Eastern-held Illyricum and Epirus with Alaric, not sending troops north to Gaul. Indeed, court resentment at Stilicho's behaviour was stirred up by the courtier Olympius and caused the killing of him and his military partisans, who would have included quite a few competent officers in a violent purge in August 408.

This then left the West with a demoralised and faction-ridden army to face Alaric's next attack, while the lack of state help to Gaul had led to the commander of Britain taking charge of the defence and proclaiming himself Emperor (Constantine III). The resulting civil war paralysed the West further, Alaric's success in blackmailing the Western government into paying him off in 408–9 and then sacking Rome and ravaging Italy in 410 thus owed much to internal Roman politics not inevitable German military superiority. The West recovered after 410 under a competent new general, the later Constantius III, but the Goths under Alaric's heirs had to be bought off with another 'federate' state (in Aquitaine) and the Vandals and other tribes remained at large in Spain. After another Western Roman civil war in 423–5 the Vandals were able to move on into Africa and revive the old threat of a naval power based at Carthage to Italy. Had there been no civil war then due to Constantius III not dying in 421, he would have been at liberty to attack the Vandals in the rear in Spain or even also reinforce Africa when it was attacked. The actual course of events saw the West's two post-425 generals, Aetius and Boniface, at loggerheads in these years to the detriment of any counter-attack.

The major Germanic invasion-crisis on the Rhine of 406–7 was not the first such attack, and though its scale is unclear it involved several peoples and probably tens of thousands of fighting men. There were enough of them to spread out across Gaul and to move into northern Spain as mercenaries hired by Constantine III's ex-general Gerontius and divide the peninsula up. Large-scale German invasions had been halted by the Emperor Probus in 276–7 and by Constantius II's nephew, the 'Caesar' Julian, in 355–6. But this time Roman weakness enabled the invaders to remain at large within the Empire thereafter. The gradual loss of outlying provinces to the invaders meant loss of their tax revenues and a spiral of diminishing Roman resources, out-of-control Germanic kingdoms facing a weakening Imperial army, though strong leadership under Constantius III and Aetius delayed military-political collapse until 455, and a situation where each barbarian success emboldened more ambitious war-leaders to defy the Empire.

As of circa 420 the Empire had been stabilised by Constantius III, though analysis of the 'Notitia Dignitatum' indicates that 97 of the West's 181 regiments had been raised since 395 and only 84 'originals' from the C4th survived – an indication of disruption to half the army. The Rhine was worst hit. This stabilisation was then hit by the deaths of Constantius and Honorius, and the struggle between Aetius and Boniface to be Western commander-in-chief in the late 420s – leading to the Vandals invading Africa. The latter could not be expelled, and delivered the devastating blows of seizure or Rome's grain-supplies and in 455 the second sack of the city. After Gaiseric's attack, the new Emperor Avitus had to be provided by the Goths and his successor Majorian was chosen by the German general Ricimer – both signs of the West's catastrophic decline in 454–5 (when it finally lost control of central and northern Gaul). Anarchy undermined trade and security, the State lost its ability to impose order outside Italy, and by the 460s the government was at the mercy of its German allies and riven by coups. Much of this could have been averted with strong and continuous Roman leadership, which was lacking at court for most of the period after 395.

This was not inevitable. Theodosius the Great, for example, died aged 47 and could easily have survived for another decade or two as sole ruler of the Empire. Given his military successes against the Goths (limited) in 379–81 and Western Roman rivals in 388 and 394, he was unlikely to have faced or been defeated by a challenge under Alaric (his loyal subordinate as of 394). Alaric or his followers may have revolted against Theodosius – suspected of exposing them to heavy losses in battle deliberately in 394 – in any case. But victory was unlikely. A competent military leader of the East in 395–7 could have defeated Alaric, which Stilicho failed to do; but the Empire had a feeble young ruler who never left his capital and a circle of vicious, feuding ministers like Rufinus (renownedly corrupt) and the eunuch chamberlain Eutropius. Stilicho's murder and the Western military collapse in 408 owed much to the distraction of the Eastern crisis; though he might not have tackled the Germans in Gaul himself if he was free (to avoid being undermined at Court in his absence) he could have sent a capable subordinate.

The Western civil war of 407–12 was thus avoidable, and if Constantius III had not died in 421 he would have succeeded his brother-in-law Honorius in 423 and the West avoided a civil war then. Constantius was probably under fifty when he died; he could easily have ruled the West as 'stand-in' for his son Valentinian III into the 440s. A long-lived Theodosius, Stilicho, or Constantius would still have had to face the threat from the Huns on the steppes, which developed into a new 'empire' of anti-Roman tribes raiding the Empire in the 430s independent of Roman politics. But the West would not have lost control of the manpower or taxes of Britain, parts of Gaul and Spain, and later North Africa, and would have been in a much stronger position by the 450s.

Ultimately the first breach in the Empire's defences and major blow to its prestige was the East's military humiliation by the Goths in 378, in which the incompetence of its Emperor Valens played a major part. He owed his position to the fortuitous election of his brother Valentinian, who then chose him as his colleague, to rule the Empire in 364, following the sudden deaths of Emperors Julian and Jovian, and indeed Valentinian had been warned against choosing him.[32] Moreover, the influx of Goths across the lower Danube, fleeing the Huns on the steppes, led to corrupt Roman officials mishandling them, extorting payments for inadequate supplies, and driving initially peaceful if armed incomers into revolt. As seen above, the venal black marketeer Roman commander Lupicinus then failed to decapitate the

Gothic leadership and turned Gothic suspicion into rebellion. Valens was preoccupied with Persia, and unlike the situations in 331 and 359 was unable to handle the influx of militarily coherent, armed immigrants personally or to send enough troops to outmatch them.

Once rebellion broke out he marched into Thrace to tackle the Goths without waiting for reinforcements from his nephew Gratian in the West, though the latter was held up by trouble on the Rhine so Valens may have been anxious to strike before winter fell. The resultant battle was on 9 August. Valens was asked not to attack by the cautious Western general Richomer, commander of the advance-party sent to aid him by Emperor Gratian, but listened to the more confident Eastern general Sebastian instead.[33] But Valens could have been deposed earlier. If a well-supported Constantinople revolt by Julian's cousin Procopius had succeeded in toppling him in 365–6 he would not even have been Emperor at this point, though Gratian was unlikely to have assisted a usurper who had deposed his uncle. A different ruler in the East who was more interested in the Danube than in Persia in the 370s, better handling of the refugee Goths in 376–8, or a victory instead of defeat at Adrianople would have prevented the Goths establishing an autonomous state in the Balkans, which the East had to concede in 382. It would thus have prevented Alaric's career of unchecked defiance within both Empires.

Chapter 3

Long-term Problems, the Nature of Roman Instability in Transmitting Power, and What Could Easily have Happened

Earlier 'What Ifs': the crises that led to the creation of the 'Later Empire'

In a similar manner to the disaster at Adrianople, a victory against the Goths in their earlier incursion of 251 – when Emperor Decius was killed and the Balkans opened to ravaging – would have avoided sparking off a round of 'copy-cat' invasions by emboldened Germans. An experienced commander who his troops had hailed as Emperor after he defeated earlier attacks and forced him to turn on his master Emperor Philip (or so he claimed), Decius had had problems in bringing the Goths to battle in Thrace in 250–1. Logically the invaders had spread out over too wide an area to be confronted quickly in one grouping and had to be confined in a manageable area. This was an inevitable result of the time lag between them crossing the Danube and the Emperor arriving from Italy. There had been trouble on the Danube from the Carpi through the 240s, so a major attack was not that surprising, but placing a local commander in the area with a large enough army was politically dangerous, as he might use his troops against Decius as Decius had done to Philip. The delay in tackling the Goths probably owed much to Decius' caution after recent revolts. A stable and unchallenged ruler could have risked having a senior commander or more troops in the region or both. This is with the caveat that manpower was available and had not been diverted to face Persia, we simply do not know. In any case, both Decius and his elder son were killed in battle. A bout of internal Roman revolts followed Decius' death, with his surviving son Hostilianus, young and inexperienced, being superseded by one general after another.

The wave of German attacks, at sea across the Black Sea as well as on land, was followed by another invasion by the opportunistic Sassanids and the diversion of Emperor Valerian and many of his troops to the East to fight them in 260. The Emperor's disastrous military failure there and capture at a parley by Great King Shapur's troops broke the Empire up into chaos and opened many more provinces to ravaging. The humiliation was played up by Shapur, whose ambitions seem to have been to restore the ancient Achaemenid Empire of Darius and Xerxes that had reached to the Aegean. Reviving the ancient tradition of rock-cut glorification of the Persian Great King for all to see on the main road from Iraq up onto the Iranian plateau, he created a carving of Valerian kneeling before him as a suppliant, and was rumoured to have stuffed his body as a trophy when he died. In practical terms, the Persian invasion of Syria had to be driven back by Odenathus, the Roman client-ruler of Palmyra, as the shattered Roman army in the East retreated into Asia Minor and became split up in claims of Imperial power by its commanders. A wave of rebellions left Valerian's son Gallienus with control of the central Roman lands but the West (Gaul, Spain, Britain, the Rhine) lost to a breakaway regime under Postumus and the Levant controlled by the autonomous city-state of Palmyra under Odenathus and later his widow Zenobia. Both states were reconquered by Aurelian after 270, but the multiple crises led to the emergence of a much more centralised, bureaucratic, and tax-heavy Roman state.[1]

Would this form of state have ever emerged had the Empire not faced disaster in the 250s? Or was the loss of Roman manpower in the plague of the 250s sufficient to embolden attackers and fatally weaken the Roman army anyway? Indeed, it can be argued that the nature of copycat revolts, one successful rebel general's example encouraging another to challenge him later, means that the chronic and disastrous instability of the mid-third century Empire owed a lot to recent political failure. The Empire had been invaded by large-scale German tribal forces at a time of plague in the 160s, but Marcus Aurelius had fought them off and the Empire did not collapse. Was this because the Empire of the 160s did not have to cope with the Sassanid state too, or was it due to mid-second century Roman political stability? It is noticeable that the Emperors whose death and capture sparked disaster in 251 and 260 (Decius and Valerian) were both usurpers, not secure long-term rulers from an established dynasty.

Would the Empire have fared better had it had a stable line of unchallenged rulers after the extinction of the Severan dynasty in 235?

There were no long-lived rulers or secure successions from this event until the creation of Diocletian's new system of government after 284. It is possible that the loss of both Emperor Septimius Severus' adult sons in 211–17 (Geta murdered by his brother Caracalla, the latter a tyrant murdered by his most senior commander) was what ushered in this dangerous instability, given the inadequacies of their distant cousins and successors Elagabalus and Alexander Severus. The tyrannical Caracalla was murdered for self-preservation by his competent Praetorian Praefect Macrinus in 217, but the latter was seen as dynastically illegitimate by his mutinous troops; some of the latter duly acclaimed Caracalla's cousin (and reputed son) Elagabalus, the teenage High Priest of the Syrian sun-god at Emesa. Macrinus was defeated in battle and killed, and the victor and his entourage moved to Rome, taking the sacred stone (was this a meteorite?) of the god with them. A transvestite bisexual exhibitionist, Elagabalus was murdered in 222; Alexander, his cousin and successor, was seen as dominated by his mother and was murdered too on a Rhine campaign (235). A round of coups commenced, with the troops' capable but lowborn choice of sovereign, the Thracian ex-ranker Maximin, facing revolt in Rome and Africa.

After 235 no Emperor could secure stability, even the militarily competent Maximin and Philip the Arab. Arguably, the fault for all this lay with Septimius Severus for not killing his violent, and fratricidal elder son Caracalla, who had possibly already plotted his murder, and ensuring that the less dangerous Geta succeeded him; the latter and his capable adviser Papinian could have secured stability for a vital period of the early-mid third century. Severus' stated plea to his sons on his deathbed to live at peace with each other, keep the troops happy, and not bother about anyone else was wishful thinking. If he did not want to kill his son he could have despatched him to a remote island, as Augustus did with his allegedly violent and politically dangerous grandson Agrippa Postumus.[2]

The Empire's problems in the third and fourth centuries. How might they have been reduced by earlier military successes?

In the longer term, it is also arguable that the nature of the German-threatened Empire's outer defences in the later fourth century, easily crossable rivers, the Rhine and Danube, weakened its defences. In the first decade of the millennium Augustus' generals had attempted to annex the lands between Rhine and Elbe, bringing many of the local tribes into the Empire, only to meet with disaster in the Teutoberg Forest in AD 9. The conquest of lower Germany had then been abandoned. Even if it had succeeded, a combination of Roman parsimony about garrisons and the ever-likely civil wars could easily have occasioned a successful revolt before the fourth century. In the 100s Trajan had responded to repeated Dacian attacks on the middle Danube by advancing his frontier to the eastern Carpathians, and in the 170s Marcus Aurelius had temporarily overrun the Czech lands.

Maintenance of all three occupations would have brought many of the tribes who threatened the Empire under its rule, with their warriors serving in the Roman army, like the previously hostile Gauls from the 50s BC, instead of raiding Roman lands. The remaining Germanic territory South of the Carpathians, that of the Iazyges between middle Danube and Theiss, could have been occupied or left as an allied kingdom under pro-Roman chieftains. The military occupation of a slice of territory was in any event less important than its neutralisation as a threat. Rome had long operated through a cheap system of allied kingdoms that did not entail direct rule, as with the Germanic tribal realm of Maroboduus on the Danube and the multiplicity of Levantine Greco-Aramaic states. Provided that a territory was not immanently hostile to the Empire, occupation usually occurred when a Roman ruler needed to prove his military credentials by an impressive conquest, as with rising politician Caesar in Gaul in 58 BC and ageing new Emperor Claudius in AD 43. Indeed, it is worth remarking that despite the disastrous defeat of a large Roman army in the German forests East of the Rhine by Arminius in AD 9 the situation had been partly rectified by Tiberius' nephew Germanicus before he died in 19.[3] The latter was ambitious and arrogant, and made much of his physical resemblance to Alexander the Great.

Had Germanicus succeeded Tiberius as planned, could he have decided to add to his reputation by invading and annexing territory beyond the Rhine or Danube? Doing this would have entailed either moving part of the garrison of Lower Germany (four legions on the Rhine) into the area, risking revolt to their rear, or raising more legions. Augustus had had trouble in finding new troops after losing three legions in the German disaster of AD 9, having to arm slaves, so would it have been difficult to create even two new legions to help hold down the lands to the Elbe?[4] There was a political advantage in creating this new force for a new province (Transrhenus?), as it would serve as a check on the ambitions of the military commanders in Lower Germany. In AD 69 their commander Vitellius rose in revolt against new Emperor Galba and fought his way to Rome; could he have done so had he faced a local rival who was still loyal?

The precedent of Roman occupation of a similar agriculturally based tribal society in Gaul shows that local rebellion was still a problem (occasionally) in Tiberius' time, seventy years after Caesar's conquest, and there was to be a major eruption under Julius Civilis in northeastern Gaul once Rome fell into civil war. The latter revolt in 69 was aided from beyond the Roman frontier on the Rhine, and had the Empire advanced to the Elbe some time after AD 9 or had Varus defeated Arminius then and saved three legions for use in an occupation, revolt was still probable later. Crucially, the Empire kept existing tribal units as administrative sub-provinces in Britain and Gaul, and would probably have done the same in Germany. This aided a sense of identity among the locals, as shown in the tribal-based nature of revolt in Gaul in the early 20s and 69. Breaking up the existing tribal landowners' landed power-base by atomising the social structure would have been more effective in preventing revolt, which would have entailed mass-deportations as in Dacia under Trajan after 100. Was this the successful policy that the Romans adopted in keeping the Iceni quiet after Boudicca's revolt in 60–1? The name of the Iceni never re-emerged in the fifth century, unlike other British tribal kingdoms. And could a similar break-up of Germanic tribal polities between Rhine and Danube in the first century AD have produced an invaluable long-term German boost to the Roman army that aided it in its third and fourth century wars?

Such territory may not have been fully occupied as a province (like Germany west of the Rhine and the Gallic Belgica) but just dominated by legionary outposts, leaving open the chance of revolt at times of weakness, as with the Batavian region of the Rhine-mouth in AD 69–70. The rule of this region had been left to its own local chieftains, provided that they supplied troops to the Empire; the same strategy was followed for allied British kingdoms beyond the frontier in the 40s and 50s, e.g. Cartimandua's Brigantes and Prasutagas' Iceni. The main aim of the Antonine occupation of Bohemia in the 170s seems to have been to prevent more invasions of Italy, and this aim may have been achieved without creation of a formal province. In the event Marcus' death in 180 and Commodus' withdrawal meant that Marcus' war-aims of around 177 are unclear.[5]

The effect of military domination and partial occupation would still have been the same: to prevent the emergence of the new super-tribes, the coalitions of disparate German peoples under single dynamic leaders which invaded the Empire in the mid-third century. The use of new names to identify them in place of the terminology of the first century AD suggests new tribal groupings emerging, probably under active warlords who forged coalitions. The regular recruitment of their menfolk to the Roman army would have kept the latter as allies to, not preying on, the Empire. The Germans would have been sent to serve well away from their home territory to minimise the chances of revolt, as with the Empire's Sarmatian nomad allies from the lower Danube.

Holding down such an extended dominion would have had its problems, not least revolt. Romanization of tribal peoples was a slow process and some of the Gauls revolted in the early 20s AD , followed by the major Rhine revolt of Civilis in 69–70. But a mountain frontier eastwards from the Elbe Gap near Leipzig to the Iron Gates on the lower Danube, broken only by a few passes and occasional low-lying regions like the Ostrava Gap/Beskids, would have been easier to defend from penetration than the river frontier, and would certainly have required no more troops. The main danger would have been of a still-restless tribal population hankering after its freedom and ready to revolt at times of crisis with help from beyond the frontier, as with parts of northeast Gaul as late as AD 69, over a century after Caesar's conquest. That problem, however, had not been insurmountable once Rome regained its military cohesion and Vespasian could send troops to suppress the Gallic revolt under Civilis; using the same argument, the Danube-Carpathian lands were no less controllable for the period after 180. There would however have been longer distances involved, hampering quick reaction. Also, the poorer soil of the north German plains and the forests would not provide useful produce for the Roman economy; costs would have been high.

The numbers of invasions that the Empire faced from the 170s onwards would thus have been reduced, though attacks from Wallachia across the lower Danube (e.g. the Gothic invasion of 251 and Gothic refugee-movement of 376) would have been unaffected. The Persian threat from the 230s would have been equally serious, though the disaster of 260 (when Emperor Valerian was captured and the East dissolved into chaos) owed much to the distractions of the Rhine and Danube invasions that resulted in an under-manned Eastern army. The third century Empire would still have been subject to major losses from the plague of 252, though not necessarily as many civil wars given the absence of certain domestic crises such as Commodus' reign, the civil war of 193–7, and the successive coups and revolts from 235 to 260. Internal stability would have decreased the distractions of civil war, which aided the invaders, enabling an unchallenged Emperor to meet the main attacks head-on with his army as Marcus Aurelius did after 169.

State structures and the succession: from 'First Citizen' to hereditary autocrat

It can be argued that each successful coup or revolt from 192 had a cumulative effect on the Empire's stability, and thus on its long-term chances of survival. No arrangement for the political succession is of course infallible, though a rigorous selection process or a definitive genetic right of heirship can present distinct advantages. The most stable political systems have relied on a collective leadership rather than one individual, as with the oligarchy of medieval Venice with its figurehead Doge, but this was unrealistic for an age of monarchy and military leadership, particularly in the Greek-Middle Eastern areas of the Empire.

The whole tradition of government in Rome had evolved from the concentration of political and military power in two annually appointed senior magistrates, with a temporary dictatorship for emergencies but a taboo on any notion of kingship; it was Augustus' genius to introduce a hidden monarchy while avoiding the open single rule which Caesar had not troubled to disguise. The vital role of military power in a far-flung state needing large armies that the government had to control to avoid the turbulence of the late Republic made one man's ascendancy inevitable. There was a need for a visible individual as the centre of control (and of cultic worship), as Caesar, Antony, and Augustus duly recognised. The last attempt to re-create a stable collective aristocratic leadership, by Sulla in 82–80 BC, had foundered on patrician feuds and powerful provincial army commanders. The same would have been likely to happen had Pompey and the Senate defeated Caesar in 48 BC or Brutus and Cassius defeated the Caesareans in 42 BC.

There was not yet the necessary structure of government, or acceptability for it, to create a rigid, top-down bureaucracy in the early Empire. In this case a cabal of ministers heading permanent departments would rule the state and the Emperor be its nominal front-man, whose personal failings and possible removal did not affect the viability of the state. This sort of regime emerged in centralised dynastic China from the middle Han period, under a succession of weak Emperors. Ultimately, in China this did not prevent failure of leadership; inter-ministerial feuds erupted, civil war and revolt followed, and repeated break-ups into rival provincial polities followed that. But China had by then evolved a tradition of centralised bureaucracy, as created in the state structure of the kingdom of Jin in the 'Era of Warring States' and imposed on the entire country by the unifying 'First Emperor' Jin Shih Huangdi. The nearest bureaucratic equivalent in the Mediterranean world was the complex governmental structure of Ptolemaic Egypt, which carried on functioning irrespective of the incompetent sovereigns and bloody feuds within the ruling dynasty. In traditionalist Rome, government had been a simpler and more ad hoc affair with the small number of senior officials assisted by their private households and their groups of personal 'amici'.

It had only slowly adapted to the massive political and economic demands of empire in the last two centuries BC, with its resistance to change aiding the political chaos of the Late Republic. Even with power and Mediterranean-wide official business concentrated on the Emperor, Augustus and his successors governed through the traditional means of a senior magistrate's personal household. There was contemporary criticism of the emergence of low-class freedmen household officials wielding immense power under the later Julio-Claudians. There was always something ad hoc about the early Empire's Imperial government, as analysed by Fergus Millar, and much was left to local self-rule by governors and city councils who sought Imperial advice and instructions when necessary, as shown by the famous correspondence between Trajan and Pliny the Younger.[6]

The creation of a large-scale and intrusive bureaucracy had to wait until the later third and early fourth centuries, and is plausibly ascribed to a specific political strategy formulated by the administratively minded Diocletian. This bore some resemblance to the hierarchic governmental systems of Sassanid Persia and China, and notably had a Persian-style formal court based at a 'Sacred Palace' instead of the more democratic courts of most early Emperors. The Emperor was cut off from direct contact with his subjects, surrounded by a hierarchy of court officials and Persian-style eunuchs, and in an increasingly religious age an effort was made to have the court reflect the order and ceremonial of Heaven (firstly in its Olympian guise, but soon in a Christian context).

It may be significant that Diocletian, unlike his militarily successful predecessors Claudius II, Aurelian, Probus, and Carus was a civilian (Greek) bureaucrat not a general. He may have decided to trust in a foolproof state system, not personal charisma as the Illyrian soldier-emperors from 268 to 284 had done. The system of a godlike Emperor isolated at court, which he created, was then kept on by the next long-ruling Emperor, Constantine, who could have reverted to a less formal mode of ruling. It is not sufficient to claim that a huge court was the inevitable accompaniment of autocracy, as the Illyrian Emperors, and even Septimius Severus much earlier, had ruled by naked force rather than in tune with early Empire deference to the Senate.

Megalomaniac Emperor Caius 'Caligula' had seen himself as a god and used the Temple of Castor in the Forum as the entrance to his palace. Nero had built a colossal statue of himself as the sun-god Helios and ruled as a sun-king from his 'Domus Aurea' in the mid-60s, and Domitian in the 80s had ruled as 'dominus et deus' ('lord and god') and built a large throne-room in the Imperial residence on the Palatine.[7] This fitted in with Eastern notions of the ruler as semi-divine but not with Roman practice; it was a different matter from so-called 'Emperor-worship', a universal practice in the Early Empire which was more a matter of a cult of respectful loyalty to the status of the ruler than treating him as divine. On all three occasions this innovation had been reversed by their successors, so the same could have been done to Diocletian's 'Oriental' Court.

But instead Constantine continued the process, and made a further break with tradition by creating a new Christian capital, inaugurated in 330: 'New Rome' (later called 'Constantinople') on the Bosphorus. The idea of a permanent Imperial capital in the East for a locally resident Emperor had been Diocletian's, but he had chosen the established Bithynian city of Nicomedia. Constantine set up a much more radical project, with a new and carefully planned city (based on a previous, smaller Greek town) with the facilities that were to become appropriate for medieval Christian cities (e.g. a cathedral). He also set up a Senate and encouraged aristocratic families to move to the city, going further than his predecessors had done; the new capital was clearly meant to supersede the old one.

It was also linked to a huge and dominant court and a regular round of Imperial ritual that added mystique to the Imperial office, though the unique and non-Roman nature of this may owe more to hindsight, as Constantinople was the only Late Roman capital to survive for centuries. Constantine still kept the senior role of Western Emperor for his eldest sons, Crispus (killed 326) and then Constantine II, who were based at Trier. The literary evidence certainly hints at him having a form of megalomania in his later years, which may have influenced the boldness and grandiosity of his plans. His family life ended up replaying ancient Greek myth, as he killed Crispus at the behest of the latter's stepmother Fausta and then killed her for false accusations, an echo of Theseus, Hippolytus, and Phaedra.[8]

Augustus had laid claim to the loyalty of the troops of his late great-uncle's armies from 44BC as his genetic heir, the new Caesar, and duly outmanoeuvred the more experienced senior general Antony. The new system focussed loyalty on the 'Princeps' in his role as 'Caesar', with a family surname turning into an administrative title, and the hereditary basis of power was established. Significantly, the ailing Augustus' designated heir in 23BC was his young and untried genetic heir, nephew and son-in-law Marcellus, not an experienced political and military lieutenant like Agrippa; in later years the choice fell on his equally inexperienced grandsons. The unique position he had created for himself became a hereditary monarchy, though with the technical caveat of confirmation of powers by the Senate. When the latter attempted to choose their own (or no) candidate for ruler after Caligula's murder in January AD41 they were swiftly reined in by the Praetorian Guard.[9]

Augustus eventually attempted to lay down a form of succession by the most experienced member of the Imperial family rather than by father-son descent, arranging for his stepson Tiberius to be followed by Tiberius' older, militarily senior nephew Germanicus, who was married to Augustus' own grand-daughter, not by Tiberius' son Drusus. Drusus (maybe two years younger than Germanicus) would then be followed by Germanicus' sons. Tiberius kept to this faithfully, and put Germanicus' sons ahead of Drusus' (under-age) son Tiberius Gemellus in the queue to be Emperor. Arguably, Claudius did the same in putting his stepson Nero ahead of his own, younger son Britannicus. This system then evolved to father-son descent in the second century, when an Emperor had a son or brother, which was not the case from 81 to 161.

But a wholly hereditary system of rule, whereby the next eligible adult male (son, brother, or cousin) inherits irrespective of capability, introduces the risk of incompetence or insanity. This is followed by the overthrow of the incumbent by a more competent but illegitimate successor, who can then be challenged by ambitious relatives or military commanders. One coup leads to another, a minority is the inevitable opportunity for adults to overthrow the under-age sovereign, and prolonged instability is only ended by a strong ruler. This is what happened to the English monarchy in 1399, 1461, 1470–1, and 1483–5, though other kingdoms (such as France in 987–1328) had a luckier run of unchallenged capable heirs (usually adult) in direct succession.

If a state dominated by its officer-corps or provincial generals turns into a hereditary monarchy, any succession of an inexperienced minor can lead to coups by the military, as seen by the repeated fate of Sultans' under-age heirs in Mameluke Egypt after 1260. This fate happened to Gordianus III of Rome, teenage ruler in 238–44, at the hands of his Praetorian Praefect Philip. If there is an heir entrusted with a governorship and army outside the capital, they can then overthrow their sovereign, as Julian did to Constantius II in 360–1, and as occasional Ottoman Sultans did, e.g. Selim I to Bayezid II in 1512. If a state is split among a multiplicity of eligible adult heirs as co-rulers, mutual assistance is less likely than endless struggles for supreme power, of which invaders then take advantage, as with Carolingian Francia among Louis the Pious' sons in the 840s. If the state is lucky, one heir can quickly destroy his rivals and reassert central authority, as Bayezid II and Selim I did in the Ottoman civil wars of 1481 and 1512. If it is not, a standoff and permanent division ensues as in Francia post-843.

In Rome's case, the split of power among multiple heirs in the fourth century often led to civil wars among the rivals which only ended with one candidate's victory, as after Diocletian's abdication in 305 and Constantine's death in 337. The division between Valentinian and Valens in 364 was better managed. It was not fatal to a militarily strong Empire, despite the loss of manpower in internecine warfare; but after the split of 395 the mutual mistrust of Arcadius' East and Honorius' West was to give Alaric's Gothic armies a crucial opportunity to play one Emperor against the other and militarily overshadow both.

In the case of Rome's principal contemporary equal, Han China and its heirs, a succession of weak rulers in thrall to a feuding court bureaucracy and the repeated accession of minors led to instability and decline at the centre of power and ultimately to successful military challenge from the provinces. Once a regular succession of competent adults to the throne failed, central power weakened and the Emperors became puppets of their ministers, as with several initially successful Chinese dynasties after the Han, most notably the T'ang in the ninth century. In Japan, the powerful court dynasties surrounding the throne in the ninth century and afterwards even kept the throne restricted to under-age rulers in order to secure a succession of lucrative regencies. In Sassanid Persia from 226, a more centralised state with a more unified army than that of its Parthian predecessor, a long-lasting dynasty survived under rulers of varying merits with only a few internal non-dynastic coups, e.g. in 590. This was probably due to the overwhelming power of the central as opposed to provincial armies, which coup-prone Parthia had lacked.

No provincial warlord would think it worth challenging a State with overwhelming military superiority. That factor probably kept most ambitious Roman provincial commanders from challenging the Emperor in Rome until the rule of Nero deteriorated and made the central authorities vulnerable in 68. Once there was a hiatus in Rome or one commander dared to rebel, it was open season for would-be rebels to join in, as in AD 69, 193, and 260.

The reliance of the Roman political system on the merits of one man, as introduced by Augustus, had ended earlier instability. The repeated politico-military struggles and usurpations of the period from the Gracchi to Actium had been caused primarily by the feuding over power of the rival senior noble families and ambitious new men of the late Republican patriciate, and centred on the senior provincial governors' possession of armies. Ultimately, with Julius Caesar and then Octavian-Augustus, only one political leader was left with full control of all the Republic's armies, and the latter, as 'Princeps', ensured that the armies remained loyal to him and his family and that the political system was unobtrusively turned into a monarchy while remaining technically a republic. Unlike Caesar, he did not flout the cherished 'mos maiorum' and he enabled the Senatorial aristocracy to live within the fiction that the traditional constitution was being maintained, once he had slaughtered all real or potential serious challengers.

The succession problems of his dynasty are well known, and were survived by luck as much as by good judgement in the case of two mentally unstable rulers (Caius 'Caligula' and Nero) who were murdered and one civil war (AD 69). Luck could have been better and there have been no tyranny, for example if Tiberius had been succeeded by his original heirs, but his nephew Germanicus, his son the younger Drusus, and the former's son Nero Caesar all predeceased him, possibly violently. Caligula was only Germanicus' third son and was an unlikely successor until the destruction of his elder brothers, Nero by the jealous Sejanus and Drusus (II) by Tiberius for betraying his family to Sejanus. Nor did Caligula's worst traits become apparent until after a serious illness months after he succeeded Tiberius in 37; did this illness emotionally unbalance him?

Britannicus was only in his early teens when Claudius died, and the latter had political reasons for advancing his older stepbrother Nero as senior heir.

Nero was more closely descended from Augustus and his mother's family were popular with the troops.[10] Possibly Claudius even suspected that Britannicus' nymphomaniac mother Messalina had used one of her lovers to father the boy, or that his enemies, led by Nero's mother Agrippina, would say that. But an older and more viable Britannicus could have succeeded his father as an adult around 60–62. Claudius might not have adopted his stepson Nero as senior heir, or Claudius discovered Agrippina's poison plot in time in October 54. The Julio-Claudian succession system would have worked then and not have seemed inferior to that of the Antonines in retrospect. The Empire would not have had to wait to 96–180 for a run of good Emperors.

Thereafter the Roman Empire had been lucky in its transmission of the succession from 96 to 180, no ruler except Marcus Aurelius having an adult close relative to succeed him. But the succession was not always smooth, as with the mysterious political executions of four consuls early in Hadrian's reign and the early death of his chosen heir Aelius Verus. It was unlucky thereafter. There was not a conscious system of choosing the best man as Edward Gibbon and other historians believed; if an Emperor had a son of whatever age or quality, as Marcus with Commodus, the choice of heir was clear, and the army would probably have baulked at accepting any substitute.[11] Marcus would have had problems had he proposed to set his incompetent son Commodus aside, assuming that the latter's faults were already visible by the time of Marcus' death; the most blatant acts of Commodus' misrule occurred after some years in power. The new Emperor (aged nineteen) was taken advantage of by flattering Court favourites such as Saoterus and later Cleander, a perennial problem for a vain and impressionable young autocrat (as shown by the initially good Nero).[12] For that matter, it should be remembered that Commodus had a twin and a younger brother, both of whom died young; had either of them replaced him on his murder in December 192 there would not have been a succession crisis and civil war then either. Instead the chosen new ruler, the competent but brusque and disciplinarian general Pertinax, alienated the over-indulged Praetorian Guard and was soon murdered too.

The run of poor or easily challenged rulers in the third century was not inevitable, and some Emperors ducked their responsibility to provide an adequate and unchallenged heir, most crucially Septimius Severus with Caracalla and Geta in 211. It should also be remarked that the Empire had been lucky in that a new civil war did not erupt in 97–8 after the unexpected extinction of the Flavian dynasty. The shaky regime of the elderly, obscure, and heirless Nerva, defied by its own guardsmen, swiftly adopted a powerful and charismatic military commander (Trajan) as its heir to ward off another civil war. Nerva was fortunate to avoid the fate of the similarly placed Galba thirty years earlier. There was no certainty in 193 that Pertinax would not be able to control the Guard, or that he would be killed rather than just defied as Nerva had been in 97. Had he been more careful or tactful, this veteran commander (aged sixty-six in 192/3) could have averted murder and civil war and passed on the throne to his chosen heir, either Septimius Severus, an earlier protégé, or the latter's rival Clodius Albinus. Instead, the son-less second and third century Emperors sought to bolster legitimacy by adopting their heirs, which was bizarre at times, as when Elagabalus adopted his cousin Alexander Severus, four years younger than him. Septimius Severus retrospectively had himself adopted posthumously by Pertinax.[13]

The habit of provincial military challenges to the centre of power had been a threat to the Roman polity ever since the emergence of powerful provincial armies. Sulla had used his armies in Greece to overthrow the regime of Marius' heirs in 83–2 BC, Caesar had marched on Rome from Gaul in 49 BC, and in 43 the Senate was helpless before the triple alliance of Antony, Octavian, and Lepidus. It recurred throughout the early Empire at times of crisis and uncertain leadership in Rome, potentially (though aborted) with Gaetulicus in AD 39 and Scribonianus in 42 and fully with the civil war of 69. Augustus, lucky in the possession of a large family, had where possible kept the armies in his loyal and competent male relatives' hands. It resumed with the instability following Pertinax's murder in 193 (though there was an abortive revolt as early as the rumours of Marcus' death in 175), and became endemic after 235. But once the chances of a revolt succeeding had become greater, with the lack of an recognisably dominating ruler and stable dynasty in Rome, the temptation to challenge the Emperor became greater. One successful revolt bred another, and in turn the preoccupation of the current incumbent with survival meant that external enemies were emboldened.

The safest military solution to this was that adopted by the late Roman state, probably through a deliberate plan by Diocletian which Constantine reinforced; the central army at the Emperor's disposal, the 'comitatus', outnumbered any provincial army and the old Augustan provinces were split into many smaller ones so that no provincial commander had enough men to risk challenging the government. Each province also now had a separate civil and military governor. This did not stop some bold commanders, as with Maximus in Britain in 383, a desperate man like Silvanus in Trier in 355, or a junior Imperial prince commanding a 'comitatus' on a threatened frontier, as with Julian in Gaul in 360; but it made revolt more risky and so halted the epidemic of risings in the 250s and 260s.[14]

In the 250s the instability at the centre, coherent military challenge from Persia, and opportunistic attacks from Germanic tribal coalitions across the Rhine and Danube – all feeding off each other – came together at a time when the Empire's manpower was being undermined by plague. The results were catastrophic. But what if there had been greater political stability within the Empire at this juncture?

The 250s and after: dynastic mischance and its exploitation

Apart from the military advantages of a firm and continuing response to outside threats, greater political stability from a secure succession process would have enabled the Empire to call upon its full revenues for and troops from all unaffected provinces to aid the government and military. The plague of 252 would still have diminished both, making the chances of defeat and a civil war higher, particularly with the opportunistic Persian Great King Shapur I ready to invade. The defeat of the Eastern armies, sack of Antioch, local power-vacuum, and seizure of the politico-military initiative by Odenathus and Zenobia of Palmyra in the 260s were probable if the Rhine or Danube wars had tied down the Western armies. If the Emperor marched East and had no capable colleague to guard the threatened Rhine, a revolt on the latter was probable. In real life the local commander Postumus deposed Gallienus' young son and set up a breakaway Gallic-Spanish-British realm in 260 and it was not reconquered until Aurelian had dealt with Palmyra in 272–3.

Recovery should have been quicker without the multiplicity of revolts in 259–67, and the strain on resources to pay for the enlarged Diocletianic army and civil service less without the economic dislocation caused by ravaging across many provinces. The efforts usually attributed to a bureaucratically minded Diocletian to secure adequate manpower for vital professions (the military and agriculture in particular) centred on the solution of making them hereditary, while economic problems were tackled by similar legislation. Inflation was solved by being banned, the reaction of a despot like a modern Third World dictator. Diocletian's crucial lack of a male heir led to an ingenious attempt to solve the endemic problem of the succession by another administrative solution. The two new Emperors, of East and West, would each adopt a competent adult heir who would serve as deputy ruler or 'Caesar' under him before succeeding to the throne. Was this only suggested because Diocletian had no son? This idea was unworkable given human nature and the desire of the men involved to pass on their power within their families, and it was duly wrecked by a complicated power struggle among Diocletian's heirs after he retired in 305.

The outcome was the personal ascendancy of Constantine as sole ruler in 324, followed by his own attempt to divide up the Empire among his sons and nephews, which also collapsed in bloodshed in 337. The successive bouts of political instability and civil wars which followed saw no dynasty surviving with stable adult male rule for more than a few decades, although the loss of manpower in civil war did not immediately affect the Empire's survival when it lacked external challengers. But indirectly the effects of dynastic strife commenced the process of political disintegration; Valentinian I's unwise choice of his brother Valens as his co-ruler in 364, criticised at the time, presented the East with the man who mishandled the Gothic crisis of 376–8 and was killed in Rome's first serious military defeat at German hands since the 250s. After the death of Valens and destruction of the Eastern army at Adrianople in 378 the Goths, initially a flood of refugees from Hunnic incursions into their steppe homeland not a hostile invading army, were able to maintain their own polity within the borders of the Empire. Nominal military vassals at first, after their accommodation with Theodosius in 381, their Gothic-commanded forces were outside the Roman chain of command, and were able to exploit the vacuum in leadership that followed Theodosius' death in 395.

At this point, the Empire's physical loss of control of the provinces, and their manpower and revenues, commenced, and the Germanic warlords within its borders began to be a serious military challenge. The spiral of Decline and Fall, began, more specifically meaning a growing loss of resources and military power in the West at a time of rising challenges from unchecked Germanic warlords who could not be intimidated or bought off indefinitely. There has been much argument over the size of the barbarian hordes, the amount of damage and economic dislocation, and the possible exaggeration of their depredations. But the loss of Imperial political control of the outlying provinces, leaving a rump state at the mercy of its German-led armies in the 460s, speaks for itself.

The survival of the Western Empire: feasible with better luck?

A larger state: a match for the Germans and the East?
The survival of Theodosius I, only forty-seven at his death in 395, for another decade or two, putting him in the position to combat the Germanic

crossing of the Rhine into Gaul in 406, should have made that attack containable like the previous invasions of the mid-270s and 350s. Probably Alaric the Goth would not have risked his attacks on Italy from 402. Even if the Empire had faced at least one of these challenges, an experienced adult Emperor would have been in a stronger position to meet them than the regent Stilicho. The Germans would not have had the opportunity to spread unchecked over Gaul, Spain, and later Africa from 406, detaching rich provinces from the Empire and so reducing its ability to pay for a militarily superior central army that could defeat tribal based armies led by opportunistic German warlords. Barbarian kingdoms would not have coalesced around successful warlords in Roman territory and become more powerful than the Imperial armies, or the central Imperial army been reduced to over-reliance on king-making German generals with their own loyal entourages, e.g. Ricimer and Gundobad. Crucially, the Vandals would not have been able to set up their kingdom in Africa from 429 and deliver the major blow of the sack of Rome in 455, ravaging the Italian (and other) coasts for decades thereafter and undermining trade. The Goths would not have been able to operate freely in Italy against an undefended city of Rome and a militarily weak government in Ravenna after Stilicho's assassination in 408, or set up a kingdom in Southern Gaul in 418.

Thereafter, a more powerful Western Roman army, though probably still with a major autonomous allied German contingent, would have been available under Aetius to meet the attacks of the Huns. The latter might still have been undefeated until 451–2, due to earlier concentration on the weaker East, but German refugees from Attila's empire fleeing to the West would have reinforced the Roman army. Even in the circumstances of a weakened Empire that had lost control of its African corn-supplies and much of Gaul, Aetius, who had usefully lived in exile among the Huns earlier and knew their tactics, was able to muster a Romano-German coalition to defeat Attila's incursion into Gaul. How much better would he have fared had the Empire not already lost much of its revenues and power?

The assassination of Aetius by his jealous sovereign Valentinian III in 454 led to a vacuum in Roman military leadership, a new power-struggle at court, and Gaiseric's physically and psychologically damaging sack of the capital in 455. It also led to Aetius' successor Petronius Maximus, allegedly implicated in his murder, seeking alliance with the Goths, which Rome had avoided since 408, and the latter securing a free hand to operate in Spain and extend their power there. What if Aetius had escaped the attack and overthrown his monarch? (He was already rumoured to be intending to install his son

Gaudentius as the next ruler, married to Valentinian's daughter.)[15] As praised by his contemporary and panegyricist Merobaudes in his laudatory poems of around 439 and 443, the indefatigable Aetius had restored order to Gaul in the 430s and defeated Germans and 'bacaudae' alike – and even held up Gaiseric's advance in Africa temporarily by bringing in Aspar and Eastern troops in 435. The relative stability he brought after three decades of chaos speaks for itself, as does his successful leadership of the Romano-German coalition to defeat Attila somewhere near Chalons in 451. The collapse of Roman power in Gaul and Gaiseric's attack on the capital only followed his death, so what if his rule had continued?

The defeat, containment, and death of Attila in 451–3, followed by Aetius' continuing ascendancy at court, would have enabled Aetius to recruit many of the subject tribes who revolted against the Huns in 454 to be allies of Rome. The Western Empire would have continued as a major military power into the later fifth century with most of its provinces intact, and Aetius had competent officers to succeed him in power such as Aegidius and Majorian. In real life Aegidius ruled parts of northern Gaul as a Romano-Gallic warlord after 455, and Majorian became Emperor in 457. Such competent and energetic rulers, with appropriate armies, would probably have dissuaded or defeated further provincial revolts, and if North Africa and its corn supplies had still been in Vandal hands reconquest would have been a priority. The Empire would have been manageable without outlying regions of Gaul (lost to Goths, Burgundians, and Franks) and Spain (lost to the Suevi).

Either a strong military leader or a legitimate Theodosian would have served as a focus for stability in the 460s and after. With or without the continuation of the dynasty of Theodosius, the Empire's military leadership and control of resources would have been adequate for survival on the politico-socio-economic basis of the state of the fourth century. It would have been the military equal of Justinian's Eastern Empire provided that it was not undermined by further civil wars. Therafter it would quite possibly have been an unviable target to conquer. Indeed, the notion of an Eastern attack on the West owed much to the aggressive (and ultra-Christian) ambitions of Justinian himself, a conqueror, builder, and would-be theological arbiter on the scale of Constantine the Great.

But what if this humbly born Balkan peasant-boy had never become Eastern Emperor? He did not take the throne by obvious military talent as had the humbly born Balkan Emperors of the later third and early fourth century like Claudius II, Aurelian, Maximian, Galerius, and Constantius I.

His introduction to the capital, Court, and politics was due to his (childless) uncle Justin becoming an ex-ranker Guards officer and inviting him to the capital around 500 as his protégé. The disputed succession to eighty-eight year old Emperor Anastasius in July 518 then saw Justin, commander of the 'Excubitors' guards regiment, selected as a compromise candidate instead of the ambitious civilian minister Celer or Anastasius' nephew Hypatius.[16] The latter was the 'legitimist' choice of the Nika rioters to replace Justinian in 532.

Justin, then aged around sixty, may well have been seen as a stopgap by his selectors, less dangerous and strong-willed than Celer and a respectable Catholic in place of the unpopularly pro-Monophysite Anastasius. The latter had recently had to abandon his pro-Monophysite policies due to a Catholic military revolt led by the charismatic general Vitalian, who still had an army to hand in 518 and so was a potential Emperor. Instead, Justinian took control of the administration as his semi-literate uncle's civilian strongman, had Vitalian bought off with a consulship and quietly murdered, and was duly made co-Emperor. In 527 he succeeded his uncle, despite tension over his marrying the ex-actress and alleged prostitute Theodora. But would the West have been invaded in 533–7 had Celer, Hypatius, or Vitalian secured the throne in 518?

Had the Vandals been kept or driven out of Africa, the only significant military challenge the West would have faced after Attila's death would have been the armies of Theodoric the Ostrogoth (encouraged to leave the East after defying its rulers through the 480s) around 490–3. In real life Theodoric was able to overthrow the post-Imperial regime of Odovacer in Italy, but a strong Western central army could have held him at bay as Stilicho had done to Alaric in 402. Indeed, there is a possibility that a militarily strong West could have sent troops to assist the Catholic military revolt of Vitalian against Anastasius around 513 and helped to save the cause of orthodox religion in the latter's capital. The West had intervened successfully in the East before, as Constantine had defeated the suspiciously lukewarm pro-Christian Licinius in the name of orthodoxy in 324 and Julian had attacked his uncle Constantius II in 361. A Western Empire controlling most of its provinces (and maybe with Gothic allies from Aquitaine) was a formidable foe for an East whose armies were in disarray, and in real life Anastasius had to treat with Vitalian as his armies could not defeat him. A West that had held or restored the Rhine frontier could have militarily outmatched Anastasius' divided armies in 513–18, especially if its Catholic Emperor allied to Vitalian in the cause of orthodoxy.

A smaller state

Alternatively, if the Western Empire had been weakened by invasions and poor leadership in the fifth century, a core of Mediterranean provinces, probably minus Gaul, the Rhineland, and Britain, could have survived as a small state into the 530s. This scenario was possible from the recovery of the Empire in the 410s under Constantius III, which left a Gothic 'federate' state ruling south-west Gaul, Germans roaming at large in Spain, and the Rhineland and Britain permanently lost. Had the Vandals still managed to conquer North Africa, in which a power-struggle between Aetius and Boniface to control the regency in Rome around 428–33 aided their advance, the West would have faced a new pirate kingdom with a fleet raiding Italy, worryingly based at the ancient foe Carthage, and the loss of African corn and revenues. That need not have led to the devastating sack of Rome in 455, the result of the murder of the military leader Aetius by Valentinian III and the chaos that followed, which gave Gaiseric the excuse to intervene. But the surviving Empire would have been weakened further by regular raids and the defeat of a retaliatory expedition (e.g. that of Majorian in 462) would have been a signal for more political instability.

A massive expedition from East and West like that of 468 could have evicted the Vandals if competently led. The expedition apparently consisted of a huge armada of 1,100 ships according to Byzantine sources, and was only defeated due to skilful use of fireships by Gaiseric as the Eastern navy reached the Tunisian coast – against which the wind helped in trapping the Roman ships so they could not sail or row to safety. The Eastern commander Basiliscus was accused later by the sixth century historian Procopius of accepting a bribe to delay the attack, which enabled the Vandals to prepare and use their fireships (though nobody could have known that the wind would change and trap the Eastern ships against a lee shore). Once an army was ashore it had a reasonable chance of defeating the incumbent power, then blockading Carthage into surrender and driving resistance out into the deserts, as carried out by Scipio Africanus in 203–2 BC and Belisarius in AD 533. Had the alleged overwhelming size of the combined Eastern and Western force secured victory, the corn and tax revenues of prosperous North Africa would have been restored to the Western Empire and it could have raised the men to tackle the smaller kingdoms of German-held Spain (e.g. the Suevi).

A success by Majorian in Africa in 462–3 (his expedition was defeated en route and he was overthrown by Ricimer) would have been more useful in regaining Spain than a success by Anthemius and Basiliscus in 468, as by 468 the Goths were more entrenched in Spain. But either expedition could have regained Africa and tipped the balance of resources in the Western Empire's favour, at least securing it control of nearer parts of Spain. This would have helped the Empire to hold onto central and southern Gaul too, with or without a war against the Goths who only gained control of the Auvergne region around 470. The North was partly ruled by survivors of Aetius' Gallic army, under Aegidius and his son Syagrius, until 486 and this force (based at Soissons) was likely to rally to the Empire if the latter was in the ascendant. In that case, a revived Mediterranean-based Western Empire that Majorian or Anthemius had secured North Africa would have been viable for decades but for an external threat or civil war.

This smaller Empire could still have avoided ruinous civil war if there had been a stable succession within one dynasty, which could have been that of Valentinian III, his son-in-law Olybrius, and grandson Areobindus from 425 to around 510 or Anthemius' family, or the role could have been taken by a series of strong military leaders such as Aetius, Majorian, Marcellinus, and Julius Nepos. It was actual or potential Roman civil wars that gave the Germanic tribal leaders their opportunities, from the time when Stilicho neglected tackling the invasion of Gaul in 406–8 to concentrate on the Eastern succession to the power-struggle in Rome in 455.

Holding onto its remaining Mediterranean territory with a viable army led by Roman generals, the Empire should have avoided becoming the puppet of German officers such as Ricimer. The latter's emergence as commander-in-chief and Emperor-maker in the later 450s would have been inconceivable had Aetius been alive, and in any case he could have been overthrown by his Emperor (for instance the capable Majorian) as in the East the Germanic commander-in-chief Aspar was killed in 467 by his puppet Leo I. Majorian's defeat of the Vandals, rather than his own defeat, in 461–2 would have strengthened both him and his rump Empire, and in 467–8 the Eastern fleet could have defeated Gaiseric and reconquered North Africa for the new Emperor Anthemius.

If the Western Empire had defeated the invasion of Theodoric in circa. 492–3 the state should have had no more military challenges into the sixth century, when it would have posed a tempting challenge to the aggressive Eastern ruler Justinian. (Being orthodox instead of Arian like the Gothic kingdom of Italy would not have saved it; the East had attacked the West already in 351–2, 388, 394, 425 and 467). The likelihood is that Justinian would have sought to reabsorb the West even had it been ruled by a Roman Emperor rather than several disunited heretic German kings, but he might have regarded this as a lower priority and taken on the Sassanids for a long-term war first. The attempt at reunification would have been risky, as in real life Justinian could only spare small armies to carry it out (due to the Persian threat to the Eastern frontier) and if the West had survived he would have been facing a Roman 'comitatus'. But he could still have attempted it, particularly in order to remove a theologically unorthodox, possibly Arian, Emperor or to exploit a civil war. It appears from the contemporary accounts of the great plague that commenced in 542 that this cost millions of lives, and thus would have reduced military capability to send an adequate army West thereafter.[17] But an attack before that date was still feasible, with the caveat that independently of internal Roman politics a new wave of Germanic, Asiatic (Hun and Avar), and Slavic attacks was disrupting the Balkans by the 540s.

Assuming Justinian and his general Belisarius had succeeded in invading the West, there would have been one Empire as last seen under Theodosius I in 394–5. The Imperial writ would have run from the upper Euphrates and upper Nile valleys to Southern Gaul and the Straits of Gibraltar, with or without a surviving Rhine frontier (which even if it had not been breached in 406 could have fallen to a migration of refugees from Attila's empire in the 430s). The West could then have been given to a separate ruler in a new division of power in the later sixth century, as appears to have been considered as an option in real life by Tiberius II in 582. At the time, the possible division of power between Tiberius' son-in-law Maurice (East) and Germanus Postumus (West) would have left a weakened West struggling to hold back the Lombards in an Italy ravaged by Gothic wars.[18] But there could have been been no Gothic occupation of Italy in 493 (or any grant of land to Germans in 476), or a more decisive victory for the East by 540 without Totila's subsequent fight-back. In these scenarios, Italy would have been free from the presence of German settlers with homes to defend against the Eastern troops and a ruinous war would not have occurred.

Even in the circumstances of real-life 540, the East had driven the Goths back into the Po valley and their demoralised remnants were reduced to inviting Belisarius (evidently admired as a chivalrous foe) to become their ruler. (This did not do his reputation any good with his suspicious Emperor.) The Goths' initially successful recovery in the early 540s was partly due to the capable Totila taking on the command; partly due to

Justinian's recall of Belisarius and many of his soldiers, and partly due to Roman manpower losses in the devastating plague of 542–3. The Persian attack on Syria and sack of Antioch made the recalls probable, and the plague meant that Justinian could not send an adequate army West until his nephew Germanus' mission in 550 (aborted by the general's death).[19] Justinian, like George Bush in Iraq in 2003, seems to have been too eager to proclaim 'mission accomplished' and not alert to the possibility of revolt. But what if Totila had been won over or killed quickly, or Belisarius had not been recalled? Italy would have been in a far better condition to meet any new invasions in the later sixth century, though still denuded of manpower if the plague of 542 had occurred. As it was, the land had already been ruined by decades of Romans and Goths fighting over it before the Lombards moved in, making conquest easier, and Justinian's extortionate tax demands did not help agricultural recovery either.

The survival of the Western Empire during 476–535 would have provided a 'comitatus' to be incorporated into Justinian's army at the reconquest, and a stronger force available to hold back the Lombards. The Western Empire, possibly incorporating southern Gaul and Spain as well as Berber-raided North Africa, should have survived as a viable political entity into the seventh century. Crucially, providing there were good relations with the current Eastern Emperor it would have been able to send him troops to fight the Persian incursions in the 610s, and later to fight the Arabs. But if the plague of 542 had carried off up to half the population, as estimated by Procopius, military manpower (and tax revenues to hire troops from outside the Empire) would have been smaller in the later sixth century than in the fourth and fifth. The military challenges from the new nomad threat, the Avar empire (centred in the Hungarian basin and Wallachia like Attila's), and the mass-movements of its fleeing enemies (e.g. the Lombards) would have prevented a peaceful and prosperous future for the united or divided Empire of the period 570–600.

Part II

Consequences

Chapter 4

Western Empire:
What Would Have Been the Likely Developments for the West, the British Isles, the Vikings, and North-Eastern Germany had One of the Foregoing Scenarios Occurred?

It is reasonable to speculate on the further unfolding of the history of the Weastern Empire as follows, bearing in mind the actual developments of society in the unconquered East and in the more urbanised areas of the West that survived under Germanic rule.

A kingdom of Britain

Decline in Roman military manpower in Britain in the later fourth century is probable, with many troops accompanying rebel Emperor Magnus Maximus to Gaul in 383. Indeed, later legend asserted that he had been the final Roman Emperor to rule in Britain rather than rebel Constantine III (who took a second army to Gaul in 407). Maximus allegedly settled a large force of British troops in Armorica, modern Brittany, led by his British wife Helen's kinsmen. It is not clear how many troops remained in Britain after 383, but the frontier 'limitanei' forts on Hadrian's Wall and anti-piracy forts in Yorkshire appear to have been garrisoned into the 390s. The departure of troops under Constantine III to fight the invading Germans in Gaul in 407 was a result of the central authorities in Ravenna failing to end an army to do so, as they had done in similar circumstances in the mid-270s and 350s. But a similar crisis leading to Roman troops abandoning Britain at a later date was probable, even had a competent Emperor (for instance a surviving Theodosius I) not needed to use British troops against the invaders of Gaul after 406. By the early 440s more tribes were moving into Gaul in flight from Attila, such as the Burgundians.

Assuming that the Empire had to withdraw troops and/or authority from Britain in the early fifth century to concentrate resources in Gaul, there would have been independent authorities in the island. Another Germanic crossing of the Rhine could still have required the Empire to order most of its garrisons in Britain to intervene, as the nearest large army, had the central government been preoccupied. Much is uncertain about numbers and precise tribal identities in the chaos of the early fifth century, but it is logical to assume that had aggressive and ambitious tribes (or tribal coalitions) like the Vandals been held back from crossing the Rhine in 406 the threat from the Huns would have led to a later attempt. The Western Roman civil war of 423–5 was an obvious opportunity to exploit military weakness, though that occurrence would not have taken place had the militarily capable co-Emperor Constantius III not died young in 421. Alternatively, a usurper in Britain could have taken most of his troops abroad and left the island's provinces under-manned; Constantine the Great had launched his Imperial career from Britain in 306 and Magnus Maximus followed suit less successfully in 383. A rebel Emperor could have taken over Britain and defied the government successfully with his fleet, as Carausius did in 287–93.

Any of these events would thus have led to the British provinces breaking away from central control or being abandoned. But this did not entail an end to 'Roman' government in Britain. Roman-style civic institutions, with or without the villa economy, seems to have continued until the major Saxon attacks of the 440s (c.f. the *Life of St. Germanus* on the situation circa 429).[1] The defeat of the German invasion of Gaul from 406, leaving the roads of Gaul more settled for trade and a Roman army on the Rhine in need of British corn, should indeed have aided the survival of the Late Roman economy and farming-system in fifth century Britain. The new states that emerged in post-Roman Britain, some at least dynastically based kingdoms in the tribal areas of the west and north, would still have been threatened by invaders in any scenario and had limited economic and military resources. Once the threat of Attila to the Empire passed around 453, Rome would have been able to lend assistance but it is not likely that any massive diversion of troops for a reconquest would have been seen as desirable.

It is debateable to what extent any British over-kingship in the fifth century owes more to medieval legend than reality. It is now argued that the stories of a powerful over-king during the post-Roman period that were current in the time of the first Welsh historian, Bishop Nennius of Gwynedd (fl. circa 829), were composed with a view to inspiring contemporaries about a British revival that the Bishop's employer King Merfyn 'Frych' could lead. The legends of 'Vortigern', apparently the ancestor of the Kings of Powys in central Wales and the great war-leader 'Arthur' had a contemporary, ninth century purpose and should not be taken as an accurate record.[2] The history of a powerful fifth century British kingship written in the 1130s by Geoffrey of Monmouth was certainly couched in contemporary, twelfth century terms that reflected Anglo-Norman kingship and its international pretensions, and is highly unreliable. But it is clear from the nearest contemporary writer, the monastic controversialist Gildas in the 540s, that the British civil and military authorities after 410 had fought back against the Saxons with initial success, which would suggest a unified command.[3]

Given the structure of Late Roman governance and military command (the latter is preserved in the Notitia Dignitatum of circa 400), there was a field-army under a 'Count' operating in Britain. Most of the troops seem to have left the island with the pretender Constantine III to fight in Gaul in 407, but the command structure could well have been re-created after 410 to co-ordinate resistance. Some modern historians, following Robin Collingwood, have argued that Arthur or his predecessor Ambrosius Aurelianus were Counts of Britain, utilising late Roman military structures.[4] Novelist Rosemary Sutcliff duly used this idea.

According to Welsh tradition by the ninth or tenth centuries, the elusive ruler Constantine, possibly Custennin 'Fendigaid' ('the Blessed'), who ruled before Vortigern, may have been called in from the expatriate British military settlements placed in Armorica under Emperor Maximus in the 380s. He could have been a son of Maximus, who had commanded in Britain before his usurpation in 383, or else a descendant of Maximus' British brother-in-law Conan Meriadawc of Armorica. In 1284 the conqueror of Gwynedd, Edward I, was shown the supposed tomb of Constantine, as son of Maximus, at Caernarfon – a late Roman military fortress in Gwynedd linked to Maximus in the Welsh poem 'The Dream of Macsen Wledig'. The later Welsh genealogies placed Maximus, then a famous figure of legend as 'Macsen Wledig' (who starred in the twelfth century literary collection later known as the 'Mabinogion'), at the head of several major dynastic lines including Powys and Morgannwg-Glamorgan.[5] He was thus an important source of legitimacy to later British-Welsh royal court propagandists.

This may be due to later attempts to glorify the ancestry of important dynasties, but might genuinely reflect a real-life fifth century political role held by his Imperial descendants like Constantine. Some sort of supreme authority over parts of southern Britain seems to have been wielded by the elusive Vortigern (as indicated by his name, which means 'overlord'), Maximus' son-in-law, before the Saxon revolt which the *Gallic Chronicle* dates to 442; he and his Council called in Saxon mercenaries to fight the Picts and granted them land in the traditional Late Roman manner for 'federate' allies.[6] After Vortigern's overthrow leadership of the struggle against the Saxons passed to the 'last of the Romans', Ambrosius Aurelianus, of a noble Roman family wearing the 'purple' (would that have been consular or Imperial?) in the 470s or 480s (as stated by Gildas in *De Excidio Britanniae* in the 540s).[7]

The existence of a central military command for Ambrosius' fight against the Saxons has sometimes been linked to the survival of the earlier Roman office of Count of Britain and of a Romanised cavalry force derived from the late Roman military tradition. Cavalry would have given the British the ability to move quickly around the country on the Roman road network, as has been implied from the wide ranging placing of the elusive Twelve Battles which Nennius ascribes to Arthur, and given them a military advantage over Saxon infantry. In fact the said battles may only have been ascribed to one man in later centuries, perhaps by ninth century mythographers. It is unclear if the office of 'Count' of Britain, or a similar command on the so-called Saxon Shore of southeast Britain centred on its fortresses, existed by around 400. The theory that the chain of fortresses from Portchester to Brancaster were the centre of a coherent, long-lasting Roman defensive network is also now in dispute; if they were military bases, where were their barracks? It has been suggested that the forts were probably more collection points for corn supplies en route to the Rhine army than major centres of troop deployment.[8] It is more likely that they were mainly military. Whatever the true nature of the alleged network of Saxon Shore forts and the extent of Germanic raiding, the latter was evidently a major problem by the later fourth century, as were the descents of the Picts from modern Scotland and the Irish.

A triple attack and major destruction in 367–8 is testified to by Ammianus Marcellinus, and the few written sources for the early fifth century agree that the end of direct Roman rule in 410 was followed by another major attack which the Britons managed to fight off themselves.[9] The local authorities who took action to raise troops, mentioned by Gildas around 540, would have been the civic councils of the major towns (principally the five 'coloniae') and presumably the senior civil servants of the five Roman provinces in Britain.

The names of the final civil governors ('praeses') and their military counterparts ('duces') in each of the five are unknown, but the complicated structure of late Roman civil and military governance would not have collapsed overnight and experienced officials and officers would have been available for the first years of independence. Given the pattern of urban and rural settlement, with farms rather than Italian-style villas predominant outside the South and Midlands and most towns in the lowland areas, it would seem likely that Roman cultural and economic life was essentially a phenomenon of the south and east, with traditional tribal 'Celtic' lifestyles predominant outside these areas. Even in this area pre-Roman tribal administrative terminology survived, e.g the name of the Cantii in Kent, and may underlie the geographical limits of later Anglo-Saxon kingdoms (e.g. Sussex as continuing the 'Regni', Wessex the 'Belgae' or 'Atrebates', and East Anglia the 'Iceni'). Does this mean a survival of a sense of regional tribal identity by the local Romano-British landowners over 367 years of Roman rule, ready to emerge in 410?[10] Did they even have identifiable aristocracies tracing their lineage to the conquered nobles of the first century AD? The pre-Roman names certainly survived in Roman Gaul, frozen into neat Roman administrative districts.

The division of Britain into two provinces, Northwest and Southeast, with capitals at London and York, by Septimius Severus, probably reflects the existence of a civil, romanised area and a military, tribalised zone. Noticeably, almost all the known post-Roman British kingdoms of the fifth century emerged in the latter; the Southern kingdom of Dumnonia, in Devon and Cornwall, had a non-Roman 'Celtic' pattern of farming.)

Continuing Roman authority in Northern Gaul through the fifth century would have been a source of backing to the post-Roman civil and military leadership, and possibly in the real-life chaos of post-406 Gaul the return of some degree of order after 418 may have resulted in a degree of Roman authority in or assistance to the more romanised areas of Southern Britain for a decade or so. (The term Celtic should be taken as referring to the indigenous pre-Roman Britons; the notion of a distinct culture or race' is more contentious. The contemporary useage would have been 'Britanni'; the term 'Celt' for Britons was invented by Edward Lhuyd circa.1690).[11]

There also appears to have been Germanic settlement in southeast Britain by the early fifth century, near towns and in undefended villages so by arrangement with the residents. This has been interpreted as a sign of Germanic 'federates' settled in Britain before the end of Roman rule, possibly to help defend the coast against other raiders from the Continent or seaborne Pictish and Irish raids. Many German artefacts have been found in the region near the late Roman Saxon Shore forts from Kent to Norfolk, leading to assumptions that the owners were German troops and their families based at these places. However, one modern theory prefers the idea that the presence of such Germanic artefacts need not mean German residents brought over from the Continent, only a shift in emphasis in trade from an insecure Roman Gaul to the Germanic lands, which brought in German goods. A change in imports and fashion, making Saxon ornaments desirable objects that the rich would then bury in their graves, is thus the explanation for the arrival of such items – not a mass-invasion of land-hungry Germans.[12] But the physical presence of at least some Germans is more logical, although Gildas' ravings about massacres in mid-fifth Britain are dubious. If most post-Roman farms were left empty for new settlers as a result of Germanic attacks, why does the recently analysed vegetation record show no break in usage of the fields?[13]

If the Empire had still been extant and ruling in Gaul through the fifth and sixth centuries, Roman influence on terminology, military tactics, and institutions in Britain should have been much greater than in reality and a pro-Roman leadership in the campaigns against Saxons and Irish raiders would have been probable. In real life, by the 460s the only surviving Roman authority in nearby Northern Gaul was the kingdom of Soissons, the minor state based on the lands of Aetius' former lieutenant Aegidius and then his successor Syagrius. This was practically independent after Aetius' murder in 454 and the following year's sack of Rome, and was conquered by Clovis the Frank and absorbed into his growing kingdom in 486. But had Roman power been sufficient to contain the Germanic invasions of Gaul after 406, as it had been in the 270s and 350s, the Empire could still have wielded authority as far as the Channel – except possibly for one or more allied kingdoms of Germanic tribal settlers in Belgica and on the lower Rhine, where Franks had been settled under their own leadership as early as the 360s.

The Roman Ambrosius, and his putative successor Arthur (if he existed), would have been bolstered by Roman support, and possibly mercenary troops, and a central kingship is quite likely to have evolved, held by the military warlords. Possibly other relics of Roman administration, not least the Church with its links with Italy, would have survived into the sixth and seventh centuries in a Britain that had driven out any invaders in the 440s and could look across the Channel for support and trade. The Romans' fleets should have kept down piracy, and the larger Romano-British towns would have survived better provided that there was no widespread destruction by pirates or a catastrophic decline in trade due to insecurity.

Accordingly, there would have been Roman assistance to an independent Romano-Celtic kingdom of Britain in the sixth and seventh centuries under a line of successors of the Count Ambrosius Aurelianus (maybe including the mysterious commander later known as Arthur, the Celtic for bear) This state would have evolved directly from the Roman provinces of romanised Southern Britain, and would be run by a mixture of civic officials and a landed nobility. Conceivably some of the more self-sufficient villas might have survived as functioning economic units, with a powerful local landed class as in post-Roman Gaul. The real-life collapse of the villa economy in Southern Britain is now put down to the end of their economic viability, as providers of large-scale agricultural produce for the Western Roman government and army, rather than systematic destruction by bands of Germanic marauders.[14]

Thus, a continuing demand for British corn (e.g. from the drained Fenland or former great Imperial estates) for the Roman army on the Rhine, and a secure, brigand-free network of roads across Gaul should have enabled the majority of villa estates to continue functioning through the fifth century. The most probable scenario for a rural crisis and economic decline would have been the loss of agricultural manpower, and markets for produce, in the great plague of the 540s, which according to surviving British and Irish sources afflicted post-Roman Britain badly.[15] It presumably spread via the trade routes, archaeology showing that there were Mediterranean imports to southwestern Britain via ports like Tintagel and Bantham, and would have been worse in a politically stable Western Roman state where trade was still at the levels of around 400. As in relatively peaceful late sixth century southern Gaul in real life, post-Roman towns and estates would have been badly affected by plague and at risk of decline.

There might be independent but allied tribal kingdoms in the hillier zones of Northern and Western Britain that did not have Romanised towns or a villa economy, without loss of territory to Saxon and Irish settlers. From archaeological evidence, the latter seem to have been locally predominant in Cornwall, Pembrokeshire, and the Lleyn Peninsula in the early fifth century. The written evidence of later genealogies for the ruling dynasties of the emerging fifth century kingdoms has to be treated with caution, given that our extant information is as late as the tenth century and was compiled retrospectively for the descendants of those new kingdoms that had survived that long. Heroic saga may well have magnified, or outright invention falsified, the oral record remembered by bards at Royal courts. Later heroic mythology has been accused of inventing the whole saga of the founder of the Anglo-Saxon kingdom of Kent, the mercenary captain Hengest (whose name means Stallion), as well as magnifying or inventing the deeds of the British war-leader later identified as King Arthur who by the tenth century was supposed to have brought Ambrosius' Saxon war to a victorious end at the battle of Mount Badon around 516.[16] The same problem could apply to any dynastic founder or early ruler only known to us from written accounts centuries later.

Our nearest source, the monk Gildas around 540, deals as much in inference or allusion as in fact in his polemic against the sinful British leadership of his time. But he names one of the five rulers he condemns, Constantine, as king of Dumnonia; the others are mostly identifiable from the genealogies, e.g. Mailcunus (Maelgwyn) of Gwynedd, Cynglas of Powys, and Vortipor of Dyfed.[17] (The latter's memorial-stone has survived, giving him the late Roman military rank of 'Protector'). Other basic information vital to post-Roman history is uncertain; we have no clear idea of whether the Lothian prince Cunedda was called into Gwynedd to evict Irish settlers by the Roman government around 400 or by a later ruler (could it be Vortigern?) around 440. The claim that he arrived '146' years before the time of Maelgwyn, who died in the plague of around 547/9, is at variance with the later Welsh genealogy which ascribes only two generations from Cunedda to Maelgwyn's father Catwallaun.[18] The terminology that Gildas uses for his tyrant kings implies that they were illegitimate rulers, i.e. not legally appointed magistrates or governors but self-appointed war-leaders.[19] This is presumably the view of a legalist churchman of new men warlords flung up by military emergency.

Kingdoms that had been absorbed into other polities may well have left no record, and there is minimal information in the tenth century genealogies on the rulers of those lands absorbed by the new Germanic kingdoms of lowland Britain in the sixth and seventh centuries. Many rulers of lowland states may have been left out of the record because they left no heirs to preserve their details. Gildas makes it clear that tyrants, i.e. rulers lacking legal and legitimate authority, had sprung up all over Britain by his time, and he refers to some kings, e.g Aurelius Caninus or Conan (of Gloucester?), and dynasties (such as that of Ambrosius) which are not referred to in extant Welsh genealogies. Our picture of post-Roman government in Britain is thus partial and probably inaccurate.

Continental developments

Likely offensives with Rome's Germanic allies would have taken place to keep the Saxons in check by attacking them in the rear by land and along the North Sea coasts by sea with the continuing Classis Britannia operating from the Saxon Shore forts and Gesoriacum (Boulogne). If sufficiently Romanised, the Germanic tribes east of the Rhine could aid a Roman conquest and settlement of the Saxon territories; it would have been useful to utilise the energies of warlords such as the emerging Merovingian line of the Franks to fight for Rome so they did not gain their loot and prestige from attacking the Empire. The land hunger of the Angles, Saxons, and Jutes trapped in the coastal areas along the North Sea coasts from Frisia to Jutland (which in reality led to a migration to Britain, though of disputed extent) would have been blocked from British ventures by a strong resistance in the island. Similarly, the stronger position of the Western Empire would have meant that peoples such as the Franks were still living in the romanised areas east of the lower Rhine and would have blocked expansion in that direction. As a result, warfare with Rome leading to their military defeat on land and sea could have meant that many of them would have been enlisted in the Roman army and acquired land across the Empire on their retirement rather than forming their own political authorities under their own leaders.

The Empire could have Christianised them and used them as 'federate' Germanic allies in Roman expansion east of the Elbe. There had been Christianization of Germans beyond the Roman frontier in the earlier fourth century, by Ulfilas among the Goths, though it is unclear if his initiative was taken with backing from the civil or ecclesiastical leadership with a view to the strategic advantages of it. As he was an Arian, not a Catholic, in theology this resulted in major problems for fifth century Arian Gothic kings in dealing with the Catholic bishops of their new kingdoms. In real-life Gaul around 420–30, it appears that the local episcopate, maybe with Papal backing, saw the potential in firstly Palladius and then Patrick taking on missions to convert the heathen and hostile Irish.[20]

Accordingly, some similar mission might have been mounted by zealous clerics within Gaul or the Rhineland to convert German tribes beyond the

Roman borders. The existence of a single, charismatic leader in new kingdoms, such as the Salian Franks' real-life rulers Childeric and Clovis, would have presented a tempting target for conversion, though there would have been less urgency if such men had not been ruling Roman Christians within the old Roman frontiers. Even if the Franks had been blocked from expanding in Gaul after around 480 by the Roman military authorities, and thus driven to attack fellow-Germans in the lower Rhine valley, converting their leaders would have been politically useful in cementing an alliance. The see of Rheims took the lead in working with Clovis in real life, and in this scenario would still have been geographically close to the Frankish kingdom so with an interest in ensuring that Clovis was an ally who did not raid fellow-Christians in the province of Belgica

Quite conceivably, the Western Empire would have gone on in the seventh century to annex Jutland to prevent any further raids across the North Sea. The peninsula appears to have been divided among small tribes, traditionally the enigmatic Jutes, Angles, and possibly some Saxons in Schleswig, without major kingdoms in the real-life fifth to seventh centuries, apart from possibly the realm of the original king Offa of the Angles whose descendants ruled Mercia in England. Without a major settlement in England from around 440 there might have been overcrowding in the peninsula, or else hardship in the coastlands arising from flooding due to rising sea levels, both matters of historians' speculation.[21] Without a safety-valve for settlement overseas many more warriors might have enrolled in the Roman army for betterment, or aggressive war-leaders been as much of a menace to the Roman lands on the lower Rhine as they were to Frankish Austrasia ahead of Charlemagne's conquest in the 770s. Any continuing raiding into Roman lands would have made retaliatory invasion logical, assuming that the traditional Roman option of paying and supporting friendly tribal leaders to preserve peace on the border had not worked in the long term.

Jutland would logically be divided up among farmer-soldiers (some locals and some veterans) to form a Western equivalent of the Eastern 'theme' armies. The settlement of farmer-soldier 'limitanei' on the frontiers of Eastern and Western Empires after the late third century, providing a backbone of locally based men with military experience to support the field armies, would probably be continuing into the sixth or seventh centuries if the West had survived. It was ideally suited to utilising the social basis of society beyond the western frontiers, namely Germanic warriors used to both farming and fighting, for defence of new territories under Imperial politico-military leadership. Beyond the neutralised peoples of the Danish peninsula, loyal vassal-kings would be assisted by trade and military help against their rivals in Scania and Geatland (southern Sweden). The Danish and Geatish peoples had local kings by the sixth century if the later legends written down about their royal families are to be taken with any degree of accuracy. The later Danish historian Saxo Grammaticus wrote of the 'Scylding' dynasty, the people of Scyld, in Denmark,[22] while the famous (possibly eighth century) heroic poem 'Beowulf', its events dated to around 500 by the timing of a reference to a historical attack on Gaul, refers to king Hrothgar of the Danes and the eponymous hero, King Beowulf of the Geats.[23] The mythic events of the saga, with their lake-monsters and dragon, are clearly invented, as are the tidy back-construction of a long-ruling dynasty in Saxo's work. But, as with the British myths of King Arthur, their usage of legend and contemporary references may well hide a kernel of truth about the antiquity of kingship, though not a full, national dynastic kingdom, in the area.

As with the Roman promotion of trustable leaders beyond the frontier with Roman goods and backing to keep their turbulent peoples in order in first to fourth century Germany, the Empire would logically have served to promote kingship and stability among its Northern neighbours. Christianised kingdoms on the periphery of the Roman world would thus have evolved in Sweden and any unconquered part of Denmark at an earlier date than they did in reality, sponsored by the Empire and the Church to aid stability on the frontier. But a similar development in the divided jarldoms of pre-tenth century Norway is less likely, as the intensity of feuds among the warrior-nobility and lack of a clear dynastic authority seen in the sagas would militate against stability. Christianization or diplomatic relations with a powerful ruler may well have occurred but proved impermanent, as with the Frankish empire's attempts to sponsor Christianity and stability in Denmark after around 800.

The Roman fleet, if indeed there was one, based at the supposed Saxon Shore fortresses in Britain in the fourth century had failed to hold back Germanic or Pictish raids, possibly because the invaders' long keels were superior to Roman shipping used to the Mediterranean (perhaps using sails more than oars) or because their small groups of fast-moving vessels could elude Roman patrols. The only late Roman admiral in the Channel with a successful anti-pirate record that we know of was Carausius in the 280s, and he was accused of keeping the arrested pirates' loot for himself and revolted to escape punishment.[24] But it can be assumed that the Romans would have had to master North Sea tides and storms to tackle the Danish coastline successfully during an invasion of Jutland, and to stave off further raiding on the British and Gallic coasts. An invasion of the mainland would leave sea-raiders with no refuge unless they escaped beyond Roman reach to Norway or the Baltic, and it would be logical for the empire to take on seaborne as well as land-based German-Danish mercenary 'federates' and reinforce its fleet with local experts. Roman naval bases around the sites of Bremen and Hamburg would police the North Sea's eastern shores and the Skaggerak, aided by new military and naval bases around Aarhus and the Danish islands, and it is likely that the Church would seek to Christianise the area (as with hostile pagan Ireland) and set up monasteries as beacons of 'Romanitas'.

Ireland

The Church in Rome had sponsored the civilising missions of Palladius and Patrick in the real-life mid-fifth century. If the Western Empire had continued, Rome's interest in the project would have been greater (not least to discourage local raids on Britain and Gaul) given that the post-560s Papacy would not have been distracted by its local political role in Italy as it was in real life. The main centre of administrative expertise and organisation in the senate-less Rome of the restored Imperial Italy from the Gothic defeat in 553/4, it had an important local role backing up the civil government (which was based across the Appenines in Ravenna). The mixture of plague and devastating war had reduced the personnel available to man the administration of Italy, and from 568 the region was afflicted by a piecemeal penetration by bands of Lombards who were centred in the Po valley but by the 570s and 580s were spreading further south. The lack of a concerted invasion by a powerful Germanic army, as with the Goths in 402, 405, and 408, or of a permanent centralised Lombard war-leadership did not prevent the Lombards from serious disruption. Assorted local duchies were set up usually with autonomy from the emerging Lombard kingship based at Pavia by the Po; a major one was at Spoleto in Umbria, within striking-distance of Rome.

The estates of the remaining Roman nobility and the Papacy were being raided, thus diminishing their resources, and Rome itself was threatened by the time of the reign of Pope Pelagius II (579–90). The Lombards were a major preoccupation for Gregory the Great and his successors. A stable and peaceful Imperial government in Italy would have avoided this distraction and enabled the better-resourced Papacy to concentrate on useful missions like converting the Irish to aid the Empire's foreign relations. Conversely, however, the political and military weakness of the Eastern Empire's viceroys in Italy, the 'Exarchs', and the absence of the Senate meant that the Papacy had to assume local civil leadership in central Italy. Lacking this stimulus to its administrative development and initiation of its own foreign policy, the post-550s Popes would have been less powerful than Gregory and his ilk, and under closer Imperial control even if the Western Emperor still ruled from Milan.

The emerging Christian Church organisation across Ireland would have received more aid from Italy had the central Church authorities had more resources. Patrick is unlikely to have been the only (recorded) mainstay of the conversion-mission, and the Church in Britain or Gaul would have been directing his mission and supplying priests. It is also probable that local customs at variance with those of the Roman Church, the different form of the priestly tonsure and the divergence in the date of celebrating Easter, would have been slower to develop, if they had done so at all. In real life the Church in Ireland and its offshoots, including Aedan's mission in post-634 Northumbria, was allowed to develop without a stream of instructions delivered by zealously conformist officials sent from Rome. The result was a major divergence in practices which provided inconvenience, though not any theological split between a (supposedly more liberal) Celtic Church and Rome as some anti-Catholic historians have interpreted this problem. As Rome asserted its influence in Celtic-influenced Christian lands in the mid-late seventh century, commencing with Britain, it made efforts to enforce its own agenda and practices.

Thus the representatives of the two parties in the Church came to argue out their cases before the civil leadership of Northumbria at the synod of Whitby in 664, with Rome's representatives led by St. Wilfred winning; the clinching argument was the role of Rome as heir to the senior apostle St. Peter, at least as Bede recorded it.[25] The triumph of Roman practices in the morer remote Dalriada and the Pictish lands in Scotland, let alone in Ireland itself, had to wait until the eighth century. A surviving Western Empire would have provided the political weight, and probably the greater Roman missionary manpower, to bring about earlier submission to the Papal practices, though the 540s plague and local military preoccupations might logically have delayed efforts to bring Irish and Scottish missionary Churches into line with Rome.

The Empire would also have been keen to aid civic order and a central control over potential raiders from Ireland. It had backed up centralised rule by pro-Roman leaders to control their warlike inferiors on the Rhine and in Britain in the early empire, as well as making these alliances with local kings the mainstay of its eastern Mediterranean and Middle Eastern foreign policy from the late Republic onwards. For a start, it was cheaper than annexation. As has been seen earlier, it is probable that Valentinian I (via Count Theodosius) resorted to this expedient beyond Hadrian's Wall after 367. Indeed, it was late Roman practice to build up supposedly controllable and Romanised kings to control the threatening Germanic peoples, including Alaric as the Gothic ruler before 395. The Irish were part of the coalition that attacked Britain in 367, whether or not any High Kingship existed at that time to direct raiding, and the archaeological evidence shows that they were settling in the Lleyn peninsula, Pembrokeshire, and Cornwall in the fifth century. The traditional Dyfed royal pedigree linked the southwest Wales Irish leadership to the royal house of Leinster.

Backing a pro-Roman kingship in Ireland, or at least in provinces whose inhabitants were raiding Britain, in the fifth century would have followed normal practice. According to John Morris' theory, the British ruler Vortigern' of the 430s established this sort of link with the 'High King' Loeghaire.[26] Thus a surviving Western Empire would have seen the value of supporting the fifth and sixth centuries High Kings of the 'Ui Niall' dynasty, at least once the threat posed by Attila had passed and such alliances could be considered at leisure. This is subject to the caveat that we cannot be certain how powerful the High Kingship based at Tara-Temhair actually was in the fifth and sixth centuries. Did it really establish a form of control or leadership of the sub-kings of the Five Provinces, or was its real power restricted to the eastern province of Midhe where it was based?

It was subsequently claimed that the line of Niall 'of the Nine Hostages' (d. 405?) had been powerful over-kings until the eclipse of the central kingship in the 550s, when a coalition of provincial rulers aided by St. Columbcille (Columba) brought down Diarmait mac Cerbhall and reduced his successors to nominal national power. But modern historians would prefer to contend that the centralised power of Niall's line had always been ephemeral beyond the plains of central Ireland and the kingdom of Midhe. Their alleged control of their allies was an anachronistic myth promoted by tenth and eleventh century writers who wanted to look back to a Golden Age of royal power.[27] The Church, too, found it useful to claim that one centralised kingship had served as the ally of the national apostle St. Patrick, thus presenting a template of secular-religious co-operation for later kings to follow. Did later writers create the myth of a powerful fifth century High Kingship for contemporary rulers to follow, as they undoubtably exaggerated, or maybe invented, the earlier kingship of the Golden Age of Cormac mac Airt in the third century?

It is possible that a Roman military expedition would assist a pro-Roman client High King in defeating his rivals and becoming a reliable ally in return for aid in ending all raiding on Britain. This political and military support could have proved crucial in mid-sixth century High Kings of Niall's line in resisting their dynastic and provincial enemies successfully, and securing domination for their kingdom of Midhe over its neighbours with the aid of Roman troops and/or weaponry. The Roman Church could order its local Catholic bishops to assist the King and promote the kingship's role, as in seventh century Britain. As in reality, tribal dynastic families would provide a number of the leading clerics; powerful abbots would gain land and influence for their monasteries. But a Roman-influenced British state(s) and Church would still be in existence across the Irish Sea, and British clerics would play a part in encouraging the Irish Church to develop on Roman lines (e.g. adopting the Roman dates for Easter). Ireland did not have towns to serve as the seats of bishoprics in the Roman manner, however, so a Roman pattern of urban sees could not develop; the bishops would still have been attached to the tribal royal courts.

Thus it is possible that in the crucial confrontations around 560 Diarmait mac Cearbhall would have prevailed over decentralising provincial rivals, not least St. Columba and other Ui Niall princes, and preserved the High Kingship as a strong force for the coming decades. It is less certain that a hereditary kingship could have emerged, due to the comparative strength of the provincial under-kings who would have resisted that. A dynamic ruler would have had to establish a centralised army to enforce his will, possibly with Roman or British mercenaries. The main provincial kingdoms of Leinster (under the two rival lines of the 'Ui Dunlainge' and 'Ui Cennselaig'), Munster (under the descendants of the mid-fifth century king of Cashel, Cormac Corc), Connacht (under the family of mid-fifth century High King Aillel), and Ulster (under a branch of the 'Ui Niall' based at Ailech), should have survived as the main political units, with a mass of minor local tribal kings. Unless the Roman Empire had annexed southern Scotland permanently, under Agricola around 80–4 or Septimius Severus in 208–11, the lands of Argyll ('Coast of the Gael') would still have been available for settlement in the fifth and sixth centuries by eastern Ulster peoples pushed out of their homeland by the 'Ui Niall'. The Irish settlers' kingdom of 'Dalriada' would thus have evolved as in reality, though a powerful central British kingship ruling to Hadrian's Wall would have restricted southern raiding or conquest by them or their Pictish neighbours.

Dalriada and the Irish overseas

It has been suggested that the post-367 Roman military recovery in the North involved setting up pro-Roman border kingdoms of Celtic allies in Strathclyde and Lothian (Gododdin) to block Pictish raids, as implied by the Roman names of their alleged dynastic founders (maybe Clemens and Paternus) and late fourth century dating.[28] Lothian had a strong military tradition, with its prince Cunedda being called South to drive the Irish out of Gwynedd (in 400 or 440?) and a famous heroic campaign led by its warriors against the invading Angles at 'Catraeth' (Catterick?) around 600 commemorated in the poem 'The Gododdin'.[29] If so, a strong post-Roman authority in Britain should have been able to assist these kingdoms as a buffer to Pictish and Dalriadan power. Alternatively or in conjunction with this, Roman Church missionaries would have sought to convert the Pictish and Dalriadan kings to Christianity and to make them reliable, non-raiding Roman allies. An imposition of central control and order on Ireland by a pro-Roman dynasty in the fifth or sixth centuries would have encouraged those chieftains and warriors who did not wish to co-operate to emigrate to free Argyll and bolster the manpower of Dalriada. An ambitious Irish princely missionary like St. Columba would have been a logical choice for the Roman Church to use in converting his fellow-Irish-speakers in Dalriada.

Lacking the large-scale legionary forces to hold down both Ireland or the Saxon-Jutish lands in the long term, the Empire would naturally co-opt the missionary zeal of the Church to civilise its potential enemies as the figures in the actual Church did with lands beyond the fifth and sixth century Christian frontier (Ireland, Anglo-Saxon England, and the Goths) in reality. The military power of the Empire would help to tie the new bishoprics in Ireland and Denmark into the fabric of the Western Imperial Church administrative system. But in semi-independent vassal Ireland, local tradition would assist in the continuing evolution of powerful monasteries rather than urban-based bishoprics as the centres of Christian civilization.

In real life, the Irish clerics provided a major stimulus of manpower and enthusiasm for re-converting Western European lands that had once been Christian but had now reverted to Germanic paganism. They were active across both Britain in the sixth century and newly Anglo-Saxon England in the early-mid seventh century, as hagiographies and Bede's account make clear. In due course they moved on to Gaul, with St. Columbanus' mission extending as far as modern Switzerland. Had the Western Empire survived, southern Britain and Gaul as far as the Rhine would have remained Roman Christian through these centuries. But the Roman Church had shown little or no interest in converting the Germans beyond the Imperial frontier in the fourth and fifth centuries, the crucial Arian mission of Ulfilas to convert the Danubian Goths came from Constantinople and there was no equivalent on the Rhine. Would the missionary zeal of the wandering Irish monks have led to missions beyond the Western Roman frontier in central Europe?

One logical target for conversion would have been the Saxon peoples, fiercely devoted to paganism on the Continent in real life until Charlemagne the Frank sought to convert them by the sword in the 770s and chopped down their sacred tree Erminsul. Their central German neighbours had been converted earlier in the eighth century by Germanic-speaking Saxons from England, led by St. Boniface. If the Anglo-Saxon migration to Britain had not occurred, the real-life political leadership of their kings, who sponsored the Church in seventh England, are unlikely to have emerged to provide invaluable backing to such missionaries. As Bede makes clear, the adherence of the local king to conversion was crucial to its success; where a new king returned to paganism, as several times in Essex, and nearly in Kent in 616/17, the mission faltered. But as far as can be judged it was the political and military needs of the new Germanic polities in Britain which gave the real-life Anglo-Saxon dynasties the opportunity to emerge. On the Continent, the only royal line to have held any sort of prestige or power was that of Mercia's 'Icelingas' under shadowy rulers such as Offa of Angel. If the patriotic Danish historian Saxo Grammaticus was using genuine tradition in his later accounts, there may also have been Danish overlords for zealous Christian missionaries to approach.

Western Christianity – Emperor and Pope

A Roman Emperor ruling in Italy would necessarily have meant that the Church in Rome of Gregory the Great's time was more like the real Church in Constantinople, submissive to the politics of the Court and theological whims of the Emperors. But the solid Catholic theology of most of Western Europe means that once Arian German rulers had been persuaded to recant by Imperial military power under a concerned Emperor, in this scenario probably Justinian after 536/40, it is less likely that Western Emperors would have sought to interfere theologically in high Church politics as the Eastern rulers did in the sixth, seventh, and eighth centuries. Without the usurpation of local power by an Arian German tribal elite, the leadership of the West would have continued to be Catholic. Catholicism had been unchallenged as the dominant Western theological doctrine at Court since the end of the Arian regency of Justina for Valentinian II in Italy (375–87), when Bishop (St.) Ambrose of Milan had earned heroic status for defying her attempts to assist her co-religionists. The final pagan Emperor had been the usurper Eugenius in 392–4, and even then the alleged assault his regime had launched on the Church was probably exaggerated in retrospect by his defeaters.[30]

The triumph of Catholicism and creation of one state doctrine had then been finalised by Theodosius I, with his legislation against pagan temples and worship accompanied by similar orthodox moves to marginalise Christian heresy. Any residual sympathy for pagan religious practices, apart from rural conservatism in customs, would have centred on the pull of centuries of tradition, and the good luck pagan religious observance had brought the Romans, among the aristocracy. The latter had led religious observance in the annual round of ritual observance in Rome, due to monopolising the priesthoods, and their conversion to Christianity was clearly a gradual matter over generations despite official legislative prodding by zealous Emperors, principally Theodosius. Pagan resentment of the latter had played a part in the revolt of 392–4, in which great aristocrats like Nicomachus Flavianus had had a leading role, though it has been exaggerated. The cause of the 'Altar of Victory' in the Senate House, whose removal on Imperial orders was resisted by leading aristocrats in the 380s, was an example of the physical separation of the worlds of the Senate and the (non-resident) Christian Emperors.[31] Most of the Senate appears to have adapted to the new religion during the early fifth century and the ban on old rituals enforced the change of the old Rome to the city of Ss. Peter and Paul, but the survival of the Senate would have aided the notion of a traditional aristocracy at a distance from the Court.

The new attacks on official doctrine about Grace and Predestination by Pelagius in the early fifth century had never been popular enough with those possessing influence in court or in the clergy to stand a chance of Imperial support and protective legislation, and had eventually been banned after intensive orthodox lobbying. In the East, in contrast, the rival Nestorian theology had been a serious threat around 430, with a risk of Imperial backing from the easily influenced Theodosius II who shortly before his death (450) took up Monophysitism. His sister Pulcheria quickly re-asserted Catholic control of State Church dogma and office in 450–1, but two further Emperors backed the Monophysites, Basiliscus in 475–6 and (tentatively) Anastasius in the 500s, causing orthodox revolts. The Monophysites remained predominant in Syria and Egypt, and Justinian was apparently on the point of enforcing his own third way to reunite the two hostile dogmas when he died in 565. He would probably have infuriated both parties and achieved the hostility of both. Heraclius and Constans II attempted a similar theological reconciliation by Imperial fiat and doctrinal innovation in the 630s and 640s. But this problem did not exist in the West, where even Pelagianism only seems to have been rampant beyond the Imperial frontier, in Britain, if Constantius' near-contemporary life of St. Germanus is to be believed, by the 430s.[32] Catholicism would have maintained a theological dominance aided by State power, and it is unlikely that a Western Emperor would have been keen to support an Eastern Monothelete or Iconoclast enthusiast by calling a Church council to change Western doctrine in his support.

Eastern Orthodox theologians offended by their Monothelete or Iconoclast ruler's heresy would have been likely to call on a Catholic Western Emperor to invade and depose the blasphemer, particularly determined persecutors such as Constans II in the 650s, Constantine V in the 760s and 770s, and Theophilus in the 830s. It is not impossible that an ambitious adult Western Emperor with no pressing military problems and hopes of unifying the Empire would have listened to them, though two of the three most determined Iconoclast Emperors (Constantine V and Leo V) were good generals which would have discouraged this sort of adventure. Bearing this threat in mind, the Eastern Emperors would have been likely to secure their Western counterparts' neutrality before embarking on major doctrinal changes, and the practical requirements of military alliance against the Arabs between the Empires in all doctrinal controversies.

The Western Emperors might well have intruded court favourites into the Papacy, although the absence of the Emperors from Rome made their interest in the state's principal see less than was occurring in contemporary Constantinople. Constantius II was the only fourth century Emperor to actively interfere in papal appointments; the see of the Court residence, Milan, was more at risk. Imperial nominations to sees of the fourth century had been stimulated by a need to support the Emperor's own doctrine against its rivals at a time when the Catholic victory over Arianism was not assured, as seen in Constantius' and the regent Justina's Arian appointments and Theodosius' Catholic reaction; this conflict was now over. But an Emperor with interests in theology or Church personnel would undoubtably have interfered with Church promotions to favour their own court candidates, at least in areas close to the Imperial residences.

A great Roman aristocrat with diplomatic experience such as Gregory the Great would have been a natural choice as Pope in 590, but he would have had less of a political role as there was still an Emperor in Rome, Ravenna, or Milan and and there would be no Lombard invasions of Italy. An ambitious and talented Pope such as Gregory would have been more of a court adviser like Ambrose of Milan in the 380s, encouraging the Emperor against heresy and able to send out more missionaries (e.g. to Saxony, Denmark, and Dalriada and Pictland). But whether the Emperor was resident in Rome, Ravenna, or Milan the Popes would have been under his eye and incumbents who defied his wishes would have faced the deposition which Constans II inflicted on Martin I in 649 for opposing the 'Type'. In real life the weakening Imperial power in Italy led to Pope Sergius defying attempts to evict him by Justinian II's troops, the arresting officer allegedly had to hide from the Rome city mob under the Pope's bed, and in the eighth century the Popes defied Iconoclasm openly.[33] This divergence between Emperor and Pope added to Imperial inability to defend Rome from the Lombards, and led to the Papacy calling in the Carolingians from Francia as its new, Catholic military ally from 751. This would have been inconceivable in a continuing Western Empire with an Emperor still resident in Italy.

There would certainly have been no succession of disreputable ninth and tenth century Popes set up and deposed by noble factions in Rome with accompanying poisonings and massacres, as the city would have been under continuing strict Imperial governance. At the worst, there would have been factional intrigue and rioting on the occasions of disputed Papal elections when the Emperor was preoccupied elsewhere, as in the 360s. The continuation of the great Senatorial dynasties of the fourth and fifth centuries, now fully Christianised, could have led to the sort of struggle between them over the Papacy that occurred between similar wealthy Roman dynasties in the fourteenth to seventeenth centuries, at least when the Emperor was not sufficiently interested to impose his own candidates. The later Orsini, Pamphili, and Barberini Popes would have had their dynastic equivalents; the most powerful and wealthy dynasty of fifth century Rome was the Anici.

What of secular power and influence in Rome? The great dynasties survived the collapse of the Western Empire in real life, with the Senate functioning, and consuls being appointed, under Odovocar and Theodoric. The Gothic kings had adopted a Roman court lifestyle and titles and continued to be advised by great Roman aristocrats, most famously by Cassiodorus and the executed philosopher Boethius. Ironically, it was Roman reconquest not Gothic rule that fatally damaged their world, as the Gothic army managed to recover from its defeat by Belisarius in the 536–40 campaigns and launched a fight-back under Totila that led to Italy's devastation. This commenced before the great plague and the combined threats of Persia and Balkan raiders had already caused Justinian to reduce his military commitment to Italy by 542, but the loss of manpower and revenues in the epidemic made the war longer and more ruinous. The Senate seems to have ceased functioning in the 540s as a result of the dislocation and flight caused by the Gothic wars, when Totila captured Rome and drove out the inhabitants in 546. The landed aristocracy and many rural estates were ruined; this would not have occurred in a continuing Western Empire without a Gothic war, or in an uninterrupted Justinianic reconquest. Justinian's suspicious character and alleged miserliness, made much of by the savage pen of Procopius in the 'Secret History', hindered the Empire's ability to tackle Totila, or contemporary rebels in North Africa, quickly in the 540s.[34] But without adequate manpower, or money to hire Germanic or nomad mercenaries if the Empire was short of troops, even a fully-trusted Belisarius would have had to rely on luck and his strategic genius to kill Totila and wipe out his main army quickly and limit the damage to Italy.

Monasticism would have continued to grow in peacetime, but with more secular careers open to ambitious and/or literate civilians it would have attracted fewer able candidates and it would have had to rely on Emperors and local landed aristocrats for donations of land and money. It would not be the only centre of learning, as a continuing urban Roman society would have kept secular schools open. In real life, many leading aristocrats in Gaul and Italy chose ecclesiastical careers after the fall of the Empire, there being no functioning bureaucracy in the post-Roman German kingdoms and civil government now being under the control of a German elite. Towns in the more Romanised south of Gaul fell under the leadership of aristocrats of ancient lineage as the local bishops, and their dynasties monopolised the senior clerical offices (c.f. Gregory of Tours' family).

This would not have occurred had the Empire continued. Estates were transformed into monasteries by devout aristocratic laymen, such as Cassiodorus in Italy; this phenomenon was underway already before the end of the Empire, as seen by the career of Paulinus of Nola, but if the Empire had continued it would have been one among many options. Certainly the sense of a world coming to an end in invasion and chaos, which benefited the otherworldly preoccupations of the emerging monastic movement, would not have been so strong had Imperial government continued. Monasticism was well underway across the West by around 400, e.g. at Lerins and Tours in Gaul, and would have continued to exert a pull for devout Christians, but would probably have had fewer adherents. The absence of major wars in Italy in the sixth century, though not the absence of plague, would probably have given St. Benedict fewer recruits, and arguably a great Roman noble like Gregory would have had less certainty of following a Church career.

Military matters

There would have been less risk of a major barbarian threat to Roman military power in northwest Europe in the seventh or eighth centuries, a period of relative stability between the major movements of Germanic peoples in real life. The caveat here is that a Western Roman military block to westward and southward Germanic incursions in the period after 406 would have prevented the emergence of at least some of the emergent German-led kingdoms of the real sixth and seventh century, most notably the settlements in Spain (Vandals and Suevi from circa 410, and later Visigoths from the 460s), Italy (Ostrogoths' and their allies from 476/93 and later the Lombards from 568), and Africa (Vandals from 428).

The pressure of Attila's empire on the peoples of Germany in the period around 433–52 might well still have led to the Rhine frontier being overwhelmed by refugees then, and to a surviving Western Roman 'comitatus' under Aetius after 454 having to accept Germanic peoples west of the Rhine. But a still militarily powerful Western Roman state, with a larger and better-equipped army than the disunited tribal forces ranged against it, would have kept the Empire in the militarily favourable position of Theodosius' forces around 395. The Empire would have been likely to cede control of northern Gaul and the lands from Upper Danube to Alps as indefensible, leaving them open to the creation of Germanic kingdoms (logically created by the real-life fifth century founders of new states such as Gaiseric, Athaulf and Wallia, the Goths, and Theodoric). Given a lack of ruinous civil wars, the inner provinces should have remained under Roman control, and the new Germanic kingdoms would have been the Empire's inferiors in resources and military strength.

The Empire had already adapted to the presence of coherent barbarian polities and armies within its old frontiers, with Theodosius' rapprochement with the undefeatable Goths in Thrace after 381; and Stilicho was able to hold back and make use of Alaric in the period 395–408. Indeed, as a fellow-German he was to be accused of being suspiciously unwilling to destroy Alaric when he had the chance.[35] Similarly, Aetius was able to use the Gothic kingdom of Toulouse and other Germanic states and warbands in Gaul as his junior allies against Attila in 451. Logically, a stable Western Roman polity in the fifth, sixth, and seventh centuries would have preserved this favourable political and military position with regard to its new neighbours. Had the Rhine frontier been preserved by a line of long-lived and vigorous Roman commanders (Theodosius, Stilicho, Constantius III, Aetius, and perhaps Majorian or Aegidius) the Germanic kingdoms would then have emerged within Germany to its east, at least once the empire of Attila had broken up after 454. East of the Oder line poor soil would inhibit the growth of prosperous kingdoms; in real life the proto-Slav villages have yielded poor archaeological remains. It was no viable centre for resistance.

This would enable Romanization and Christianization of the more coherent Germanic peoples, probably the Franks, clearly from Gregory of Tours' account already ruled by tribal kings (not only the Merovingian line) in the fifth and sixth centuries. Salian and Ripuarian (i.e. those on the Rhine river) Franks, in real life forcibly united by Clovis and his sons from about 480 to 550, already lived in territory within the Roman frontier at the mouth of the Rhine by about 400 and in real life expanded across Belgica in the next decades. If the Western Empire had lost control of that area after the invasion of 406 it could still have evolved into a separate kingdom under the vigorous Merovingian line, but if the Empire kept control of the Rhine area the Franks were the likeliest of the local peoples to cohere into a kingdom east of the river. As with allied German tribal states from the first century, the Empire would have an interest in establishing a friendly dynast who could control his people as its ally on the Rhine; the Empire could thus have backed the Merovingian dynasty as it established an allied kingdom in what became the eastern part of the real-life Frankish kingdom, Austrasia.

Rome could have been fighting and forcibly converting the disunited tribes of Saxons in the lower Elbe area in the eighth century as Charlemagne did in reality, with more troops so easier success despite the swamps and forests. It could then have moved on to annex other decentralised, badly-armed tribes towards the Vistula, probably encouraged by a mixture of Church missionary zeal and a practical desire to stop independent tribesmen beyond Roman control aiding their resentful conquered relatives.

The Viking threat

In due course, a Roman clash with the Scandinavian Vikings ('men of the viks/fjords'?) over control of the North Sea and raiding on Britain would have occurred. A united Romano-British kingdom in Britain that had been spared the real-life collapse of the fifth century, using Roman tactics and weaponry and cavalry to defeat raiders, would have put up a successful co-ordinated defence against all but isolated Viking raids and scared the latter off, particularly if they had a fleet and Roman naval aid. The first Viking attacks on the real-life small Anglo-Saxon kingdoms in the 780s and 790s appear to have been individual raids by opportunists, gathering in intensity and scope to a full-scale invasion by a large army under Viking kings in 865/6. In real life, the successes that the Vikings were having in moving up the great river-systems of France to pillage towns and monasteries encouraged the attacks on Britain, and the Frankish kingdom lacked a competent fleet or (after 840) a united politico-military leadership.

These problems would not have faced Roman Gaul, which had a Channel naval base at Boulogne (Gesoriacum) and could have called on the Imperial armies for defence. Co-operating Roman 'duces' would not have been as militarily weak as the Vikings' Carolingian foes. The Vikings would have been more likely to attack an easier target, and the precedent of Saxon and Pictish raiding on Britain in the fourth century, if still remembered in Scandinavian sagas or retold by Saxon refugees, have suggested Britain as well as Ireland as a victim. Indeed, the absence of a Viking military presence in the Frankish kingdoms in the mid-late ninth century would have made it more likely that the full force of Viking expansion fell on Britain and Ireland in these decades. But some adventurous Scandinavians would have been content to take on Roman military careers, as men like Harald Hardradi of Norway did in Constantinople in real life.

A larger, united British kingdom would have had more resources to meet the challenge, including cavalry which the Anglo-Saxons lacked, and the Vikings may never have risked challenging such a well-prepared state en masse unless it was weak in its response to raids (as Ethelred II's English kingdom was in the 990s). The Romans had more sophisticated weaponry in battle than the Saxon reliance on the shield-wall, and importantly had siege-weaponry that could tackle the Vikings if, as in the real-life invasion from 865/6 with its Viking encampments at York, Nottingham, Reading, Wareham, Exeter, and Chippenham, the latter tried to rely on a defended town to defy a local army. The Saxons could not wait outside a well-defended town indefinitely as long as their troops were only militiamen called up for a fixed term of service (the 'fyrd'), a problem which Alfred of Wessex tackled after 878 by calling up his men in rotation.[36] The British/ Romans would have had a professional field-army, and also have had the siege-engines to storm a Viking-held town and the ships to blockade a longship-supplied Viking base on a river like Nottingham (868) and Reading (870–1). Only in 868 did the forces of two Anglo-Saxon kingdoms fight the Viking Great Army together, and Northumbria (866–7), East Anglia (869), Wessex (870–1 and 875–8), and Mercia (868 and 875) were tackled separately by evidently superior Viking forces.

The provinces of post-Roman Britain should have been more co-ordinated. But a minority government, civil war, or resurgence of separatism in the Celtic kingdoms would have given the Vikings their chance and a major attack by a force of land-hungry Norwegians (or unconquered Danes) by circa 850 cannot be ruled out. Any serious British defeat and/or civil war in Britain could have led to a Roman reconquest, either directly or via an expedition to back up a pro-Roman candidate for the throne of the main kingdom in the South. The joint efforts of the British kingdom and a Roman expeditionary force should have outmatched any army that the Vikings could gather for a direct challenge, particularly if there had been naval attacks on the Vikings' fleets as well. Denmark may already have been occupied by Rome, and if not it would have been an easy target for retaliation on land from Germany. Even a united Norwegian state such as that ruled by Harald Finehair (circa 920) or Olaf Tryggvason (990s) would have been vulnerable to a Roman North Sea fleet invading while the King was away fighting in Britain or Ireland.

The main Viking threat would have come from Norway, probably via the sea routes to the Hebrides and the Irish Sea to evade the Roman North Sea fleets. Rome would have been in a naval position to defeat any invasion by a massed fleet, though the manoeuvrable Viking longships would have had an advantage in evading their pursuers or in hit-and-run raids and Rome would have had to adapt its usual shipping to North Sea conditions. Rome may not have bothered to interfere with small Viking settlements in the isolated and agriculturally poor Orkneys and Hebrides. The likeliest area for large-scale Viking settlement would have been Ireland, which would have been likely to have a number of provincial kingdoms around 800 barring a major Roman military initiative to aid or conquer the High Kings. In real-life England in 865–70, the Viking Great Army picked off the Anglo-Saxon kingdoms one by one and even compelled one small kingdom (East Anglia) to lend them assistance to conquer another (Northumbria). The divided political nature of ninth century Francia was also invaluable to them. Ireland would thus have been their most tempting target. A prolonged bout of raiding or settlement, in real life, fortified bases on rivers accessible for their longships (Dublin, Waterford, Limerick), would have necessitated Roman intervention there if the local rulers proved inadequate defenders and the Church was complaining to the Pope about the sacking of monasteries.

Rome would probably have tried to impose pro-Roman chieftains in the nearer areas of Norway that their summer-time expeditions could reach from Britain or Denmark, South of Trondjheim. The serrated coastline and mountains would have impeded direct conquest and made the usual networks of roads and forts impractical, except in the Oslo plain where a Roman province could have been established to co-ordinate regular military intervention against such chieftains as continued to aid descents on Britain and Ireland. The Western Empire, like the East with their restless and potentially hostile Russian ally from 988, would have been keen to bind the Norse to them as allies. Thus the creation of the West's own Varangian Guard of ferocious Viking mercenaries is a logical possibility, together with Viking officers emerging as Roman generals (as Germans did in the fourth and fifth centuries). By the eleventh century, talented scions of Viking kingly families such as Cnut the Dane and Harald Hardradi would have been natural recuits to the Roman army and possible senior generals, even commanding Roman fleets against their kinsmen. Given a weak ruling dynasty and factional strife over power in Rome, a senior general of Viking origin could have emerged as more likely to have set up a vassal Norwegian High King, in this case imposing Christianity on him too, than to have attempted full conquest.

If the smaller and militarily weak Irish states had been unable to cope with Viking plundering in the eighth and ninth centuries, their Church if not the proud chieftains could have sought aid from Rome as the leadership of Christianity, leading to the despatch of an expeditionary force. Roman technology and numbers should have prevailed over the invaders, but Rome is unlikely to have been able to afford the troops for direct control with most of the Western army still needed in Jutland/Norway/Eastern Germany. By this date the East had the naptha-based secret weapon, 'Greek Fire', to burn flammable wooden ships. It was first used against the Arabs in the siege of Constantinople in 674–8, and the West would have used this against Viking longships to devastating effect.

Chapter 5

The Western World –
Some Further Speculation

Rome in the Americas?

It is not hard to see many Vikings considering it preferable to emigrate west along the Atlantic seaways in search of easier targets, and thus colonising Iceland earlier and in greater numbers than they did. Given the likely early Roman response to any serious Viking attacks on Britain, a conquest of Jutland and landings in Norway could well have occurred by the 830s if Viking raiding had followed the same trajectory as in reality. Many real-life explorers were adventurous exiles, e.g. Erik the Red the discoverer of Greenland.

The lack of available farmland for an expanding population in the narrow Norwegian fjord-valleys is usually accepted as a major reason for expansion overseas, with exploratory voyages showing the raiders the lack of resistance to determined attack. Summer raiding was followed by settlement, the latter first occurring on the Shetlands, Orkneys, and Hebrides, where there was little loot and the recent DNA analysis would indicate that the newcomers nearly wiped out the proto-Pictish locals.[1] The timing and scale of the Vikings' assaults on the Irish, Anglo-Saxon, Pictish/Dalriadan, and Frankish kingdoms is better-known due to the literary evidence. It seems to have built up during the first half of the ninth century, aided by the poor military response, which in the case of a surviving Western Roman Empire would have been different. It also utilised the opportunities offered by a civil war, e.g. that between Aelle and Osbert in Northumbria in 866 and in Francia in the 840s.

Used to maritime North Sea raiders since the Germanic attacks of the mid-third century, the Empire would have provided a centralised European response and it would have had a far larger fleet than the limited ones sporadically available to the real-life local defenders. The first fighting fleet of an Anglo-Saxon kingdom was ascribed to Alfred by the Anglo-Saxon Chronicle, and was later used to make him the 'father of the British navy'.[2] Charlemagne is recorded as building a Frankish fleet to thwart the Viking raids, and he and his successor Louis the Pious endeavoured to build up an allied and Christian kingship in Denmark to control the local warriors; but these initiatives did not last. Under the Roman Empire, there would have been as determined a response as met the seaborne Germans in Britain in the days of Carausius (280s) or Count Theodosius (367–70?). Land-hungry Vikings, who abandoned their attacks on Wessex for weaker targets in 878 and 896, would not have been satisfied indefinitely with Ireland, or may have been defeated there thanks to Roman intervention. Earlier and larger-scale movement to empty lands in the Atlantic was a logical alternative, with the shipbuilding technology for such voyages already extant by the ninth century.

The pressure from Rome in Europe and unprofitability of raiding Roman lands could also have led to an earlier Viking discovery and substantial settlement in America, the climate being optimal for sea voyages into the area in these centuries. The climate of Greenland was warm enough for scattered settlements well up the West coast in real life around 950–1100, though it is a matter of dispute as to whether worsening climate or Inuit attacks later weakened the colony. Little is clear about the state of the North American climate around AD 1000 and it is now linked to the ongoing climate change debate. But the Viking settlements in Greenland evidently had enough grass in summer to feed substantial cattle-herds or flocks of sheep, and Greenland could have sustained a reasonable émigré population at around this time. Similarly, Labrador and Newfoundland, and possibly Nova Scotia, are candidates to be the elusive 'Vinland' where allegedly vines could be grown. It is uncertain if this claim was merely spin by over-optimistic early voyagers in order to recruit more settlers (Leif Erikson is the suspected culprit) or a reflection of a genuinely warmer climate, but in any case pressure on land in Roman-dominated Europe would have been likely to encourage the Viking voyagers to sail as far south as they needed to find good agricultural land.[3]

The better-armed and warlike Vikings would have overpowered the resistance of the dispersed and poorly-armed 'Skraeling' tribes (the 'Athabascans') along the East coast, with a larger amount of manpower available to them than that which they possessed when they tackled the area under Leif Erikson around 1000. In real life their frequent clashes with the locals (possibly around the site at L'Anse-aux-Meadaux in Newfoundland) discouraged a long-term commitment. Blockage of their European ambitions by Rome would have provided more manpower to overcome this, even without a Roman conquest of Denmark or Norway. There was nothing to stop the Viking navigators rounding Cape Cod and experimenting with farmland in Massachusetts or Connecticut, whose forests would have been familiar from their Scandinavian homeland; their probable numbers and enthusiasm for battle would have made them as able to take on local tribesmen as the seventeenth century settlers of New England. Technologically, they would have lacked the advantage of muskets that gave the seventeenth century settlers a major advantage; but they would have been more used to prolonged fighting than the largely peaceful Pilgrim Fathers.

By 1000 there could have been a High King of Ireland backed up by Roman troops, Roman reoccupation of Britain, Romano-German settlers in Denmark and the Oslo plain, a number of pro- and anti-Roman warlords fighting over the rest of Norway, and a substantial Viking empire of independent émigré settlements stretching over the Orkneys, the Shetlands, the Faroes, Iceland, Greenland, and eastern Canada around the Atlantic provinces down to Massachusetts. The improved climate of the northern Atlantic islands around that time seems to have been able to sustain a larger Viking population in Greenland than is now possible, and it would have been an obvious staging-post for settlers en route to Canada. The Niagara Falls need not have impeded Viking exploration of the Great Lakes area, given that they had light ships that could be carried round it and they were used to portage round the rapids on the lower Dnieper in Russia. The forests of eastern Canada would indeed have been a familiar environment to the Norwegians, reminiscent of their homeland; they were more used to woodland fighting than the real-life seventeenth century French invaders had it come to a conflict over land with the 'Hurons'. The 'Five Nations' of the Iroquois to the south do not seem to have been united this early and so would have been easier to tackle than the Europeans found in the seventeenth and eighteenth centuries.

Given the survival of the Western Empire and a prosperous and politically united Western Europe benefiting traders, it is likely that some captains would have sought out routes to the rumoured Viking discoveries in America too. The Empire, if animated by traditional Roman opportunism and a missionary Catholic Church, would have followed them with official expeditions, on a more southerly route than the Vikings used. The prevailing winds would have taken them via the Canaries, possibly known to some classical sailor, to the Caribbean, which Rome would have equated with the Hesperides of classical legend as a distant paradise reachable by sea from the Pillars of Hercules. Did St. Brendan's Irish voyagers find an American Land of Promise in the mid-sixth century? In both cases sceptics have claimed that these stories' accounts of western lands are coincidental and do not reflect real voyages; but the case for St. Brendan discovering Iceland is strong with or without Tim Severin's re-creation of his voyage to Canada being used as evidence that it was feasible.[4]

Rumours of distant and colonisable lands like these, reinforced by the hints gained from traders who had dealt with the Vikings of their new lands, could have inspired ambitious captains by circa 900 to endeavour to follow the currents west via the Canaries to the Caribbean. The voyage of six weeks or so between the continents would have been well within the capabilities of sailing-ships, and if the right impression of opportunities of empire, trade and Christianization had been made on the Imperial court expeditions would have been backed (with more resources from a Roman Emperor than Ferdinand and Isabella could give to Columbus). Given the continuance of peace and prosperity in Western Europe under one polity, this could easily have occurred well in advance of 1492, possibly before 1200 given the optimal climate and a growth in population and mercantile trade-seekers. The likeliest position for early Roman settlement, given the climate, fertility of the land, and harbours, would have been the Greater Antilles. Propaganda at court could have made the most of 'emulating the labours of Hercules' in an officially sanctioned expedition to the West.

Rome and the civilizations of Mexico

It is also probable that further voyages would have followed. Then the new settlements would trade with the continental mainlands within decades, and stories of vast quantities of gold would have been as alluring to the central Imperial government and to individual captains as they were to the Spaniards. It is possible that the early Maya and Aztecs had come by sea to Mesoamerica from the Caribbean, the 'old red land' to the East being Cuba, though the former do not seem to have had any seaborne contact with the Antilles by their Classical period (circa 400 to 800) and the sketchy and mythologized references we have in sixteenth century records to Aztec migrations make it impossible to locate their whereabouts circa 800 to 1200.[5] (Their original home, 'Aztlan', has been hopefully claimed as Atlantis.)[6] Any

Roman expeditions to the mainland would probably have been opportunistic exploration rather than a result of information gleaned from the few scattered residents of the Antilles, whose cultural level was lower than that of Mesoamerica when Columbus arrived. The local tribal Caribs do not seem to have created recognisable polities or been aware of the mainland by circa 1500; unlike Aztecs, Maya, and Incas they were obliterated with relative ease by the Spaniards.

And from that arises the intriguing possibilities of what the Romans would have made of the equally belligerent Aztecs if the clash of civilizations had occurred in the fifteenth century, or the Toltecs or Mayas if it had occurred earlier. The dating of the Toltec culture in Mexico is vaguer than that of the Maya, whose deciphered records show that their feuding city-states were in decline by the ninth century and largely abandoned to the jungle by 1100. But they would seem to have been active around 900 to 1200, based at Tula near Mexico City.[7]

The half-known civilization of the Toltecs (and before them that of the massive city of Teotihuacan, built on the scale of Rome) indeed served a role for the Aztecs similar to that of the Etruscans, and before them the lost 'golden age of Saturn', to Rome, as their inspirational legendary forebears. The Aztecs looked back to the era of the Mexican culture-hero from overseas, the legendary and godly founder Quetzalcoatl, as the Romans of Augustus' era did to their own semi-divine founder from distant lands, Aeneas from Troy, who was made the son of the goddess Venus and ancestor of Augustus' family. Some past historians have sought to portray the bloodthirsty, dynamic Roman conquerors and their peaceful Etruscan forebears as the Italian equivalent of the Aztecs and the Maya. That myth has now been exploded by decipherment of the Mayas' own alphabet, which shows them to have been as predatory and fond of human sacrifice as the Aztecs.[8] The Romans did however have a long-lasting myth of a foreign, Trojan, origin like that of the Aztecs, who had wandered across Mexico for centuries before settling in the great valley of Mexico City circa 1325.

According to the scanty accounts preserved after the Spanish conquest, the early Aztecs settled at Tenochtitlan were supposed to have been looked down on as a band of servile vagabonds by their more urbanised neighbours, who they duly conquered, as 'Romulus' Rome had served as a refuge for runaways, stateless brigands, and other undesirables. Both civilizations were built on dynamic warfare, and both had an emblem of an eagle. In the Aztecs' case it survived onto the national flag of Mexico, and in the Romans' case it was adopted as the Imperial emblem of Roman, Eastern Roman, and later 'Holy Roman Emperors', and hence was taken up by the Second and Third Reichs. The double-headed eagle of the Russian Czars (apparently used by the Byzantines from circa 1325) has now been brought back into use as a patriotic pre-1917 emblem for Putin's Russia.

Would the Romans have recognised similarities between themselves and the Aztecs as they conquered them? Unless the Church had been allowed to develop its doctrines of religious superiority over godless pagans untrammelled in Rome as in medieval Europe, the destruction of Aztec, Maya and other South American culture by the conquerors may have been less than in real life. The Christian Roman Empire of real life from circa 324 was a civilization on the defensive, and so had no record of conquest and assimilation. Peoples beyond the frontier of the Eastern Empire were to be converted to orthodox (and non-orthodox) Christianity by missionaries throughout its history, from Armenia and Georgia in the early fourth century through Ethiopia to the Bulgars, Slavs, and Russians. Armenia, the first to be evangelised, was converted by private initiative while the Roman state was still pagan; Axum/ Ethiopia was converted circa 330 via a local request to the Church in Alexandria. A community of nations culturally and religiously aligned to the Empire – what Dmitri Obolensky calls the 'Byzantine Commonwealth' – was created. But this did not involve military conquest, so we cannot tell what the attitude of a militarily triumphant Christian Roman Empire to conquered 'pagans' would have been. It would seem probable that local culture would have been thoroughly Christianised and all traces of pagan religion blotted out, as with the newly Orthodox Slavs in Eastern Europe under Eastern Roman missionaries. Destruction of idols was a centrepiece of Christianization from the time of Theodosius I and Cynegius, long before Charlemagne and St. Boniface vandalised Saxon idols in Germany. But politically the Roman Empire had long been used to allowing native rulers to survive as Imperial allies, as with British and German tribal leaders from the first to the fourth centuries. Thus Aztec and Maya princes ruling dependant territories were more likely to be tolerable to a distant Roman Emperor than they were to the Spanish monarchs, and land-hungry local Conquistadors to be under closer Imperial military control than were Spain's autonomous grandees Cortez and Pizarro.

The Romans, like the real-life Conquistadors, would have had the advantage of numbers, weaponry, and Christian zeal against the primitive 'savages', with their evaluation of culture on the grounds of urbanization meaning that had they arrived too late to encounter the large Maya cities in Yucatan (or Tula?) they would have rated the local tribes as no more advanced than they rated the rural German tribes in the first century. Like the Conquistadors, they would have been vulnerable to the climate. The Mayan city-states in Yucatan (as violent and competitive as fifth century BC Greece) appear to have collapsed to over-population and famine by circa 900.

The conquest of Mexico and North America. Rome versus the Vikings?

The Roman adventurers should certainly have been able to secure the Caribbean islands, settling them as the Spaniards did in reality but with a larger state behind the enterprise. European diseases would have assisted them by decimating the local population, but deliberate genocide is less likely. Land-hunger would duly have taken the Imperial forces on to the North American mainland, with large-scale settlement of people moving from a peaceful, prosperous, and probably well-populated Europe. The lands of the southeastern U.S. would have been an obvious first choice, with the existence of a powerful central authority in Europe meaning that there should have been Roman military assistance on a larger scale than the real-life military aid given to British settlers there. Until the post-1700 'world wars' against France, England's military commitment was minimal, and the only political centralization of all the colonies was by James II. Unlike real-life colonial settlement in the Americas, there would have been one European state directing it and hence no diversion of time and resources to inter-state wars.

The local Native American tribes would have been met with force and stood no chance, but Rome would probably have pursued its usual policy with 'primitive tribes as in Scotland and granted them treaties as vassal allies once they submitted. Romanised client-chiefs would have been backed against their rivals and efforts made to create stable polities on the Empire's borders, as on the barbarian frontiers in Europe in the first centuries AD; the Church would have been encouraging missionary activity and denouncing the Aztecs and Mayas for their human sacrifices. The Church's attitude would probably have been broadly similar to that of the Spanish clergy's in the sixteenth century. The Aztecs and the Mayas may well have been regarded with the uncomprehending revulsion for their cultural practices that the Romans showed to the Druids in Britain and Caesar showed in Gaul.[9]

If the authorities in Rome were only interested in this strategic backwater as a source for trade goods rather than for creating a well-organised set of Romanised provinces, it is likely that only commercially valuable areas such as Mexico's goldmines would have been prime targets for conquest and strict control. Expansion of settlements elsewhere would have been piecemeal and disorganised, subject to individual initiatives. But gold-rich Mexico could have turned into the same sort of fertile site for greedy merchants, tax collectors, and land grabbers as wealthy Asia Minor became in the later second and early first centuries BC, with some ambitious local Mayan or Aztec client-king eventually seeking to channel discontent to throw out the invaders like Mithridates VI of Pontus did in Asia Minor in 88 BC. As with Mithridates, Rome could not have allowed its prestige to suffer and any such revolt would have been followed by major state military intervention, with outright annexation and provincial organisation. The same process could have happened on a smaller scale in North America, with a native American rising against Roman land grabbers (probably likeliest in the fertile 'Old South') being punished. As with Andrew Jackson's policies in the 1830s, Indian survivors would have been deported.

Land-seizure and exploitation in North America in the manner of what Rome did to the Iceni in the late 50s AD was as much in prospect as with the real-life British settlers in America, as was the development of large landed estates as 'latifundia' worked by slaves once this became economically attractive. It is unlikely from what we know of the Roman slave-system that the Empire would have resorted to systematic deportation of West Africans as a slave-labour force, as there is no evidence that they regarded any peoples as inferior on the basis of colour (as opposed to culture and civic development); the use of prisoners-of-war as slaves would have been more normal.

Once the Roman presence had expanded northwards there was the prospect of a clash (perhaps in the New England area) with the Viking settlements there. Any isolated Viking settlements further south would have been powerless in the face of larger Roman numbers and superior weaponry, and been subject to attacks by the Roman navy from the Caribbean. Distance and the unattractiveness of the poorer soil to Roman settlers would have helped the more northerly Viking possessions beyond Maine to survive.

There could have been a campaign fought over the Great Lakes area, as in real history between Britain and France in the eighteenth century, between Rome and the Vikings several centuries earlier. The Romans would have been using the Lake Champlain 'corridor' and the mouth of the St. Lawrence for a two-pronged advance on the Quebec area, as Britain did in 1759. They would have prevailed due to more manpower and better modern weaponry despite fierce guerilla fighting with ambushes in the thick forests if they had won the initial open battles against the Vikings. It would have been particularly crucial if the export of gunpowder westwards from China had enabled their armies to use muskets by this date.

The timing of this is uncertain, given that a prosperous and peaceful Europe in the years of the twelfth and thirteenth century climatic optimum could have enabled westwards adventuring by individual captains and then colonial expansion to commence well before it did it reality. But a substantial Roman presence could have been possible in North America before the loss of population and planning delays caused by the Black Death from circa 1350, while the worsening of the climate in Greenland would have driven Vikings living there South-West into Canada and/or New England in the fourteenth and fifteenth centuries. Thus, it would not be unreasonable to postulate a Romano-Viking war over the area by the mid-sixteenth century.

The outnumbered (and outgunned?) Vikings would have been overrun, with or without the use of hit-and-run tactics against the Romans in the thick forests aided by local Native American tribes, and Quebec and Ontario would have been annexed to the Roman Empire. But it is possible that some Vikings preferring independence would have escaped along the Great Lakes (as useful a route for longships as the Russian rivers were to real-life Viking adventurers) into the hinterland, which their fur-traders and adventurers would have been exploring for centuries, and set up new jarldoms based on fur-trading on the plains of Manitoba.

As Roman numbers and prosperity in America increased, the trajectory of expansion would have followed the real-life American expansion westwards over the Appalachians into the Mississippi valley with a probable major settlement at the river-mouth around New Orleans and another at a strategetic river-junction site upstream around St. Louis. Farming would have begun on the Great Plains, with adventurers probably escaping the bureaucratic control and taxes of the settled Roman provinces to move into the Native American tribal areas without official direction. Given the vast distances that official orders and personnel would have had to cross to reach the Americas and the cost of sending troops, it is probable that however much the Roman officials in the new provinces were legally under European orders substantial autonomy would have developed in practice.

The likeliest pattern of government would have been that of the bureaucratic, Catholic imperial state of Spain over its American empire in the sixteenth and seventeenth centuries. There was official colonial subordination and the regular despatch of top officials to head the colonial administration, but a good deal of autonomy in practice and the evasion of central governmental orders. The central viceroyalty governorships would probably have been of defined geographical areas, e.g. the southern and the northern east coastal plains, the Mississippi valley, and the Canadian areas around the St. Lawrence basin (and Mexico south of the Rio Grande, if conquered). Given the lack of inter-State and inter-faith warfare in Europe, there would have been no Francis Drakes or Dutch privateers preying on the Imperial shipping that exported loot and trade-goods to Europe. Instead, the energies of restless European coastal provincial adventurers could have been used to establishing a western trade route across the Pacific to China. The amount of state power and direction of labour available to Rome would have made it an easier matter to order the digging of a canal across the Panama isthmus than it was in reality, particularly if the survival of Ancient World documentation had enabled the preservation of details of the Pharaonic canal digging in Egypt at Alexandria. Slaves, mainly prisoners-of-war, would have been easily available to work at the project for as long as necessary and the Empire would have had as little compunction as the Spanish Viceroyalities in impressing local labour for such projects.

The existence of a continuing central bureaucratic government, and a Catholic religious structure, across Europe could well have led to an exodus of people seeking more automony from government control to the Americas and thus an evolution of more democratic local government there within the provinces (at least for the wealthy farmers and merchants), centred on advisory councils to assist the governors. Given stronger central direction from Europe than in real-life British North America, probably on the basic pattern of Spanish America, a local settler ethos would have developed on the lines of creole society in the Spanish empire, and the cultural precedents their thinkers had to study should have led to an interest in the Ancient Greek colonial' precedents of autonomous colonial societies such as republican Syracuse and city-states in the Hellenistic kingdoms. The expansionist nature of a society of rugged independent minded farmers fighting local tribesmen should also have led to interest in the precedent of early republican Rome in Italy and the cultivation of republican farmer virtues as celebrated by Livy, indeed, the interest in heroic Roman

Republican virtue of the real-life French revolutionary era and of Jeffersonian America are natural developments to have been replicated in the Roman American colonies.

Society in post-fifth century Roman Europe.
Something like the physical structure of sixth century Eastern Mediterranean life would have been the norm for a continuing Western Roman social and economic world in the sixth and seventh centuries. The only caveat to this scenario is the possible impact of the epidemics and climate, problems that seem to have afflicted all Europe for decades from the early 540s, quite independently of the military situation. Recently David Keys has constructed a theory of far-reaching political, economic, and psychological results arising from this train of disasters in his study *Catastrophe.*[10] The famines and later the plagues of the period are traced to the apparent 'dimming of the sun' for months in 535/6 reported by Procopius,[11] and connected to the effects of a massive volcanic eruption in the Krakatau islands off Java that caused dust-clouds to circle the Earth and prevented the sunlight ripening the crops across the world.[12] The overall effects of these disasters remain contentious, but even in a fairly settled Europe the loss of manpower would have severely affected urban life and trade besides causing famine in the countryside. Particular hardship would have fallen on the poorer classes, affecting the government's ability to raise taxes and to feed the cities and armies.

If a large 'Diocletianic' bureaucracy and an army on the scale of that listed in the *Notitia Dignitatum* were still in existence in the sixth century West, loss of manpower would have affected the ability of the citizenry to pay for them. It could have caused a (temporary?) flight from the towns to avoid the onerous duties of the curial classes in making up for their fellows' tax defaulting. The physical effects of this would have included a decline in the ability of the civic taxpayers and the town councils to repair civic buildings and carry out expensive new projects, with the untaxed Church and monasteries at a distinct advantage. Some villages in the rural areas could have disappeared altogether, along with smaller towns, as in the similar mixture of bad weather, famine, and plague in the fourteenth century, but it is likely that larger towns would have survived as they did then. Isolated peoples not on the regular trade routes, such as the Vikings and remote Slavic settlements, would have been at a demographic advantage. As a result, the untaxed Church could have preserved its wealth and the fabric of its properties better than the rest of society, and Church buildings could have been more dominant in the surviving towns as they were to be in those of surviving Byzantine cities that had a Classical origin (e.g. Constantinople, Thessalonica, Ephesus, and Nicaea).

It is noticeable that the public context of civic life in Byzantine cities tended to be centred around the Church rather than the secular buildings that had been the centre of life in the Classical era, most especially the public baths. The cost of maintaining the latter in a time of financial stringency, and possibly a shortage of skilled masons to maintain the fabric, must have played a part in this decline for secular civic culture. There is also the factor of the Church's disapproval of the inheritance of the ancient Greek sporting 'ethos' for nudity and immorality. Theodosius I's closure of the Olympic Games in 394 is often cited as an exemplar of the new Christian puritanism, though it is unclear how popular such spectacles still were.[13] The Church, following St. Paul, denounced Greek athletic nudity – which had not originally been a Roman practice.

It is not clear how may of the local pagan Games and other cultural or sporting competitions of civic Greece, recorded for the second century in the travelogues of Pausanias, survived the chaos and economic dislocation of the third century crisis and were still active at the time of Theodosius' prohibitory legislation. The most prestigious Games, e.g. at Nemea, seem to have survived. Even if there were dramatic contests in the theatres at Athens and Epidaurus until 394, there is no record of new drama being created; instead, the traditional repertoire continued ritually to be performed. Without the formal bans on all non-Christian festivals and seizure of shrines' property by Theodosius, it is probable that these aspects of established tradition would have continued for generations under local patronage. Important buildings vital to the practice of ancient Greek cultural practices, such as the sanctuary of the 'Mysteries' at Eleusis, which Alaric's Goths sacked in 396, would have survived but for Constantinopolitan politics and military crisis. But the major series of famines and epidemics in the mid-sixth century would have added to the strain on the curial classes' purses of maintaining these buildings, and Procopius' vehement comments on the mid-sixth century civic tax burden shows the state of the people who paid for them. The greater emphasis on private, as opposed to public life (except in religion) argues against civic buildings seeming as vital as in the classical period anyway.

The cost of government and war would have been high, particularly after the plague of the 540s, and affected these classes' ability to pay for the physical structure of 'civilized' classical life. The anti-pagan legislation of Theodosius, followed by the active persecution of all religious deviants by the obsessive Justinian, only accelerated an ongoing decline. It is noticeable that the orthodox Christian State backed vigilante actions against local pagan temple buildings, as when under Theodosius I the militant Christian state commissioner Cynegius toured Syria wrecking such buildings with the puritanical enthusiasm of the Taleban destroying statues of the Buddha. Theodosius and Justinian both sanctioned official *razzias* of destruction like Mao in the Cultural Revolution. Systematic vandalism of pagan shrines was also carried out by the Patriarchs' heavies in Alexandria in the early 390s, notably at the great Temple of Serapis.[14] But murders of blasphemous pagan philosophers are known on only one occasion, the lynching of the female lecturer Hypatia, a feminist icon, by the Patriarch's men in Alexandria.

It is unrealistic to assume that the ethos of Classical sport and entertainment would have survived unchanged if the Empire had not fallen. The developments of the fourth and fifth centuries under the Christian Emperors are instructive. The gladiatorial content of the games in Rome had already been halted before the West 'fell' in real life, initially by Constantine and finally possibly as a result of an incident after Stilicho's victory over Alaric in 402.[15] Thus there would have been no continuation of the Games familiar to the early Empire; sporting enthusiasm would have probably transferred to chariot racing as in Constantinople, with the great racing teams serving as the foci for partisanship. Rome had had a long history of racing at the Circus Maximus, and post-fifth century Rome would thus have had its own racing riots and political interventions by the racing faction demes as well as Constantinople.

As analysed by Alan Cameron, the races were an important occasion for the Emperor to connect with his people and show that he shared their interests and was available to listen to their complaints.[16] A politically astute ruler would pretend to take an interest in the races to show his affability and democratic instincts, like a New Labour minister showing an interest in football today. A disgruntled Hippodrome crowd was capable of hailing a new Emperor, as they did to Justinian at the Nika Revolt in 532. He had to send in the troops to carry out a massacre before the rioting ended.[17] The factions of rival Hippodrome race teams had a major role in city life, and it was seen as a matter of major import that Justinian's wife Theodora had a family background in the racing world as daughter of a Hippodrome bear trainer. After her father died his racing faction refused to give his family a pension, so Theodora always backed their rivals.[18] This was not merely ephemeral show business; in 532 the usually fratricidal Greens and Blues joined together to try to depose Justinian, and in 602 the factions helped to depose Maurice.

It is unclear, however, if the rigid ceremonial of the Byzantine races would have been as apparent in the Western Empire; the formality of fourth century Western state ceremonial could have been reversed at a later date by more democratic rulers. This was, however, unlikely as long as the Church, with its year-round rituals, was a major prop of the state. The evolution of ceremonial at the eastern court had a religious function to present the Emperor as the 'equal of the apostles', with religious ceremonies frequent; this 'holy' aspect of the imperial capital was developing in Rome too in the fourth and fifth centuries, but had another focus than the Emperor, i.e. the Pope as heir to St. Peter.

The Emperor at Constantinople served as the focus of religious devotion, as the heir to the 'thirteenth apostle' Constantine, and the local patriarchate was a newcomer to the religious hierarchy. The see had initially only been a bishopric, being elevated to patriarchal status relatively late, and lacked the antiquity of the venerable sees of Rome, Antioch, and Alexandria, all founded by apostles. But in Rome the religious leadership had the advantage of a first century foundation by the man charged by Christ with leading the Church, and was making the most of it to claim local disciplinary authority even in the third century. Rome had the relics of Ss. Peter and Paul, martyred in situ; Constantinople had to import its relics and was only a minor Greek town in the first century.

There was thus every political reason for the authorities at 'nouveau riche' Constantinople, which lacked the authority given by age and apostolic associations, to consciously build up an atmosphere of holiness centred on its Emperor as religiously unchallengeable. The dynamic Patriarchs Theophilus and Cyril of Alexandria had overshadowed both Emperor and Patriarch of Constantinople as chief defenders of orthodoxy in the early fifth century. But in the West there was less religious controversy over the form of official doctrine, and no rival patriarchs to challenge the bishop or Emperor in Rome. There was thus no need to build up the Emperor's role or his sacred status. An Emperor living at Milan or Ravenna might have been relatively free from the sort of religious atmosphere to his public appearances that developed in Constantinople, or even at Rome he might have played it down.

The Church would have held great power and continued to draw in able careerists, but would have had a rival in the continuing Roman civil service and been subject to secular control as in Byzantium. The Papacy would not have held more than a primary position of honour. And in due course a revival of interest in pagan culture and rejection of the Church attitude towards ancient philosophy would have stimulated a renaissance, perhaps after the military threat posed by the Vikings to the new urban centres and monasteries of Northern Europe had passed. The leisure and politically stable conditions that enabled such interests to develop would have been unlikely in a sixth centuryWestern Roman world affected by plague or an eighth to ninth century world afflicted by Vikings, but could well have emerged by the later eleventh century when real-life theological speculation began to flourish in France and Italy.

The ethnic composition of Europe would have been much different from reality, with no (or few) Angles and Saxons in England, no (or few) Franks in France, no Goths or Arabs in Spain, and no Lombards in Italy. The nature of civilization and politics in any 'Twelfth Century Renaissance' would have been much different from that of reality, not least with a powerful Emperor and a weak Papacy, though Latin would still have been the lingua franca. Crucially, the stimulus given to development by autonomous or independent local towns in Italy and Germany would have been absent. Each district would have been under an Imperial governor, whether or not the division between civic *praeses* and military *duces* introduced circa 290 had continued. These men would have continued to be bureaucrats, regularly appointed place holders under the direction of the central government, not the hereditary rulers of medieval Europe.

The nature of central control over the localities would have been beyond that of any medieval state, even late Capetian France. The role of the Church in the localities would have been smaller, as also its monopolization of career paths for the literate. Also, Church control of intellectual speculation in the universities would have depended on the backing of a still powerful secular State. In the Eastern Empire the autonomy of the university school of Athens was ended, along with the rights of pagans to teach, by Justinian in 529. This is traditionally supposed to have closed the institution founded by Plato nine hundred years before, with its pagan scholars emigrating to more tolerant Persia under the patronage of the learned Great King Chosroes Anushirvan.[19] This convenient and symbolic break with Ancient humanism and tolerance, at the hands of the belligerently Orthodox Justinian, may be an exaggeration. But Justinian seems to have been as keen to destroy incorrect thought as Stalin or Mao, though in his opinion no doubt it was his godly duty. Poor evidence makes it unclear exactly how much post-secondary teaching by acceptable Christian scholars survived in post-529 Constantinople, or even in Athens. Crucially, Procopius seems to have expected to be well read by an Empire-wide literary elite but evidence of scholarly activity crumbles even for Constantinople after 600, possibly due to the wars for survival. In Heraclius' time, local Greek took over as the 'lingua franca' at Court.

But when university teaching of Classical philosophy revived in ninth century Constantinople it was subject to constant intolerant Church interference, the pagan philosophers being regarded with extreme suspicion. Careful scholars had to genuflect before the requirements of Christian orthodoxy and make it clear that they did not accept the ancients' religious beliefs, even if (like Michael Psellus in the 1040s) they had close Imperial connections and patronage.[20] This greatest of Byzantine 'revivalist' enthusiasts for Greek philosophy had to be careful of Church hostility, and found it prudent when Imperial support waned to retire to a monastery as reassurance of his orthodoxy. Emperors were to back the Church against undesirable philosophers of dubious orthodoxy, e.g. John Italus in the 1080s, who was put on trial amidst public demonstrations of hatred.[21] Notably the term 'Hellene', with its ancient Greek cultural and religious connotations, was not back in usage in Eastern Roman culture until the fourteenth century, and even then Platonist enthusiast George Plethon could not teach in Constantinople. Ironically, he settled near ancient Sparta at the local Imperial appanage capital, Mistra. The same difficulties for unorthodox thought could have occurred in the West.

The continuation of peace and settled conditions across Northern Europe and the presence of an urban civilization as a market for produce would have stimulated agriculture, though the problems of bad weather and disease would have held it back. The existence of large aristocratic estates under the late Empire would have continued, with the peasantry as 'coloni' rather than feudal serfs but equally subordinate to their masters; freer communities would have had a better chance to develop in newly-acquired territory e.g. the north-east German/Polish plains and Denmark, or maybe Ireland. The optimal climatic conditions of the twelfth and thirteenth centuries thus could well have led to a population explosion in the prosperous Western Empire and the need for new acquisitions of territory, with secular knowledge of land management and agriculture surviving from the classical world. As a result of debateable numbers of Germanic warriors and their dependants not having been able to migrate west of the Rhine or into Britain from 406, there would have been more physical pressure on the land in Germany with the probable destruction of forests and settling of farms on a wider scale than really occurred in the 'Dark Ages'. Pressure for new lands in the East would have been likely by about 1200.

The steppes – and the Mongols

If the Empire's authorities, mariners and the commercial leadership of the Atlantic coast provinces had not yet discovered America, the likeliest area for conquest would have been the continuation of the 'Drang nach Osten' into the Ukraine as far as the Dneiper or the Don. This could not have been achieved until the defeat of the Mongols, who presumably would have arrived there in 1237–40 as in reality and with luck would have been defeated as they threatened Poland in 1241/2. The Mongols would have faced a united Europe under a military leadership used to fighting nomads from the steppes since the time of Attila, probably with Greek fire to match the Mongols' Chinese fire-crackers and certainly with all the Classical world's military technology. They would not have been allowed to rampage as far as Poland and Hungary without a major challenge, even assuming that Rome had not bothered to annex the emerging Slavic kingdom in Poland or the Slavic-Viking principalities of Russia. There was constant interest in real-life Byzantium in developments on the steppes, as shown in Constantine VII's strategic 'handbook' *De Administrando Imperio* of around 950.[22] The Empire(s) would have been aware of the Mongol threat at least since the defeat of the Sultanate of Khwarezm in 1219–20, and a large army could have moved into Russia to meet them as they arrived in 1237. If not, then the united forces of Western Europe would have been available to meet the advancing army of Batu in Poland or Hungary, instead of the Mongols being able to take on one kingdom at a time. The Romans would have been able to put together an army of 60–80,000 if necessary to meet the Mongols, whose numbers are unclear but vastly outnumbered their real-life enemies, on much more equal terms

The extent of the Mongol threat would have been such as to require military co-operation by both Empires to defeat it, and afterwards one or other Empire would have been anxious to secure the steppes from further threat to the settled lands to the West. Remaining Turkic or Mongolian tribes, such as any Volga Bulgars or Cumans/Polovtsians the Mongols had not destroyed, would have been Roman vassals. Granted the previous

Roman practice of building up reliable buffer states against major enemies, e.g. the screen of client kingdoms in the eastern Mediterranean between Rome and Parthia, the Roman leadership should have been keen to use local peoples to reduce the threat of the Mongols returning. Logically, the Empire would have encouraged any non-Mongol tribal forces remaining independent in Siberia or Turkestan to act as Roman clients, and taken a greater interest in Russian and steppe affairs.

Constructing forts to defend the Empire was not an option, as there was no easily defensible line of frontier. The Urals were too low to provide a barrier to nomadic raiding and the lower Volga too long to be patrolled. If the Mongols proceeded to set up the same subordinate Khanates across the region east of the Urals as they did in reality, the 'Jagatai' Khanate would have been emerging after the 1240s among that part of the Mongol army settled in Turkestan and the 'Ilkhanate' would duly have taken over Persia. (See next section on the Eastern Empire.) It would have been in Rome's interests to seek to stir up warfare between these states and the Great Khan in Karakorum (China after the 1260s) to keep the Mongols fighting each other, and as the Mongols were animists, to convert them to Christianity as allies. Any settlement nearer the Roman European frontier, by the 'Golden Horde' on the Don and lower Volga, or by the 'Nogaj' khanate in Wallachia, would have been a major source of concern until it was either destroyed or converted into an ally, seeming an heir to the threat posed in the fifth century by Attila.

Religion – an Imperial-led 'Reformation'?
The flux of theological speculation apparent among Christians before their religion became the state cult had seen a variety of doctrines competing for attention. Despite the simplistic view of the 'Dan Brown' school of modern writers, the fixing of a definitive, orthodox theology for all citizens to follow at Constantine I's Council of Nicaea in 325 was not an innovation by the new alliance of Emperor and bishops – or an Imperial hijacking of a multi-faceted Church debate into rigid control by a new doctrine. The now dominant Catholic doctrines had developed within Christian thought since the first century, particularly regarding the precise nature of Christ's mixture of human and divine attributes. They had always held the adherence of the senior bishoprics, among whom the See of Rome (later the Papacy) was already particularly venerated in the West and was pushing its claims as a source of authority by the third century.[23]

A majority of the Church's leadership were Catholic well before Constantine's time, holding that this was the doctrinal position established by the Apostles and St.Paul; the four Gospels and the Acts of the Apostles were already defined as the core of the emerging New Testament and most of the other books eventually included in it were already accepted before 300. The definitive list of books, and thus of acceptable teachings, was not established until Bishop (St.) Athanasius of Alexandria drew up a list in 367,[24] but the acceptance of the unorthodox writings in the 'Gnostic' Gospels, known to be second century, not from the Apostles' lifetimes, was never considered.[25] They were certainly not suppressed by the Church fathers or Constantine at Nicaea, and senior churchmen concerned for unity were denouncing such Gnostic innovation and potential for unseemly controversy (and disorder) in the third century. After Nicaea, the latest such heresy, the new doctrine of the Egyptian presbyter Arius on Christ having a human not a human and divine nature, was still a threat to the Catholic dominance, and Constantine himself made unsuccessful efforts to reach a compromise with the theologian and draw him into a state church. A desire for a tidy and ordered bureaucratic Church, an ecclesiastical equivalent of the civil and military systems established across the Empire since Diocletian's reforms, was apparent. It was not limited to Christian Emperors; Diocletian had sought to enforce precise pagan religious ritual for all citizens across the Empire and the most vehement pagan enforcer, Maximin Daia, had set up a hierarchy of State-funded pagan priesthoods like that which Constantine was to set up for the Church.[26] A disciplined hierarchy of bishops was now set up, led by the Patriarchs in the major cities of the Empire (Rome, with Constantinople added after Constantine's time as the new Imperial capital, and the apostolic sees of Antioch, Alexandria, and Jerusalem) with a metropolitan see in each provincial capital controlling the bishops of that province, and there was no room for dissent in religious as in civil life. The establishment of a state Church was duly accompanied by a definition of doctrine to be followed, the Nicene Creed, still the basis of Catholic belief, and the eviction of bishops and junior clerics who would not subscribe to it.

This centralised edifice was the religious counterpart of the late Roman secular and military state, with hierarchy and order dominant, and it was clearly designed to make religious life mirror secular affairs but in theological terms to to reflect the Heavenly order too. In due course the Emperor, now 'Equal of the Apostles' as Constantine had proclaimed himself and taking a lead in Church councils, began to participate in a round of religious rituals at his 'Sacred Palace' that reflected his semi-divine status and religious role.[27] The notion of the Emperor as a semi-divine figure had been present to some degree since the early Empire in the more religious-minded East, and had received a boost in the troubled third century when coinage had presented him as the helper or equal of the Empire's protective deities. The end of the Western Empire prevented it from continuing in the West, but it became central to the Imperial office and its round of palace and Church ceremonial in the Eastern Empire.

The potential winning of an Emperor to back a doctrine other than Catholicism was a major flaw for the new Constantinian Church system. What one Emperor had granted, another could take away. In due course, the Arians achieved the support of Constantine's son Constantius II, ruler of the East from 337 and the West from 352/3–61, and he started to appoint senior Arian clerics in place of Catholics; the Council of Sardica (Sofia) in 342–3 saw deadlock between the differing views of theologians backed by the Catholic Western and Arian Eastern rulers. Julian, a recidivist Catholic turned pagan, attempted to undermine both doctrines and issued legislation against Church privileges, thus ending the legal advantages that were inducing many citizens to convert from the traditional pagan beliefs; a further move towards a state Arian Church in the East was attempted by Valens (364–78) and in the West the regent Justina attempted to put Arians on an equal legal footing with Catholics in Italy in the late 370s to the fury of Bishop Ambrose of Milan. Catholic doctrine only became firmly established with draconian legal support, as it happened, permanently in the West, under Theodosius the Great, and the fifth century was to see the emergence of two new doctrines, Nestorianism and Monophysitism, in the East.

The first threat to Orthodoxy, Nestorianism, failed to win a foothold in Constantinople in the late 420s despite its eponymous originator being patriarch. The militant Catholic patriarchs of Alexandria secured the backing of the wavering Theodosius II, Nestorius was sacked and deported to an isolated monastery, and his doctrine secured backing in Syria and Mesopotamia but was driven underground and only flourished within Persia beyond Roman control. It later set up a mission in China, and in 1287 a Chinese Nestorian mission from Kubilai Khan arrived in Constantinople and Rome. Monophysitism secured Theodosius' backing in 448–9 thanks to Court patrons, was driven out of the capital after his death in 450, but had two subsequent Imperial patrons, Basiliscus, quickly overthrown, and Anastasius who faced Catholic rebellion from Vitalian, and became the dominant theology in Syria and Egypt. Even the obsessively orthodox and persecuting Justinian could not secure one all-embracing Imperial Church of conformists, not least due to his wife Theodora's support for the Monophysites. The state Church in Egypt, the 'Melkites' or 'King's/Royal party', appear to have been in the minority by the seventh century and some historians have argued that state attempts to crush the Monophysites encouraged them to prefer Arab rule.

The Catholic doctrine remained dominant in the West, although there was an intellectual challenge to official theology from Pelagius, probably a Briton, in the 400s which orthodox leaders such as Augustine of Hippo insisted needed suppression. Notably, the Constantinopolitan government's attempts at creating a third way theology to reunite orthodox and Monophysites in the seventh century, the 'Monothelete' doctrine and the 'Type', failed to win many adherants in Roman controlled lands in the West. The same could have been expected of any Eastern Imperial or Church innovations in a continuing Roman Empire; the Papacy in the eighth century was uncompromisingly opposed to Iconoclasm. It is unlikely that any Western Emperor would have been sufficiently interested in the relatively arcane issue of the theological meaning of religious art, (was it idolatry to venerate a depiction of Christ, the Virgin, or a saint?), to hold a council altering doctrine. Theological debate had always been a popular passion in Constantinople, as testified to in the mid-fourth century, but the Western Church was less riven by furious debate and Pelagianism and Priscillianism, a minor Spanish heresy of the 380s, were their sole contributions to late Roman theological controversy.[28] Ironically, when the Catholic St.Martin of Tours persuaded new Emperor Magnus Maximus to use state power to punish the Priscillianists the 'gulag' chosen for their exile was the Scilly Islands.[29]

This situation would doubtless have continued in a surviving Western Empire, at least until the settled socio-economic conditions and probable climactic optimum of the post-Viking era (circa 1100–1300) stimulated the equivalent of the real-life 'Twelfth-century Renaissance'. Of course, the Western Empire of that era would have been a different social and cultural world to the divided polities of real-life Western Europe. The cultural 'mix' of peoples would have been different, with the population upheavals of the fifth to the tenth centuries avoided or much altered and a much more powerful, bureaucratic secular State outmatching the Church in power. No German Holy Roman Emperor ever approached the Roman Emperors in power or the amount of territory controlled, and no Pope could have treated a Roman Emperor as Gregory VII did Henry IV, whose rebellious vassals could be used against him if he did not submit. Individual Emperors like Theodosius did humble themselves before the Church after doing wrong, in that ruler's case, after carrying out a massacre of his rioting subjects in Thessalonica on dubious evidence. But there would have been no theoretical basis for the submission of secular rulers to Church power 'per se', and no Papal legal justification for it on the grounds of a 'Donation of Constantine' abdicating secular power in the West.

The Emperors would have continued to appoint and dismiss Popes and, if sufficiently interested, to preside at Church councils. It must however be said that this different balance between secular and religious power would not in itself have led to greater freedom to propose doctrines in defiance of the Creed, or to question the basis of Christian theology. State power had decided what a citizen was required to believe and perform (in public) since the legal orders for all to sacrifice to the pagan gods by Decius in 250–1, though since Constantine the Great (apart from 361–3) the law had been backing Christianity and Theodosius I had banned pagan worship. State police powers were limited, but it would have required an Emperor who was as unusually sceptical about Christianity as Julian to reverse this legal situation. This was however a possibility from a ruler educated in the Latin and Greek classics and enthusiastic for traditional Roman culture; the survival of secular schooling in a continuing Empire would have increased the chance of an earlier than in real life renaissance of interest in the values of the classical world. An Emperor like Frederick II, interested in science and secular learning and at odds with the Church, could then have encouraged both theologically Christian and pagan speculation and refused to continue the draconian legislation imposed by Theodosius I.

One advantage for freedom of thought during an educational revival is that few Roman Emperors were likely to have gone along with any Church plans for an inquisition to root out heretics. The state would have had far more power under the Empire and so been able to back up Church crackdowns across the entire Empire if so agreed, rather than the Pope having to secure the agreement of many separate and mutually hostile secular rulers. There would be no chances of a secular state far from Rome revolting against Papal power and surviving an interdict, but the Papacy would never have achieved the prestige and independence of action that it did in the real-life twelfth century. It would have been the secular power which decided what heresies to persecute and when, as Constantine the Great did regarding the 'Donatists' in fourth century Africa, Maximus regarding the Priscillianists and Theodosius I regarding all non-Catholics. The Papacy not Honorius took the lead over Pelagians after 410, but that Emperor was a weak ruler and the state in decline since the 406–12 invasions and civil wars.

A new or weak ruler under political threat might have given in to Church pressure to act against heretics, as Constantine IX in the East was overshadowed by Patriarch Michael Cerularius in the 1050s; but this would have been the exception. Sooner or later, there could logically have been an egotistical and theologically minded Emperor who set out to reform the Church according to his own opinions as Constantine and Justinian had done earlier. Indeed, since Constantine had presided at the Council of Nicaea as the 'Thirteenth Apostle' the legal precedents were in favour of the Imperial office's interventionist role. The clerics would have had no traditions of being able to defy an errant secular authority successfully, provided that that ruler was Christian, unless by luck and good management they had been able to use a successful rebellion or civil war after the fifth century to remove a heretic Emperor.

The landed wealth of the monasteries would have been an added incentive for a financially embarrassed or ambitious secular government to act against them in a mass-confiscation and sale in the manner of Henry VIII. In real life, in the mid-eighth century East the Iconoclast 'innovator' Constantine V closed down monasteries as centres of resistance to his doctrines and held forced mass-marriages of monks and nuns. The extent of Imperial authority over a united Europe, with all its provinces subject to Imperial orders, would however have given pause to a militant reformer such as Luther. No persecuted author could take refuge from Church law and its courts in the domains of a secular ruler who shared his willingness for defiance; the safety of individual controversialists would have depended on local secular connivance and ultimately on Imperial backing. Nor could independent and godly city-states run by reformers, such as sixteenth century Geneva, be set up within an all-embracing Empire. An Emperor loyal to the existing Church order would have had a far easier job than Charles V in the real-life 1520s in putting down heresy and forcing compliance from local authorities.

But, conversely, once an Emperor decided to back the Church's opponents, as Constantius II and Valens had backed rival sects and Julian the pagans, he could throw the weight of Imperial power into the conflict in support of his protégés. Gaining the support of the secular prince would have been as vital to reform as in sixteenth century England or Scandinavia. Lacking such support, reformers would have had to develop unofficial, underground churches at risk of state harassment as in the fourth century West and East (Arians and Donatists) and the fifth to seventh century East (Nestorians and Monophysites). Such bodies may have been easier to set up in provinces further away from the centres of secular and ecclesiastical power, such as Britain, Scandinavia, and Germany, providing that there were sympathetic local governors or bishops. Many Emperors may indeed have been persuadable that multiplicity of religious belief led to anarchy, as tradition would have been in favour of 'one Church' as of one centralised secular government. In these circumstances, it is probable that unless a determined secularising ruler or a classical enthusiast had ended legal coercion an embryonic 'Protestantism' may have found it easier to develop in the new colonies in America than in centralised Europe, and Catholicism have maintained its control at the Imperial Court. A form of 'Counter-Reformationary' culture and thought would have been likely to emerge at the Imperial court, as in the real-life Habsburg Empire, with Emperors in the mould of Philip II of Spain or Emperors Ferdinand II and III. But hopefully there would have been more open-minded and enquiring rulers in the mould of Rudolf II, and the greater physical survival of classical writings would have duly stimulated a revival of interest in science.

A word of caution should be issued about thinking that a 'Golden Age' of scientific discovery could have been assisted by the survival of the information contained in the Great Library of Alexandria. Certainly, Alexandria itself would have survived as a major Mediterranean port, unless its harbours had silted up without clearance, and not declined into a backwater. Scientists could have settled in the major cities of the Eastern Mediterranean rather than emerging in the new mercantile economies of north western Europe. But it is debateable whether the Great Library still existed in the late Roman period, let alone being intact for use by scholars. The story of Caliph Omar feeding the contents to the city's baths-furnaces as being un-Islamic appears to be a late myth, though equally the warehouse of manuscripts burnt during Julius Caesar's war in the city in 48 BC was probably only an 'over-flow'.[30-31] The date of the ending of the library's existence is still debated, but the two major occurrences of destruction in the city in the third century, Caracalla's sack and the revolt against Diocletian, or the destruction of the 'Serapeum' by militant Catholic monks in 391 probably accounted for most of the premises. Many useful classical manuscripts would have survived to a Renaissance in unsacked libraries across the Empire, but much would still have been lost to neglect since the third century.

The actual term of 'Renaissance' – not a contemporary but a later one – for any revival of enthusiasm for classical art would have been unlikely, as there would have been no break in political continuity. The practical implications of less physical destruction would have preserved for more ancient manuscripts, on both art and science, to be consulted. Individual secular families' collections would have survived, in great houses in cities and countryside, and some of the civic libraries in Rome itself. The capital had been a destination for literary loot for centuries, especially from Hellenistic libraries such as Pergamum; these would have survived unless burnt in accidental fires.

In scientific matters, works by Archimedes or Hero of Alexandria would have aided inventors; in artistic matters, looted paintings and statues would still have adorned Rome. But neglect or Christian zeal would have wrecked some examples; not all the classical statuary taken to Constantinople by Constantine survived to the sack in 1204. Memorably, the great statue of Athena from the Parthonon was smashed then by a superstitious crowd.[32] Would pious Romans or Iconoclast clerics have acted similarly in the West? The surviving examples of pagan temples in the 'civilized' Roman East in the sixth xentury were shunned by the superstitious peasants and nobles alike, as seen in the 'life' of St Daniel the Stylite.

Chapter 6

The Eastern Empire, Effects of the Survival of the Western Empire

The sixth and seventh centuries, a far stronger reaction to the Avars, Persia, and the Arabs?

The Northern frontier, less of a tribal threat to the Balkans?
The survival of the Western Empire would also have had major effects on the East, which would have had an ally able to send troops in major crises but also a strategic bonus in the upper and middle Danube area. It is possible that the survival of a militarily powerful West through the third and fourth centuries, and perhaps its preservation in the fifth, would have involved a scenario where the Empire held onto or regained Dacia. Apparently evacuated at a time of military crisis in the mid-third century, probably by Gallienus or Aurelian, it might have been preserved as a province had the Empire's rulers had the will to follow through Marcus Aurelius' occupation of the Czech lands to the Carpathians in the 180s. Due to lack of firm evidence we cannot say for definite that Marcus had a grand plan of strategy in mind to advance the frontier permanently to the Carpathians, but the discovery of Roman military structures in Bohemia would indicate that a long-term occupation was planned. Lacking a determined resistance from the occupied tribes with outside assistance, the factor which led to the similar advances in Scotland in the 80s and 140s and in Iraq in 114–17 being aborted, there would have been no logical reason for a later Emperor to withdraw in the later second or third centuries.

Thus Rome would have been been defending the Carpathians not the Danube as the frontier against the German tribes through the third century; a limited number of mountain passes and gaps in the Carpathian ridges were easier to defend than a river which was crossable for all its length and needed more troops. This more viable frontier would then have been defendable through the third century, barring major defeats like that of Decius by Kniva's Goths in 251, even with the Empire's troop numbers reduced due to the serious outbreak of plague in the early 250s.

Alternatively, Dacia might have been abandoned due to reduced troop levels and the number of attacks from neighbouring tribes, if not in the third century, then under pressure from the Goths as they retreated from the expanding Hunnic empire on the steppes around 376. Roman-held Dacia would then have been an obvious destination for their refugees rather than the south bank of the Danube as in real life. Dacia might have been lost to the Huns themselves in the 430s, or fallen under the weight of attacks by tribal refugees from Attila at a time when the Western Empire could not manage a military response, maybe after the death of Constantius III in 421, in the succession crisis before Galla Placidia secured the throne for her son Valentinian III in 425. In this scenario of a surviving Western Empire, the Rhine would not have been crossed by a permanent Germanic presence in 406, and thus armed bands of warriors from 406 and refugees from the 430s–440s would not have been settling in Gaul, Spain, and Africa. The pressure of westward tribal movements on Dacia and any Roman territories in Bohemia would have been acute, leading to the same sort of demands for admission that the refugee Goths made on the lower Danube in 376. Refusing them admission to the Empire would have run the risk of defiance, armed confrontation, and a Roman defeat such as the Goths carried out in 376–8. Constantius III, who handled the Gothic problem in Spain and Gaul successfully in 411–18 and allowed them a vassal kingdom, and Aetius had the military and diplomatic skill to handle such a Romano-German crisis successfully. Valentinian III, Aetius' jealous sovereign who assassinated him in 454 and precipitated the West's fatal collapse, did not.

Even if Dacia and/or the Czech lands had been lost to the German tribes in the early fifth century, this might not have been permanent. Had the West retained a strong comitatus and control of enough provinces to fund it, its commanders had a military edge over disunited invaders. Once Attila's empire collapsed, there was a potential window of opportunity for reoccupation, or at least securing a peace with tribal leaders on terms favourable to Roman interests. Following precedent, the Empire was likeliest to require some sort of federate vassal status from the local tribal kings, the terms which Theodosius had reached with the Goths still holding out in Thrace in 381, and which kept their commanders under technical Roman command until Alaric's revolt in 395. Dacia and perhaps the Czech lands could have been reoccupied by Aetius and his armies of Romans and German allies on the death of Attila in 453, or at least secured by Aetius for a group of allied tribes who had won independence from the Huns in the revolt that the latter's subjects mounted in 454.

In order to secure Roman control of Dacia and the other lands threatening the Eastern Empire's North-West frontier, source of the major Avar threat frothe 560s, the two Empires would have had to construct a system of alliances with local tribal leaders in the power vacuum after Attila's empire collapsed. The history of the area after the anti-Hunnic revolt of 454 is obscure, but it would appear that the Huns under Attila's sons managed to hold onto a domain based around the Ukraine plains and that nomadic peoples from this Western part of the steppes were a continuing threat to the Empire. In the 490s Anastasius found it necessary to construct a massive wall across the Thracian isthmus, about thirty miles west of Constantinople, against repeated raiding from across the Danube.[1]

Indeed, this threat revived in the 540s and 550s with massive raids on the Balkans by the Kutrigur Bulgars, starting with a two pronged raid into Greece, as far as Thermopylae, and Thrace, as far as the Long Wall of Anastasius, in 540 and culminating in a massive three pronged attack on Thessaly, the Chersonese around Gallipoli, and Thrace, breaching the Long Wall, by Khan Zebergan in 559. The Empire had probably lost immense numbers of current and future soldiers, and farmers, supplying their food, and taxpayers to fund them, in the plague of 542, when Procopius estimated that half the capital's population died, and its armies were tied down in Italy, Spain, North Africa, and Armenia.

The extra threat to the Balkans from 540 strained its capacities to the limit, and during the 559 attacks the Emperor had to call Belisarius out of retirement and send him to tackle the invaders in Thrace with a hastily raised force of around 500 bucellarii (bodyguards), its size a testimony to the lack of troops available. Luckily, his reputation among the steppe nomads was such that after his initial victories in minor clashes they retreated.[2] But the extra dimension of a new nomad threat to the Balkans and the lack of troops to meet it meant that much ravaging went unchecked, undermining the prosperity, and ability to supply soldiers, food, and taxes, of the Balkans. Had the Western Empire still been in existence through the fifth and into the sixth centuries, with or without Dacia, the Kutrigur menace would have been unchanged, the raiders came from the steppes via the lowland corridor of Wallachia, and would still have crossed the lower Danube. Justinian might still have sent his armies to reconquer a schismatic, probably Arian-led Western Empire or intervened in a civil war, and so been unable to protect the Balkan heartland from which he himself came. But if he had not been fighting in the West and had turned his formidable energies on Persia, which the East had been fighting in the late 520s before the opportunity to regain the West arose, he should have had more men available despite the plague and so put up a greater resistance to the raiding from 540.

The second major threat from the steppes in the mid-sixth century, the Avars, arrived in the Ukrainian region some time in the 560s. Their epic move west from central Asia developed as a result of factors out of the Empire's control, as their first steppe empire was broken up in 552 by a revolt by their Turkish vassals and they had to flee their homeland.[3] Ultimately, this tribal revolt had the consequence of destroying the Roman Empire nine hundred years later, the rise to independent political action of the Turkic peoples touched off the migrations that led the Seljuks to Manzikert in 1071 and the Ottomans to Constantinople in 1453. With or without a victorious Western Empire, preserved by Theodosius I, Stilicho, Constantius III, and Aetius from Germans and Huns, occupying Dacia and overaweing the German tribes, the Avars would still have arrived on the steppes facing the Danube. Their threat to the East would have duly developed, with a repeat of fifth century Hunnic history as the incumbent local tribal kingdom facing the Roman Illyrian and middle Danube zone (the Gepids) was destroyed (567) and the threatened Lombards moved West towards Italy. Justinian and, sporadically, Justin II paid off the Avars with subsidies, as Theodosius II had done the Huns in the 440s, but ultimately the price of blackmail rose, 80,000 nomismata per annum as of 574, and the Avars turned on the Empire, probably assisted by the threat of a Roman-Turkish alliance against them.[4] In 579 they attacked Sirmium, key to the middle Danube, while the Lombards who had fled ahead of them were invading Italy from 568 and destroying what remained of an economy and society shattered by eighteen years of war between Justinian's troops and the Goths.[5]

If the Western Empire had still been in existence, either independent or fully reunited with Justinian's realm, as of the 560s, the Lombard invasion would have fallen on their frontiers in Dacia or the middle Danube and been met by a substantial military force in long garrisoned, unruined fortresses rather than the war ravaged Italy of real-life 568. Barring excessive losses due to the 542 plague and its successors, it should have been containable but would have prevented major Western military aid to the East against the Avar threat, or against the less centralised but no less dangerous infiltration of Slav settlers into the ravaged Balkans in the 570s and 580s. The latter ultimately lost the Empire this invaluable centre of troops, supplies, and tax-revenue and thus made it dangerously weak to face the Persian threat after 602 and the Arab threat after 634.

If the Lombards had been contained, the Western Empire should have been able to send Tiberius II and Maurice valuable troops in the 580s to deal with the Avar threat and the Slav settlers, though these smaller groups of invaders would have been more difficult to corner. Crucial fortresses such as Sirmium (lost in 582) and Singidunum (lost in 583) would have been saved, and the middle Danube line been held against major penetration. This would not have prevented the major Avar raids into Thrace from the lower Danube, which had already reached Anchialus in 583 and the 'Long Wall' in 584 and led to years of inconclusive Roman campaigns, and increasingly to worrying mutinies by the East's Balkan armies against their unpopular generals.[6]

Western military help would not have prevented a multiplicity of raids and the resultant insecurity, flight from the land, and threat to agriculture in the Balkans. But if the West, as overlord of the German tribes who had escaped from Attila's sons' control in 454, such as perhaps the Lombards and Gepids, had occupied or dominated Dacia their army would have been able to cross the Carpathian passes and take the Avars in the rear. A nomad people could easily abandon their threatened homeland and retreat across the plains with their horse-drawn waggons, outstripping their lumbering pursuers, as Darius the Great had found in this area in 512 BC. Constantine the Great had had more luck in a massive campaign North of the Danube in AD 332, aided by local allies, but lost his nerve in 334.[7] But a joint Western and Eastern advance on the Avar homeland would have served to keep the raiders on the defensive rather than perpetually raiding Thrace while their Slav allies overran the inland Balkans, and would probably have forced a temporary treaty out of their 'Khagan' until he was confident enough to resume the war.

A lesser Balkan threat, no Eastern Roman collapse after 602?
Arguably, the assistance to Maurice's forces by a Western army – meaning less pressure on the Eastern troops – would have meant less mutinies by the latter, who in real life revolted in 593, 595, and, fatally for Maurice, 602. Generals

had to be replaced, the money saving Emperor's attempts to pay his men in supplies not coin had to be rescinded, and the attempt to winter north of the Danube in Avar territory was defied successfully twice. The strain on the East's finances was obviously one cause of Maurice's careful fiscal measures, though his troops preferred to call him stingy, and after he refused to ransom the Avars' captives, who were massacred, and made a second order to winter north of the Danube, a final revolt led to his overthrow.

The resulting tyranny of the troops' nominee as Emperor, the centurion Phocas, and civil wars led to Persian intervention and the disasters of the 600s and 610s.[8] But it is possible that a less financially stringent Emperor than Maurice would not have been as hated by the troops, or faced a violent uprising in Constantinople in their support when they marched on the capital.

How much of the disastrous success of the 602 mutiny, leading to civil war as various provincial armies challenged Phocas, was due to the brusque, unpopular Emperor? What if his predecessor Tiberius II had not selected him as his chosen son-in-law and heir in 582? Maurice had been an experienced and successful general in the Persian wars before then, but he seems to have been a failure in keeping his troops' loyalty as shown by repeated mutinies in the 590s. Indeed, the chain of dubiously competent Eastern leadership can be traced back through the profligate Tiberius II to the previous ruler, Justin II, nephew and successor of Justinian. An irascible and haughty man, his refusal to continue a subsidy to the Avars is supposed to have caused their first attack on the Empire, though such a steppe empire was likely to raid the East at some point. His surprise descent into permanent mental instability in 574 led to his powerful wife Sophia (niece of Theodora and just as ruthless) taking charge of the government and choosing a senior Court regimental commander, Tiberius, as her Caesar and the next ruler. The choice of Justin as Justinian's heir was doubtful, as the old Emperor died suddenly on 14 November 565 with only his eunuch chamberlain Callinicus' word for it that he had named Justin at all. The latter was the preferred choice of the two most powerful Imperial female kin, Sophia, and Justin's mother Vigilantia (Justinian's sister). They duly hurried him to the Palace to be crowned by Patriarch John before his rivals knew Justinian was dead.[9] Without this coup, there is a chance that Justinian or his ministers would have preferred another Imperial nephew called Justin, the militarily experienced son of the late Germanus, who in November 565 was away commanding troops in Bithynia. He was sent off to Alexandria as governor and later murdered, probably at Sophia's orders. Would this other Justin have proved a better Emperor than his namesake, passed the throne on to his heirs, and thus reduced the possibility of a disastrous civil war after 602?

It is probable that the extra bonus of Western aid could have staved off this disaster to the Empire, which ruined its strength and unity ahead of the Arab attacks, though the piecemeal Slav settlement of the Balkans was more difficult to halt than attacks by Avar armies. Hopefully, though the flight of Roman farmers from the land would have transformed the social and economic basis of the Balkan peninsula, and brought in pagans to replace Christians, major towns within reach of the Black Sea and Aegean coasts could have been held and the decentralized Slavs, small groups of settlers lacking warlords or kings, been brought under Roman military control after the Avars had been vanquished. Their menfolk could then have been recruited to the Roman army and settlers moved to under-populated areas elsewhere in the Empire, as Justinian II carried out after 685 in real life, and the pagan tribes been Christianised once the Church interested itself in missionary work.[10]

The lesser strains of a Balkan war in the 590s might have saved Maurice from overthrow in 602, though losses of manpower and financial capacity due to the plague would have been serious even had the West survived. Maurice, apparently loathed in Constantinople and the object of a massive rising by the united circus factions in 602, or his inexperienced young son Theodosius (III?) would still have been at risk of overthrow at some point. To that extent the Empire would have been luckier had the vigorous if spendthrift Tiberius II (who died in 582 in his early fifties) lived longer or had a son, or had Justinian been survived and succeeded by his competent and popular cousin Germanus, who had sons. Once Maurice's dynasty had fallen, there was an excuse for his old ally King Chosroes II of Persia, who he had restored to the Persian throne in 591, to invade the Empire out of hostility to his usurping successors. In real life, Chosroes used a pretender to the identity of Prince Theodosius, whose death in the bloodbath of November 602 was less certain than that of his younger brothers. The claimant seems to have had some impact in winning over Roman commanders to ally with Persia in the threatened frontier zone of Mesopotamia, as with 'Domestic of the East' Narses at Dara in 603, though dislike and fear of the low-born and increasingly bloodthirsty Phocas would have been other factors.

Arguably, a domestic revolt in Constantinople against Maurice in favour of a more acceptable usurper from the traditional ruling classes, most obviously Theodosius's father-in-law Germanus, who Maurice accused of treason in 602, or Phocas' dubious ally Priscus, would have been more likely to command the loyalty of most Eastern army commanders and so kept their command united.[11] The Persians would have had less success in breaking through the frontier during Phocas' reign and thus presenting his replacement Heraclius with disaster in 610: even with the real-life civil wars in the riven Empire, Persia did not gain Dara until 606, Theodosiopolis (the north-eastern frontier key) until 608, and Edessa (key to the upper Euphrates) until 609.[12] The nature and beneficiary of the anti-Maurice revolt were thus crucial, but had the Western Empire still been in existence in 602–10 their army would have had the potential to invade at an early stage and remove the usurper. Heraclius, as son and nominee for the throne of the rebelling Exarch of North Africa in Carthage, would have been well placed to use Western aid to reach Constantinople earlier than the real-life autumn 610. The successful invasion of the East by the West had last been carried out in 361 by Julian, though his rival Constantius II had opportunely died before the outcome was decided by battle; Constantine the Great had removed Licinius in 324. Thus Heraclius, or another Western nominee, would have been able to assume the command in the East against Chosroes at an earlier date, and to use Western troops to drive him back.

It is possible that Chosroes, an ambitious ruler who by the 610s was seemingly intent on reconquering all the Levant lost to Persia in 334–1 BC but also potentially open to Persian aristocratic resentment for being installed by Roman armies in 591, would have invaded the Empire opportunistically at any point of domestic crisis. The overthrow of his benefactor Maurice was the real-life excuse, but there could have been others; in 540 his predecessor-but-two and namesake Chosroes Anurshirvan (Immortal Soul) had invaded Syria while Justinian was preoccupied in the West. Assuming that a domestic Eastern crisis after 600 led to a Persian invasion and that a long civil war had enabled Chosroes to take the major Mesopotamian defensive fortresses as in real life, the new Emperor installed securely in Constantinople (Heraclius?) could have called on Western aid to drive back Persia. There is a caveat in that the Empire was hit by plague and famine independently of the civil war in 608–9, thus diminishing its ability to raise troops to fight Persia, but we need not doubt that the civil wars in Syria and Egypt between Phocan loyalists and Heraclian attackers in 608–10 aided the Persians' success in overrunning this war-ravaged area a few years later.[13] Antioch and Caesarea-in-Cappadocia only fell to Chosroes' generals in around 611, Melitene and Damascus in 613, Palestine in 614 (notoriously aided by a Jewish revolt), and Egypt in 617–19; meanwhile the Persians could raid across Asia Minor to Chalcedon in 614 and in 616 two attacks reached Chalcedon and Sardes.[14]

Thus the major disasters in loss of territory only followed Heraclius' accession, and they were aided by a renewed Avar war in the Balkans; finally in 626 the two powers were able to attack Constantinople together. Had the Eastern Emperors defeated the Avars decisively, hopefully with Western aid, or Heraclius secured the throne with Western aid at an earlier date the Persian attack should have been blunted before it reached this critical stage. The Eastern Empire would have been fighting on one front not two whenever the Persians attacked, and the latter would have been unlikely to have secured Syria or potentially rebellious Palestine let alone Egypt. The main war between Heraclius, probably with Western aid, and the Persians would have centred on the fortresses of the upper Euphrates and Armenia, sites of the previous Roman-Persian wars in the 520s and 570s, or at worst on an invaded Syria and Cappadocia. Crucially, the amount of damage done to crops, towns, and fortresses ahead of the Arab attacks would have been substantially reduced and there is less chance of the collapse of Roman power leading to inter-communal massacres in Palestine. Thus the area would have been able to meet the new challenge from the desert from a stronger position in 634–6, instead of in the aftermath of thirty years of war and over a decade of foreign occupation.

Assuming a major Persian war to have taken place during an Eastern civil war in Chosroes II's reign (591–628), the Eastern Emperor, for the sake of argument, Heraclius, could still have lost control of the Euphrates fortresses and faced invasion of Syria. Without the Avar threat as a problem nearer his capital, he would have been able to take the offensive earlier than real-life 626/7. But it is still logical that he would have chosen to invade the Persian heartland via the Caucasus uplands rather than across the Iraqi plains. The Persians and their Parthian predecessors had been able to utilise the latter to harass Roman armies with their hordes of cavalry archers since the disastrous Parthian rout of Crassus at Carrhae in 53 BC. The Romans' nomad Arab ally in Eastern Syria, the Ghassanid confederation, had been destroyed by the pro-Persian Lakhimids recently, so the Emperor could not use their cavalry to protect his army's flanks against harassment. Quite apart from the uncertain numbers of troops that Chosroes' generals Shahin and Shahbaraz had at their disposal to oppose a Roman advance, it would have been a wise strategic move for the Emperor to avoid the open plains and march on Chosroes' capital Ctesiphon via the mountains, and, as in real life, to join up with the new steppe power of the Khazars in the Tbilisi area en route and secure their cavalry. As in real life, the Romans would then have descended on the Iraqi plains from the north (the intended route of Mark Antony in 34 BC) and assaulted Chosroes' heartland. The speed of the Persian collapse in real-life 627–8 indicates that there was war weariness in their empire as well as in the Roman lands, and it is probable that (as in real life) the humiliated Chosroes would have been deposed and murdered by ambitious relatives and the latter then sued for peace.

Long-term results in the Middle East, effects on the Arab invasions?
The collapse of the war-weakened Persian polity in 628 resulted not only in the evacuation of Roman lands by the undefeated Shahbaraz (who then joined in the competition for the Persian throne) but a prolonged civil war and serious instability. The eventual winner of the conflict, Yazdegerd III, faced Arab invasion in 637 and after losing Iraq, not easy to defend from the Southern desert, as seen by Saddam Hussein in 1991 and 2003, abandoned the fight and fled to the Iranian plateau. Had the area not recently suffered foreign invasion and a prolonged civil war, as with the Roman Levant, Arab occupation would not have been so easy, though the state of the defences of the cities and the morale of their defenders can only be inferred. In the field, the exaggerations of later Arab writers make accurate assessments of Persian numbers impossible. The contemporary Armenian Sebeos put numbers at Qaddisiya at 80,000. One hard-fought battle over several days won all Iraq. Indeed, it is possible that a victorious Eastern Emperor (with Western reinforcements?) could have imposed a treaty on Persia that saw further advances of the Roman frontier from the favourable terms of Maurice's dictat to the newly-installed Chosroes in 591. The obvious field for Roman expansion was the Caucasus, which had Christian kingdoms in Iberia and Lazica/Abasgia (later to merge in 1000 as Georgia) and the divided Christian land of Armenia. Long torn between Rome and Persia, most of Armenia had passed to Persia in the favourable treaty of 387 and then back to the Empire in 591; the latter treaty had also secured Roman domination of Iberia and a number of valuable fortress-towns in the salient between Euphrates and Tigris (e.g. Nisibis).

The real-life exhausted Empire of 629 was content with a restoration of the 'status quo' on the Persian frontier, but an earlier and more crushing victory, aided by Western troops and possibly by vanquished Avar and Slav 'federates' from the Danube, could have secured the Empire full control of all the Caucasus region as far as the vital Darial Pass. This invasion-route was the Khazar highway from their steppe homeland to the Kur valley, where Heraclius met their army in real-life 627, and thence on to attack either Persia or Roman Armenia; its control would be vital for the Empire and could have been secured with extra troops. There were also local Christian 'Alans' (Ossetians) available to be used as allies, with titles given to their rulers as was the Roman practice for friendly Caucasian notables. It would not be an innovation for Roman policy to extend their rule or influence this far northeast; it had been considered by both Pompey (who had invaded it in person in the mid-60s BC) and Trajan. Nor was Eastern interest in the 620s a unique result of Heraclius' situation, Justinian had fought hard to keep the Persians from the Black Sea, the two empires clashing over Iberia and Colchis.

Given the previous Roman occupation of Iraq by Trajan in 114–17, it is possible that Heraclius would have annexed it from a supine Persia once Chosroes was dead and his heirs fighting over the throne. The Persians were as vulnerable, perhaps more so, to well-armed, large Roman armies as to the small army, perhaps 7,000 strong, of Arab nomads who invaded in 637, if lacking their concentrated archery. Heraclius used propaganda to stress the religious element of his Persian war and inspire zeal, as the Caliphs did. The Romans would not have had to rebuild an occupied and war-shattered Levant in this scenario, though Syria might well have suffered heavily as in the previous Persian invasions of 260 and 540. But loss of men and tax resources to the plague and Balkan wars would make this extension of Roman territory improbable, and it is more likely that Heraclius would have contented himself with backing up his client Shahbaraz as Maurice had previously backed Chosroes. It is arguable that if the experienced Shahbaraz, soon overthrown in real life, had lasted as Great King he would have made a better job of holding back the Arabs in Iraq than Yazdegerd, with no known military experience, did in 637, defeating the lightly-armed invaders once they moved away from the desert to attack the major towns. A Persian ruler who had no dynastic legitimacy was, however, at risk of overthrow by princely pretenders, though Chosroes' noble rival Bahram Chobin had lasted until removed by Maurice's armies. It is possible that Shahbaraz and his successors could have held onto the Iranian heartland by building fortresses and defending the passes that crossed the Zagros, at least for a few decades; in real life the plateau was lost in 650. It is unlikely that a Roman Emperor after Heraclius, in real life his consumptive son Constantine III and under-age grandson Constans II, would have had strategic appreciation of the danger of the Arabs wielding Iraqi manpower and Persian military skills against them, the only reason why the Empire might have been willing to lend its troops to a counter-stroke against the Arabs for Persia's benefit. The Romans in the 640s had no awareness that the Arab conquest was permanent. The new state could have proved as ephemeral as the last successful desert state, the empire of Palmyra whch Aurelian had destroyed in the early 270s.

Within a few years of 630 the Empire would have faced a rising gradient of Arab incursions into Palestine and Syria, as in real life. This developed independently of the Roman-Persian war, following the Prophet's uniting of the Arabian Peninsula, as the warlike Arab tribesmen turned their energy from mutual conflict into attacks on their war-weakened nighbours. The consequences for the Empire's survival of a militarily improved situation in the Levant in the 620s have been covered elsewhere. But the same argument holds as made there, in that no major conflict for the region around 602–29, or an earlier Roman victory would have left fewer towns and fortresses damaged, more troops garrisoning the area, a less ravaged countryside, less mutual antagonism of Jews and Christians in Palestine, and greater will to resist. It would not have prevented military defeats in hostile terrain or bad weather, as at Yarmuk in 636, or the piecemeal undermining of agriculture and isolation of towns by repeated raiding that Roman troops could not prevent. Isolated towns, their trade reduced by insecure roads, could have fallen one by one and farmers have fled the countryside as new settlers took over their lands by force, as the Slavs achieved in the Balkans. But the number of Roman defeats should have been less, and towns, not taken by the Persians, so with undamaged walls, should have held out longer, except when struck by earthquakes.[15]

It is worth noting that in war-ravaged Italy after 568 the persistent but small and poorly-armed Lombard incursions only gradually overran the isolated towns, and failed to conquer the Southern coastal towns or fortified Rome and marsh-bound Ravenna. Inland, the countryside could be overrun and isolated towns surrounded and starved-out. Could the Arab armies have had a similarly limited effect at first in Syria and Palestine had they faced stronger resistance and the Caliphs diverted their main efforts against the weaker Persia?

Coastal towns should have held out longest as they could be supplied by sea, at least until the Arabs had acquired siege-machinery from Persia; in the thirteenth century the well-defended coastal towns of Palestine and Syria defied the inland Moslem powers for decades. The maximum danger would have come had walls been levelled by earthquakes. Logically, the availability of troops from the Western Empire to assist the Eastern army should have made the latter more formidable, and reinforced their garrisons' ability to hold out. The one caveat to this is that a Catholic Western Emperor might have take issue with Heraclius or Constans II over their heretical proposals to reunite Nicaen orthodoxy with Monophysitism by a new theological dogma, and thus broken off the supply of military aid for several crucial decades from around 640.

Inland Syria and Palestine were difficult to defend from the desert, although a stronger and well-funded Eastern army should have been able to defeat most lightly-armed Arab armies until the latter had superiority of numbers from the conquest of Iraq and the Iranian plateaus. The threat of Arab archery to Roman infantry or cavalry, as from the Parthians at Carrhae and of inclement weather or incompetent generalship would have aided the Arabs. Roman fear of encounters with their Middle Eastern enemies in the open plains was more noticeable at times of military inferiority. Trajan in the 110s, Lucius Verus in the 160s, Septimius Severus in 197–8, Carus in 283, and Julian in 363 all tackled the open plains of Iraq and the Persians chose to retreat before them. Possibly a major defeat like Yarmuk would have made them as wary of the Arabs as they had been of Persia in the plains in the 620s, or poor leadership after Heraclius died undermined a coherent resistance and led to piecemeal conquest of the Levant. But the Romans had held onto well-fortified Antioch against Parthian attack after Carrhae in the late 50s BC, thanks to decisive leadership by Cassius, later Caesar's murderer, and superior defensive capability. Could the will to resist and more troops have saved Antioch again in the 640s?

With regular military assistance from the West, not available to the heretic Constans, in real life in conflict with the Papacy, the local outposts of the Eastern Empire could have held out for several more decades, at least on the coast. A fortified 'limes' across the line of the Isthmus of Suez and ships, aided by the allied Christian power of Axum, which had had the naval power to hold the Yemen in recent decades, in the Red Sea, could have preserved Egypt for several decades, until the Arabs managed to infiltrate the local deserts and join up with local tribesmen around the Nile valley. It is quite conceivable that the Romans could have halted the Arab advance westwards at the Red Sea or the 'narrows' of Tripolitania and preserved most of North Africa for Christianity, at least until some civil war gave the invaders their chance. Western troops from Europe would have aided the resistance around Carthage, though if the Arabs had managed to convert the desert tribes the always latent threat of Berber raids could then have made the province economically unviable and led to eventual evacuation. The limited archaeological evidence in Tunisia for the seventh century shows poor agriculture and declining towns (aided by Berber raids?), so resistance would need outside help.

Most probably, the Eastern Empire would have retained Antioch and the fortresses of upper Iraq for some decades from circa 640 but faced a Caliphate that had taken over all the Iraqi plains and all of Persia and could throw the manpower of the latter and of Arabia against it. The threat would have been more acute than that of Persia, with the prestige of 'jihad' encouraging each Caliph to wage war on Rome rather than the Persian Great Kings who were only sporadically aggressive. It is unclear but possible that some of the Arabs living on the Syrian Desert frontier who joined in the invasions were former auxiliaries in the Roman army, which regularly used Arabs, who knew the area well and coveted its land for their herds. An apocryphal story has it that Arab tribes who were normally paid off to avoid raiding Syria by the Roman authorities were refused money by the cash-strapped government and so joined the attack.[16] Persistent Arab pressure from a united state keen to win lands and loot is probable.

For the moment, any Roman military success and the frustration of Caliphal plans to settle Arab tribesmen in Syria and Palestine, later in Africa, would have resulted in a heavier settlement by them within conquered Persia. Their military energy, used against each other if there was no external enemy to attack, as seen in successive civil wars in the late 650s and 680s, would still have needed a focus. The new post-civil-war regime of Mu'awiya in the 660s was particularly aggressive in ranging across Asia Minor in real life. Accordingly, Caliphs concerned to direct their troops against an external foe would have had reason to launch them against their Eastern neighbours at times of truce with the Romans. Would this have led to an earlier conquest of Transoxiana and the Indus valley, or even a concerted attack on the Indian sub-continent far earlier than the real-life efforts of Mahmud of Ghazni in the early eleventh century and the Ghaznavids in the later twelfth century?

The military adventures of probing and, if successful, conquering Spain and the Indus valley in the early 700s were taken on by local commanders in North Africa and Iran with minimal direction from the Caliph in Damascus, logically to keep their restless troops occupied in the same manner as Attila constantly sought new targets in the mid-fifth century.[17] With stronger Roman-led resistance in the Mediterranean, military adventurers could have concentrated on the East.

After the seventh century

More or less permanent Romano-Arab war would follow, on a far more regular basis than Roman-Persian conflict, and duly undermine the Empire's military and economic capacity. But the Empire would have possession of the Balkans and, usually, Western military aid, and it would be in a better position to resist, and to hold onto Asia Minor and Armenia without major raiding, than the real-life Empire of the later seventh and eighth centuries. It could also take the offensive more easily when the Caliphate began to decline and break up, and if it had held onto Egypt or Tripolitania to block an Arab advance westwards the main area of conflict would have beeen Syria.

Indeed, arguably the successful defence of the Balkans from the Avars and a Western military presence in Illyria and Dacia might have enabled the Eastern Empire to hold the Danube against the Bulgars in the later seventh century. Previous large-scale crossings had been held back by a powerful Eastern army, or at least contained in Thrace, as would have happened with the Goths in 376–8 had Valens not tackled them so precipitously but waited for Western reinforcements. Aided by Western attacks on the Bulgars in the rear from Dacia, Constantine IV might have managed to push out the newcomers in the initial clash of 680. In real life, the Bulgars established a permanent base in the lower Danube valley and threatened the rest of the Balkans. Had the Arabs distracted the Eastern armies from a Balkan war in 680, a stronger Empire could still have blocked the Sredna Gore and Haemus ranges' passes to more than occasional Bulgar raids. Constantine V's long campaigns against the Bulgars in the mid-eighth century might then have been successful in evicting them.

Disasters such as Nicephorus I's defeat and death in a mountain pass trap in 811 would have been less likely in a better-resourced Empire, if still possible in cases of incompetent command. In real life the disaster of 811 brought Bulgar Khan Krum's armies to the walls of Constantinople and lost most of Thrace and the inner Balkans, a valuable source of Eastern military manpower; a similar Bulgarian domination of the peninsula followed under Czar Simeon in the 920s. Had the East held onto the peninsula, or contained the newcomers north of the Great Balkan range in the Danube plain, it would have had extra resources of manpower and supplies, although arguably not taxes, given that this rural area was not then a monetary economy. It was however likely that large-scale and disruptive raids south would have continued to undermine the economy, send farmers fleeing, and reduce the viability of isolated towns. This had occurred during the sixth century at the hands of Kutrigur Huns and Avars despite all the Empire's armies. All this would aid the Slav settlement that occurred in the devastated Balkan vacuum in the real-life later sixth and seventh centuries. But logically a more powerful Imperial army would have had the means to coerce these divided and poorly-led settlers into supplying valuable troops to the Empire as Justinian II did in Thrace in the 680s and Irene and Nicephorus I did in Greece around 800.

The Eastern Empire might still have faced a depopulated Balkans. But it would lack the distraction of successive Bulgarian wars as it regained the military initiative during the early to mid-tenth century. The Arabs would have held only a part of the south and east Mediterranean coasts, and been less likely to have had the disruptive advantage of naval power had the Empire held onto Egypt, with Alexandria, or the Syrian coastal ports or both. Crucially, the new Arab fleets which threatened Constantinople in the later seventh century used the forests of south-western Asia Minor and Cyprus for timber; a more powerful Empire holding most of the Levantine ports would have prevented this. The Arabs would not have conquered Sicily and Crete from the 820s, thus releasing the Empire from another military distraction during the following centuries. Even if Egypt, vulnerable to raiding of the Nile valley from the deserts, had eventually been occupied, possibly by a dynamic Caliph with armies from Persia, the Western army would have been able to assist the defence of provinces further west, delaying any advance to Carthage.

Much would depend on whether the East was distracted by a civil war at a time of Arab unity, e.g. under the first Abbasids from around 750 to the 809–13 civil war, and if the restive Berber tribes of the north-western African interior chose to attack a weakened Imperial defensive system. The extent of Roman losses of manpower to the plague, rural disorder or both in the African provinces would have been crucial; it is probable that the cities of this area were in steep decline before the Arab invaders arrived. Carthage, the regional administrative capital, was already shrinking in size before its conquest in 698. The Abbasid polity of Al-Mansur or Harun al-Rashid would have been as great a military threat to the Empire as was the Sassanid Persia of Chosroes II two centuries earlier, but once the Caliphal state was in decline and its outlying provinces were breaking away their military advantage would have ended.

It is not unreasonable to speculate that a competent Eastern military leadership in the tenth century, perhaps Nicephorus Phocas and John Tzimisces, as in real life, would have had the time and resources to reconquer Syria more easily in the 960s and move on against Jerusalem or Baghdad. The Empire was in real life far inferior to the Caliphate in manpower and other resources through the later seventh century into the ninth and had to conduct a holding operation in Asia Minor. It only achieved local military superiority when the Islamic Middle East had broken up into rival states. The enemies who tenth century generals and Emperors, most notably Nicephorus Phocas and John Tzimisces in around 955–76, routed to reconquer Cilicia and Syria were the small if militant Hamdanid emirate of Aleppo, backed up by its allies in Mosul, not a major Caliph-led Iraqi state. Even then, they were distracted by successive Bulgarian wars and the Russian incursion into Bulgaria after 968.

An Empire with full possession of the Balkans, and its menfolk as recruits for its armies from the seventh to the tenth centuries, would have been in a better military position. The Emperors could even have met large Caliphal armies in the field at the time of a united Caliphate without such humiliating defeats as that which Theophilus suffered at the hands of Al-Mutasim in 838. By the mid-tenth century, they would have been able to launch reconquest without Balkan distractions, except perhaps the Russian invasion of the late 960s, launched from an area far beyond Imperial control. It is possible that the remorseless aggression of Basil II, not distracted by the Bulgarians as in real life, would have turned him to Eastern conquest and taken him to advance on the weak regimes now ruling Baghdad. The latter's Caliphs were under the military control of the aggressive, but usually disunited, new state of the Buyid family, Zagros mountain warlords ruling Western Persia, from the 960s, and hence a new Roman-Persian confrontation over Iraq was likely. The Empire would have had the edge in terms of manpower, but faced serious military difficulties if it had managed to take and hold the Iraqi cities and plains, a familiar problem for Western aggressors from Trajan to George Bush.

The Eastern Empire versus the Turks in the C11th – any difference from reality?

Backed by Western troops and 'federate' Russian and steppe nomad allies, the Empire could have advanced its Eastern frontier between 960 and 1025 to conquer all the Levant and Iraq. It would come up against the Turks on the Iranian plateau, the new local nomad power as the Buyid confederacy declined, and face the same military threat there around 1050 as it did in real life further west in the following decade. The Turkish nomad cavalry archers would have been a menace to Roman infantry, in the tradition of desert and steppe opponents since the time of Crassus' defeat at Carrhae (53 BC). Had the Empire not taken the risk of overrunning Moslem territory beyond its old frontier and restricted its reconquest to Syria and Palestine in the tenth century, then the Turkish advance would have taken the same course as in real life. The Seljuk dynasty, rallying Turkish nomad military resources as the new power on the Iranian plateau and controlling the powerless urban centres, took over control of the Caliphate in Baghdad around 1055, with their ruler as the first Sultan, technically 'slave of the commander of the faithful'. In reality they reached Armenia and Syria around 1060–70, and this was the probable time-scale for a military confrontation with the Empire had this not occurred earlier over Baghdad.

The Empire would have had more resources than it did in reality, but still been at risk of a major defeat by the Turks' nomad horsemen, the same type of foe which they had been routed by at Carrhae. It would also have had the same problem in military confrontation as in real life faced Emperor Romanus IV in 1068–71, namely a large, lumbering Roman army, moving at the pace of its baggage-train, endeavouring to deal with small groups of mobile cavalry. Both Byzantines and Crusaders had cavalry in real life, but were seriously harassed by the more manoeuvrable Turkish steppe ponies and by long-range archery. This problem would have faced a hypothetical Eastern Roman army from a larger Empire too, unless a skilled Imperial commander had used his finances to recruit a rival force of nomads such as Magyars or Pechenegs from the Empire's allies on the Ukrainian steppes. In real life, the Empire did attempt to recruit such troops to face the Turks in the 1050s but they lacked military discipline and often deserted, a probable scenario in any event.

The Eastern and the Western Empires confront the Mongols

As with the Mongol descent via Russia on the West in 1237–41, the sheer numbers involved in the Mongol assault would have made it more formidable than the Turkish invasions and the invaders would also have had Chinese military technology. The latter included siege engines and gunpowder projectiles, which had a psychological as well as physical impact. Even stone walled towns were vulnerable to outright storming or prolonged blockade, as faced by the Moslem frontier towns on the Oxus in 1220 and Baghdad in 1258. The Great Khan, unlike Attila, was interested in submission rather than in being bought off, whether or not his interest in world conquest can be attested reliably. The Empire would have been a prime target although it would have been more unified and better resourced than his real-life victims, the disunited Moslem states of Persia and the Christians of Russia and then eastern Europe. There was also a possibility of this latest incursion of steppe conquerors driving its victims to flee into or attack Roman lands, as the Goths had done ahead of the Huns in the 370s. The Mongol conquest of their first Moslem foe, the Shahdom of Khwarezm in Iran and Transoxania, in the early 1220s drove Shah Mohammed's son and his armies into seeking new lands in the Levant and Georgia, and any such flight of Moslem forces would have posed a threat to the Empire.

The real-life timing of the Mongol attacks would suggest that the first major Mongol 'probe' would come in 1227, with the campaign across Azerbaijan and the Caucasus. Even if the Empire had not been in possession of the former, any attack on its Christian allies in Georgia would have been likely to lead to an attempt to intercept or punish the attackers. A clash was more probable with the Mongol assault on Asia Minor (1243 in real life) or the Baghdad campaign in 1256–8. At the latest, the Mongol move on Syria in 1259–60 would have brought confrontation, with the need of Persian Ilkhan Hulagu to keep his huge armies occupied making long-term co-existence unlikely.

Assuming that the Western Roman Empire had aided the East to defeat the invaders, the Empire would have been freed of its neighbouring Moslem rival with the fall of Baghdad but faced an aggressive new neighbour in the Mongol Ilkhanate in Persia. In real life the Mongols required Christian as well as Moslem rulers, e.g. the kings of Georgia and the Emperors of Trebizond, to become vassals but sought a Christian alliance against the remaining Moslem power, Mameluke Egypt, after their check by the latter at Ain Jalut in Palestine in 1260.

Had the Empire held onto Egypt or regained it before the eleventh century, there would have been no Sultanate in Egypt at war with the Ilkhanate and the probable remaining Moslem power after 1258 would have been centred in Arabia, an even more distant and risky target for a Mongol army. But the danger posed by the aggressively expansionist Mongols to the Roman state would have made the Mongol successor states a major source of anxiety to the Eastern and Western Empires even when the main attacks westwards had ceased around 1260 and the rival Khanates were at odds with each other. A placatory trading mission could have been sent to the remote Great Khan Kubilai in China in the 1260s to establish more friendly relations, and even have involved traders with experience of the Silk Route such as the Polos. But ultimately it is possible that the shock Rome had experienced from the Mongol attacks, a threat of overwhelming force by uncouth barbarians comparable to the assault of the Gauls in 390/87 BC or the Cimbri and Teutones in the 100s BC, would have impressed itself on the Roman imagination as much as the appropriately-named Tatars did on medieval Europe, and produced an argument to take over a declining Persia after circa 1300 to prevent a recurrence.

The past traditions of Roman military action, at least at a time of strong resources, suggest that a pre-emptive attack on a recently hostile polity was logical. This had been seen in the time of Roman pre-eminence, with past attacks on the Gauls in the 50s BC, British (including Caledonian) tribes beyond the current frontier in the first to early third centuries, Dacia in the 100s, and Parthia whenever an Emperor found glory to be politically desirable. The temptation for an ambitious or insecure ruler to prove his military prowess was another factor in recurrent Roman aggression, and the likelihood is that the Empire would not have rested content had the Mongol push westwards been halted with a major battle around 1227 in Iraq or the Caucasus, 1258 in Iraq, or 1260 in Palestine. Co-existence with the Great Khan, the Ilkhan or both by a formal treaty was advisable while they remained militarily strong, as the heirs of the Sassanid state, a military power virtually equal to Rome after around 230. The mutual mistrust of the Mongol states in Persia and the Volga steppes in the later thirteenth century would have made any co-operation between them to fight the Empire unlikely. Luckily for any neighbours, the Golden Horde state on the lower Volga never resumed its aggression against the West of 1237–40 after the death of Great Khan Ogodai in 1241 called its leader Batu back to the steppe to deal with the election of a successor.

But the disunity of the Mongol successor states and decline of the Ilkhanate after around 1300 would have posed a temptation to take over Persian military resources and deny them to another hostile state. Militarily, the declining Mongol state in Persia under Abu Said lacked the leadership to defy its Western neighbour, or any hope of aid from China, and would have fallen, though the Empire might have preferred to rely on local Moslem dynasts as its proxies to expensive outright conquest.

Much would depend on the ambitions of the current Emperor, and the lure of repeating the legendary feats of the conquering Alexander the Great in Persia. But if the frontier was moved eastwards to the Oxus or the Hindu Kush it would pose the problem of how a state based in Constantinople could control lands so distant long-term in an era before telegraph or rail travel, the indispensible aids of the British in their equivalent rule of a far-flung Asian land empire. Might the Empire resort to the expedient proposed for Eastern conquests by Constantine the Great, who had also had a large number of male relatives to provide for? In the early 330s he had proposed to hand over conquests from Persia, like Armenia, to his nephew Hannibalianus as one of a number of junior Emperors ('Caesars') subject to the overall authority of the supreme 'Augustus' in Constantinople. If local dynasts, the real-life Mongol successors in the 1330s such as the Jalyirids and Karts, were not to be made client kings of Persia, an Imperial prince could be enthroned as junior Emperor for the region. The Empire could thus have expanded into Asia on land, and portrayed itself as completing the work of Trajan and Alexander. The size of the Mongol attack could justify 'pre-emptive' war.

Notes

References to Edward Gibbon's *The Decline and Fall of the Roman Empire* (Everyman edition, 1966) are given as Gibbon, throughout. Other references to sources are Agathias, Ammianus, Avitus, Cassius Dio, Evagrius, Gildas, Herodian, Latomus, Orosius, Priscus, Socrates, Sozomen, Zonoras, Zosimus

Chapter 1
1. *Lives of the Later Caesars*, pp. 90, 98–9, 112–3, 139; Dio, book 69.
2. *Lives of the Later Caesars*, pp. 163–4.
3. *Lives of the Later Caesars*, pp 187–9; Dio, book 73, chapter 9.
4. Anthony Birley, *Marcus Aurelius: A Biography*, pp 108, 114, 128, 147, 149, 162.
5. *Lives of the Later Caesars*, p. 208.
6. *Lives of the Later Caesars*, pp. 211–12.
7. Dio, book 76, chapter 16.
8. Dio, book 75, chapter 8.
9. Dio, book 76, chapter 15.
10. Dio, book 75, chapter 8.
11. Dio, book 75, chapter 14; Herodian, book 3, chapter 11.
12. Herodian, book 3, chapter 7.
13. Dio, book 76, chapter 14.
14. Herodian, book 3, chapters 11–12; Dio, book 76, chapters 3–6.
15. Herodian, book 3, chapter 15; Dio, book 76, chapter 14.
16. Dio, book 76.
17. Dio, book 74, chapter 1.
18. Herodian, book 4, chapters 3–4.
19. Dio, book 78, chapter 4; *Lives of the Later Caesars*, p 256.
20. *Lives of the Later Caesars*, pp 300–1.
21. Dio, book 80, chapters 1–2; Herodian, book 8, chapters 1–8.
22. Zosimus, book 1, chapter 23; Zonaras, book 12, chapter 10.
23. As analysed by Bryan Ward-Perkins (see chapter 2, note 10).
24. Dio, book 80, chapter 20; Herodian, book 5, chapter 8.
25. Herodian, book 6, chapter 7–8; Zosimus, book 1, chapter 13.

Chapter 2
1. Procopius, *Buildings*, ed. and tr. H.B. Dewing, (London/Cambridge Mass., 1940), book IV, ch. 1.

2. Orosius, book 7, ch. 23 on Athaulf – a story related by an émigré citizen of Narbo to St. Jerome in Palestine. See Gibbon, part 3, pp. 261–5. For Alaric's invasions, see Zosimus book 1, ch. 5.

3. Priscus' embassy: P. Heather, *The Fall of the Roman Empire: a New History* (Macmillan 2005), pp. 449–50. Princess Honoria: Jordanes, *De Rebus Getica*, chapter 42: Gibbon, chapter 30.

4. Ammianus, book 31, chapters 12–13.

5. Analysis of the Gothic war: Heather, *The Fall of the Roman Empire: a New History* pp. 151–8. For Augustine and the arguments over the sack of Rome, see G.P. O'Day, *Augustine's City of God: a Reader's Guide* (Oxford 1999). For Alaric in Greece: Zosimus, book 1, chapter 5 and Gibbon, chapter 30.

6. Claudian, *De Bello Getica*; Gibbon, chapter 30.

7. For the 408–10 campaigns: Zosimus, book 1, chapter 5; Sozomen, book 2, chapter 10; Gibbon, chapter 30. Analysis in P. Courcelle, *Historie litteraire des grandes invasions Germaniques* (Paris, 1964), pp. 45–55 and in J. F. Matthew, *Western Aristocracies and Imperial Court 364–425* (OUP, 1975), chapter 11.

8. For the events of 455: Priscus, fr. 2, ed. Blockley (1982); Sidonius, *Panegyric*, Avitus pp. 441–50; Evagrius, book 2 , chapter 11; and Gibbon, chapter 36.

9. *Life of St. Severinus*, translated by G. W. Robinson, Harvard, 1914.

10. See the thesis in Bryan Ward-Perkins, *The Fall of Rome and the End of Civilization* (2005). This is a powerful rebuttal to the modern arguments for basic continuity. The archaeological evidence shows a drastic localization of resources and decline of architectural standards in and around Italy during the fifth century.

11. See Ian Wood, *The Merovingian Kingdoms 451–751* (Longman, 19740, pp. 28–32. Bede, *The Ecclesiastical History of the English Peoples*, ed. Judith McClure and Roger Collins (OUP, 1969) book 4, chapter 1.

12. See H. Chadwick, *The Church and Ancient Society*, pp. 658–74; J. C. Cavadini (ed.), *Gregory the Great* (Notre Dame, Indiana, 1995). For the events of 546: Procopius, *Gothic Wars*, book 4.

13. See A. H. M. Jones, *The Decline of the Ancient World* (Longmans, 1966) chapters 12 and 16. Also, Stephen Williams, *Diocletian and the Roman Recovery* (Routledge, 1997), chapters 8 (government), 9 and 10 (society and economy). It is now less certain that there was a bureaucratic master-plan by Diocletian himself, and how much Constantine contributed.

14. Alaric Watson, *Aurelian and the Third Century* (Routledge, 1996), pp. 191–6.

15. H. Chadwick, *The Church in Ancient Society*, chapter 28; Charles Odahl, *Constantine and the Christian Empire* (Routledge, 2004), chapter 7 and 11.

16. Gibbon, chapter 37 (part 4, pp. 27–31), quoting Victor Vitensis *De Persecutione Vandalorum*.

17. e.g. in J. Wallace-Hadrill, *The Barbarian West, AD 400–1000* (Blackwell, 1967), comparing Catholic Francia to Visigothic Spain.

18. See Robert Browning, *The Emperor Julian* (Berkeley, 1976) and Gibbon, chapter 23 (part 2, pp. 330 ff.). Julian himself banned Christians from office or teaching, so he was as guilty of prescribing intellectual conformity as his predecessors; and in retaliation for his aggressive personal promotion of pagan shrines at Antioch Christians were suspected of arson at the local shrine of Apollo at Daphne. For the events of 468, see Procopius, *Vandal Wars*, book 1, chapters 5 and 6.

19. See Michael Grant, *Fall of the Roman Empire*. For the size of Egyptian monasticism c.300, see H, Chadwick, *The Church and Ancient Society*, pp. 401–2.

20. For Ablabius, see Odahl, *Constantine and the Christian Empire*, p. 248; for Rufinus, see S. Williams and G. Friell, *Theodosius: the Empire at Bay* (Batsford, 1994), p. 165. Zosimus, book 4, chapter 32 on Rufinus' oppression and the plot to ruin Tatian.

21. Ammianus, book 16, chapter 8 on Constantius' tyranny and paranoia; and see book 28, chapter 1 and book 29, chapter 1 on Valens.

22. Ammianus, book 3, chapter 6.

23. J. H. Ward, 'The *Notitia Dignitatum*', in *Latomus*, no. 33 (1974), pp. 397–434. For the probable size of the late Roman army before the collapse, see A H.M. Jones' estimate of up to 600,000 in his *The Later Roman Empire: a Social, Economic and Administrative Survey* (3 vols, Oxford 1964), pp. 679–86. How battle-ready both the mobile 'comitatus' and the frontier 'limitanie' were is another matter. Ramsey Macmullen , *Soldier and Civilian in the Late Roman Empire* (Cambridge, Mass., 1963) disparages the latter. The latest arguments are in P. Heather, *The Fall of the Roman Empire: a New History*, pp. 63–5.

24. Zosimus, book 6, chapter 3; Orosius, book 7, chapter 40. See Heather, *The Fall of the Roman Empire: a New History*, pp. 115–16 citing the work of Georges Tchalenko in the 1950s on the prosperity of Late Roman Syria.

25. See Heather, *The Fall of the Roman Empire: a New History* pp. 199–202. Also see discussion of the numbers involved in Heather, *Goths and Romans AD 332 489* (Oxford, 1991). The most exaggerate figures were by some near-contemporaries but not witnesses. Augustine *City of God*, book 5, chapter 23) claims Radaigaisus had 80,000 followers in 405, civilians included; Orosius says 200,000 (book 7, chapter 23). On the 406 invaders, Procopius in the 540s reckoned there were 80,000 Vandals and Alans fighting *Vandal Wars*, book 1, chapter 5), but Victor *De Persecutione Vandalorum*, book 1 chapter 2) has this for the total Vandal population. St. Jerome later reckoned the Burgundians at 80,000 (including civilians), *Chronicle* 2389; Orosius (book 7, chapter 32) reckoned their warriors at 80,000.

26. Tacitus, *Germania*, book 7. chapter 1; S. Bassett, *Origins of Anglo-Saxon Kingdoms*, pp. 40–4. For the mass-abandonment of German settlements north of the Danube, see Heather, *The Fall of the Roman Empire: a New History* pp. 199–201; this would suggest that there were mass-movements of entire peoples into Roman territory either in the attested invasions or more gradually.

27. Heather, *The Fall of the Roman Empire: a New History* pp. 86–8 and 90–2. Ammianus (book 9, chapter 10 and book 11, chapter 12) makes it clear that in 355–6 the Alemanni had multiple leadership.

28. Gregory of Tours on Clovis suppressing rival kings, book 2, chapters 40–2.

29. See especially coverage of the 441–2 attacks on the East (Olympiodorus, Zosimus, Count Marcellinus) as assessed by Gibbon, part 3, pp. 343–53; and in general, Jordanes *De Rebus Getica* chapters 34–50. Sidonius Apollinaris also used extravagant language for the 451 attack on Gaul, though he was a poet. Roman writers had heard a story that Attila owned the 'sword of Mars' and boasted that it would give him world conquest.

30. The term was probably invented by the later seventeenth century French historian Du Cange.

31. Procopius, *Vandal Wars*, book 6, chapters 10–16.

32. Ammianus, book 26, chapters 1 and 4.

33. Ammianus, book 31, chapter 12.

Chapter 3

1. In general on 251–84: Zosimus, book 1; Zonaras, book 1; Aurelius Victor, *De Caesaribus*, translated H. Bird (Liverpool University Press, 1994), chapters 28–39; Gibbon, chapters 10–12. For the crucial extra problem posed by the aggressive, centralised Sassanian state and army, see M. H. Dodgeon and S. Lieu, *The Roman Eastern Frontier and the Persian Wars, AD 226–363: a Documentary History* (London, 1991), and review in Heather, *The Fall of the Roman Empire: a New History*, pp. 58–61

2. On 211–35: Cassius Dio, books 27–30 and Herodian, book 1, chapters 3–6. Severus' advice to his sons: Dio, book 27 (edited E. Cary, Harvard U.P. 1955, pp. 271–2). Dio relates (ibid, p. 269) that Caracalla had already nearly attacked his father once so his disgrace would have been justifiable.

3. Tacitus, *Annals*, ed. M. Grant (Penguin, 1969) pp. 61–79. There is still the possibility that Germanicus would only have raided, not annexed the area, using war for prestige as Domitian did against the local Chatti in the 80s.

4. Dio, book 56, chapters 18–24, translated by Ian Scott-Kilvert, Penguin 1987.

5. Dio, book 71, chapters 33–4. See Anthony Birley, *Marcus Aurelius: a Biography* (Batsford, 1987), pp. 207–9.

6. See Fergus Millar's analysis in *The Emperor in the Roman World* (Duckworth, 1977), section II, part 3, chapters 4 -6 on Imperial freedmen and secretaries.

7. See the character-portraits and individual incidents in Suetonius' Lives of Caligula, Nero, and Domitian, translated by Robert Graves and revised by Michael Grant (Penguin 1979).

8. Victor *Epitome*, book 41, chapter 11; Zonaras, *Epitome* book 2, chapter 13 (for the parallel with Theseus' story); Patrick Guthrie, *The Execution of Crispus* in *Phoenix*, vol., 20 (1966), pp. 225–31; Odahl, *Constantine and the Christian Empire*, pp. 205–7.

9. Suetonius, *Claudius*, chapter 10.

10. See Barbara Levick, *Claudius* (Batsford 199x), pp. 69–75. Claudius was following Augustus' precedent after his grandsons' deaths in putting age above genealogical closeness in the order of succession.

11. Gibbon, chapter 3 (part 1, pp. 73–8) , with its famous statement that the human race had its most happy and prosperous period under the Antonines.

12. See the non-contemporary and partly fictional biographies of the brothers in the Augustan History (a.k.a. *Lives of the later Caesars*), translated by Anthony Birley (Penguin, 1976) and Birley, *Septimius Severus: the African Emperor*, pp. 57 ff.

13. For the adoption by Elagabalus, see *Lives of the Later Caesars*, p. 299 For Severus and Pertinax, see Birley, *Septimius Severus: the African Emperor*, p. 208.

14. Ammianus, book 15, chapter 5 (Silvanus) and book 20, chapter 4 (Julian). In both cases they revolted for their own safety under an unpredictable and suspicious sovereign.

15. For Aetius and Gaudentius, see Gibbon, part 3, pp. 403–4.

16. For the events of 518, see John Malalas, *Chronicle* (trans. E. and m. Jeffreys and M. Scott, Melbourne, 1986), book 17; also book 16 on Anastasius. Analysis in Vasiliev, *Justin the First*, pp. 52 ff. Possibly Hypatius' recent military incompetence counted against him. But would Justinian have succeeded Justin but for his luring his more experienced rival Vitalian into a murder-trap later? What if his foe Empress Euphemia (who loathed Theodora) had not died?

17. See Procopius, *Persian Wars*, books 22 and 23 with a caveat that he seems to be consciously echoing the description of the Athenian plague of 430 BC in Thucydides. Analysis in William Rosen, *Justinian's Flea*, Pimlico, 2006.

18. See Warren Treadgold, *The Byzantine State and Society* (Stanford University Press, 1997), pp. 226–7.
19. For the events of 550, see the final section of Procopius, *Gothic Wars*, book 4. For the course of the wars in the 540s, see Procopius, *Gothic Wars*, books 3 and 4 and analysis in J. A. S. Evans, *The Age of Justinian*, pp.151–80. It is unclear how much of the small number of troops sent to Italy in the 540s was due to Justinian's fear of another massive Persian attack, as opposed to miserliness (Procopius' disillusioned opinion) or losses in the plague.

Chapter 4

1. Constantius, *Life of St. Germanus*, chapter 12.
2. See Nicholas Higham's work on Nennius , e.g. *Arthur: Myth-Making and History* (Routledge, 2002) His theory is that the writer presented Arthur as a national saviour for the chosen people in the manner of Joshua in the Old Testament. Hence the ascription of twelve victories over the pagans to Arthur, as for Joshua. For a sceptical view of the value of Welsh historians' Arthur as a historical figure, see Oliver Padel's work, e.g *The Nature of Arthur* in *Cambrian Medieval Celtic Studies 27*, 1994, pp. 1–31. The other main recent sceptic about the authenticity of the chronicle references to Arthur is David Dumville, e.g his 1977 article on *Sub-Roman British History and Legend* in *History, vol.62*, pp. 173–92. The thrust of recent arguments is that Arthur was a mythological figure, used post-800 for Welsh literary and political purposes.
3. Gildas, chapter 25. Gildas is also assessed by recent literary experts as writing Old Testament-influenced polemics, not history. See P. Hanning, *The Vision of History in Early Britain* (Columbia U.P., 1966).
4. R. G. Collingwood and J.N. Myres, *Roman Britain*, OUP 1932. The 'Count of Britain' theory was invented by U. Zimmer, a German historian, in 1896.
5. For the tomb, see the *Chronicle of 'Matthew of Westminster'* sub ann.1283, quoted by J. Lindsay in *Arthur and His Times*, p. 69.
6. *Gallic Chronicle*, sub ann. 441/2; ed. Mommsen 1882.
7. Gildas, chapter 25. Some recent historians speculate that Ambrosius not only won the battle of Mount Badon but was 'the' Arthur, the name being a nickname connected to the epithet 'bear'.
8. See A. Pearson, *Construction of the Saxon Shore Forts* in *British Archaeological Report no. 49* , Oxford 2003, and his *The Roman Shore Forts: Defences of Coastal Britain* (Tempus, 2000). On one crucial dig, see Barry Cunliffe, *Excavations at Portchester Castle: I. Roman'* in *Society of Antiquaries Research Report, no.32* (London, 1975). A general summary of current thinking is in Francis Pryor, *Britain AD* (Harper Collins, 2004).
9. Ammianus, book 27, chapter 8.
10. See Stuart Laycock, *Britannia: a failed State* (History Press, 2008) for an extreme recent view of the revival of tribal identities in post Roman Britain. It is certainly logical that the council that aided Vortigern the British king in inviting in the Saxon mercenaries c. 428 (Nennius) or 449 (Bede) was an equivalent of the Gallic council of the Roman provinces of Gaul extant in the fifth century, and, like it, representing the ex-tribal administrative regions.
11. See Geraint Jenkins, *The Foundations of Modern Wales 1642–1780* (OUP, 1987), pp. 218–19, 241–5. The Welsh scholarly enthusiasm for reviving pre-Roman culture in the eighteenth century duly extended to a romanticised cult of the Druids, mainly due to Henry Rowlands, and in due course to Edward Williams ('Iolo Morgannwg')'s revival of the Druidic-led eisteddfods.

12. See the most (but too?) hopeful interpretation of a peaceful fifth century cultural transition from British to Anglo-Saxon in Catherine Hill, *The Origins of the English* (Duckworth, 2003). The extinction of proto-Welsh as a language in England is surely an indication that more than a dominant Germanic elite arrived. English survived the takeover by such a linguistically alien elite in 1066.

13. Petra Dark's work on specific agricultural sites (e.g. in the Fenland) where there was continuity in the fifth century, quoted by Francis Pryor in *Britain AD*, (Harper Collins, 2004).

14. See Garret Mattingley, *An Imperial Possession: Britain in the Roman Empire.*

15. Procopius, *Persian Wars*, book 2, chapters 22–3, and discussion in William Rosen,*Justinian's Flea* Pimlico, 2006.

16. *Annales Cambriae*, sub ann. 518.

17. Gildas, chapters 27–32.

18. *Harleian Mss. 3582* (Oxford), and P.C. Bartrum *Early Welsh Genealogical Tracts* (Cardiff U.P., 1966).

19. Gildas, chapter 27.

20. See John Morris, *The Age of Arthur: Britain AD350–650*, pp. 345 and 347–9.

21. Gildas, chapter 20.

22. *Saxo Grammaticus, History*, ed. P. Fisher and Hilda Davidson (Cambridge, 1979). The idea of a respectable long lineage for an aspirant dynasty ultimately came from Vergil's Aeneid and its Trojan royal ancestry for the Caesars; the precedent for Saxo was probably Fredegar's seventh century mythical early French royal line.

23. Trans. G. Garmondsway and J. Simpson, (London, 1968). The Scandinavian attack on Gaul referred to in Beowulf is dated at 524 in Frankish sources.

24. See Pat Southern, *The Roman Empire from Severus to Constantine*, (Routledge, 2001), pp. 138–43. The original details of Carausius are in Aurelius Victor, *De Caesaribus* (trans. H.W. Bird, Liverpool U.P., 1994). p. 43.

25. Bede, *Ecclesiatical History of the English People*, book 3, ch. 25.

26. Morris, *Age of Arthur*, p. 65.

27. For the 'maximalist' view of a genuinely powerful Irish High Kingship pre-560, see Morris, *Age of Arthur*, chapters 8 and 9. This is now discounted by modern Irish historians, e.g. T. O'Rahilly, as wishful back-dating by later chroniclers.

28. Morris, *Age of Arthur*, pp. 17, 19, and 66.

29. See John T. Koch, *The Gododdin of Aneirin* (University of Cardiff Press, 1997). Did the Votadini/Gododdin's horse-using elite inherit a Hadrian's Wall frontier cavalry unit, as suggested by Alistair Moffat?

30. See S. Williams and G. Friell, *Theodosius: the Empire at Bay* (Batsford, 1994), pp. 130–3.

31. See Prudentius, *In Symmachum*, book 1, chapters 1 and 2, Gibbon chapter 28, and discussion by J.T. Matthews, *Western Aristocracies and the Imperial Court AD364–425*, p. 204

32. *Life of St. Germanus*, chapter 12.

33. See *Liber Pontificalis*, vol 1, pp. 371–82.

34. Procopius, *Secret History*, book 8, chapters 22 and 24–6. In contemporary terms of supernatural belief, he claimed that the Emperor was possessed by a demon and wandered around the Palace at night without a head. But how much of this was stock rhetoric or later disillusion, not intended for publication?

35. Gibbon chapter 30.

36. See *Anglo-Saxon Chronicle*, sub ann. 893: edited by Michael Swanton (Dent, 1996), p. 84. Discussion in Richard Abels, *Alfred the Great: War, Kingship and Culture in Ninth Century England* (Longman, 1993), pp. 195–203.

Chapter 5
1. See Stephen Oppenheimer, *Blood of the British* (Constable and Robinson).
2. Anglo-Saxon Chronicle, ed. Swanton, pp. 77–8.
3. See H. Lamb, *Climate From 1000 BC to AD 1000* in M. Jones and G. Dimbleby, *The Environment of Man, British Archaeological Report 87* (Oxford 1953–65).
4. See Hesiod, *Theogony*, verses 214–16 and Pliny, *Natural History* book 6, chapter 36 for the western location of the 'Hesperides' (beyond the Canary Islands?) and Andrew Collins, *Gateway to Atlantis* (Headline, 2000), pp. 87–92 for the possible interpretation of this. The whole question of Roman coins or ships found in the New World remains controversial and unproven. For the interpretation of St. Brendan's voyage, see Geoffrey Ashe, *Land to the West: St. Brendan's Voyage to America* (Collins, 1962) and Tim Severin, *The Brendan Voyage*.
5. Their mythic land of origin, the 'tlapallan' (red land), could logically have been Cuba from its direction from Yucatan and the colour of the soil. The complex nature of Mexican and Maya myth makes it unclear if the founder cult-hero of the Toltecs around 900, who bore the same name as the god Quetzalcoatl, genuinely came from overseas or was a white man (?European) as interpreted by the Spanish in the sixteenth century.
6. See Nigel Davies, *The Aztecs* (New York, 1973), *The Cambridge History of Latin America*, vol. 1 (ed. Leslie Bethell, Cambridge 1980) and Hugh Thomas, *The Conquest of Mexico* (Hutchinson, 1993) chapter 1.
7. See N. Davies, *The Toltec Heritage* (Norman, 1980).
8. See Michael Cox, *The Mayas* (Thames and Hudson, 1999 edition).
9. See Tacitus, *Annals*, ed. Michael Grant (Penguin 1996) p. 327 for the Roman attack on Mon. Caesar also deplored Druidic practices.
10. David Keays, *Catastrophe: An Investigation into the Origins of the Modern World* (1999), and review by E. James, *Did Medieval History Begin with Catastrophe?* in *Medieval Life* vol. 12 (2000), pp. 3–6. Further evidence for unusual phenomena in the mid-530s, interpreted differently, is in M. Baillie, *Exodus to Arthur: Catastrophic Encounters with Comets* (London, 1991).
11. Procopius, quoted in ibid, and Antti Arjava, *The Mystery Cloud of 536 CE in the Mediterranean Sources* in *Dumbarton Oaks Papers no. 59* (2006), pp. 73–93.
12. As n. 98; and see J.D. Gunn, *The Years Without a Summer: Tracing AD 536 and its Aftermath* in *British Archaeological Report International Series*, (Oxford, 2006).
13. See Williams and Friell, *Theodosius: the Empire At Bay*, pp. 120–5 on the Emperor's suppression of paganism; and Zosimus, book 1, chapter 4 on the iconoclastic purge by Cynegius.
14. Socrates, book 4, chapter 18; Gibbon, chapter 28 (part 3, pp. 129–32).
15. Original story in Theodoret, *Historia Ecclesiastica*, book 5, chapter 26. Now thought to be a myth.
16. Alan Cameron, *Circus Factions: Blues and Greens in Rome and Byzantium* (Oxford, 1976).
17. Procopius, *Persian Wars*, book 1, chapter 24.
18. Procopius, *Secret History*, chapters 1–5. See Averil Cameron's discussion of Procopius' attitude to Theodora in *Procopius and the Sixth Century* (Routledge, 1985), pp. 67–83.

19. Original source for the story of the closure: John Malalas, *Chronicle*, book 18, chapter 47. Discussed in Michael Maas, *Cambridge Companion to the Age of Justinian* (Cambridge U.P. ,2005), pp. 330–3.
20. See Psellus, *Chronographia*, translated (as *Fourteen Byzantine Rulers*) by E.R.A. Sewter (Penguin, 1966) pp. 254–8 for Psellus' own account.
21. See Anna Comnena, *Alexiad*, trans. E.R.A. Sewter (Penguin 1969), pp. 174–80.
22. Constantine VII, *De Administrando Imperio*, ed. Romilly Jenkins (Dumbarton Oaks, 1967), chapters 1–13.
23. See H. Chadwick, *The Early Church* (Penguin, 1967), pp. 40–4, 81–2.
24. See Philip Rousseau, *The Early Christian Centuries* (Longman, 2002) p. 67; and discussion of the emerging definitive canon in pp. 64–9. One probably late second or early third century list, the 'Muratorian Fragment', left out 1 and 2 Peter and included the 'Apocalypse of Peter'; Irenaeus, main proponent of a finalised list, probably excluded James and 2 Peter; the Roman Church at first left out the Epistle to the Hebrews (Chadwick, p. 81). The Shepherd of Hermas was eventually removed as not by an Apostle.
25. The centrepiece of the Gnostic (hidden) tradition was probably the collection of writings of which a copy was found hidden in a jar at Nag Hammadi, Egypt, in 1945. These 'Nag Hammadi' gospels (edited James Robinson, Leyden, 1977) and similar writings were more of a collection of wisdom literature about Jesus' teachings than the letters of Apostles which were included in the eventually definitive canon. Modern scholars disagree over their dating, though some place the theologically non-Catholic Gospel of St. Thomas around 100. Their early date, and thus authenticity, as well as theological positions were seen as suspect by the mainstream Church Fathers (eg Irenaeus and Tertullian) by 180–200; their exclusion'was not the work of Constantine or the Council of Nicaea as Dan Brown et al. would have it.
26. See A.H.M. Jones, *Decline of the Ancient World*, p. 60.
27. See Odahl, *Constantine and the Christian Empire* (Routledge, 2004), p. 168 ff.
28. As stated enthusiastically by Athanasius.
29. See Lindsay, *Arthur and His Times*, pp. 70–87.
30. For the original myth of the burning of the library by Omar, see Gibbon, part 5, pp. 275–6 and J. Butler, *The Arab Conquest of Egypt* (Oxford, 1978). P. Hitti, *History of the Arabs* (Macmillan, 1970 edition, p. 66,) traces the story to Abd-al-Latif al-Baghdadi, who died in 1231; Gibbon cites 'Abdulpharagius'.
31. Caesar does not mention the incident as including manuscripts at the relevant point in his Civil War (book 3, chapter 112). Recently, J. Empereur in *Alexandria, Jewel of Egypt* (2002) thinks it archaeologically clear that the building survived into the Empire, but was it extant as late as 391?
32. As recounted by contemporary writer Nicetas Chroniates.

Chapter 6
1. See Paul Lemerle, *Invasions et migrations dans les Balkans depuis le fin de l'epoque romaine jusqu'au VIII siècle*, in *Revue Historique 21* (1994) pp. 261–308.
2. See Owen Moorhead, *Justinian* , 1994, pp. 145–53 on 540. For 559, see Agathias, book 5, chapter 14.
3. There were indeed Romano-Turkish diplomatic contacts from 568, at the latter's initiative, halted by the Turks due to Roman co-operation with the Turks' Avar enemies c. 576.
4. Treadgold, *History of the Byzantine State and Society*, p. 224.

5. John of Ephesus, *Ecclesiastical History*, trans E.W. Brooks (1936), book 6, chapter 28.
6. M. Whitby, *The Emperor Maurice and His Historian* (Oxford, 1988); Treadgold, *History of the Byzantine State and Society*, pp. 232–5.
7. Origo *Constantinis Imperatoris* trans. J.C. Rolfe in his *Ammianus Marcellinus* (London 1964), book 6, chapter 32. Eusebius, *Life of Constantine*, book 4, chapter 6 trans. E.C. Richardson in *NPNF, 2nd series*, vol 1, (Grand Rapids, 1986).
8. See Whitby, *The Emperor Maurice and His Historian* (Oxford, 1988) pp. 24–7 and Treadgold, *History of the Byzantine State and Society*, pp. 235–6. For the disastrous reign of Phocas and its implications, see David Olster, *The Politics of Usurpation in the Seventh Century* (Amsterdam, 1993), pp. 1–21. The basic details of Phocas' reign are in Theophanes, *Chronicle*, ed. H. Turtledove, (Univ. of Pennsylvania Press, 1982) pp. 1–8. Maurice's Balkan campaigns are covered in detail by Theophylact Simocatta, *History*, ed. M. and M. Whitby, (Oxford, 1986) see book 6 on the 602 mutiny and books 9–10 on the overthrow of Maurice.
9. See Averil Cameron, *The Empress Sophia* , in **Byzantion**, vol. 45 (1975). pp. 5–21.
10. See Constance Head, *The Emperor Justinian II of Byzantium* (Univ. of Wisconsin Press, 1972); and Theophanes, *Chronicle*, ed. Turtledove (Univ. of Pennsylvania Press, 1982) p. 62.
11. Theophanes does not mention the false Theodosius; see only local West Syrian chronicles. His survival is unlikely, but was rumoured as he was sent away to safety by Maurice in 602 and caught and killed separately from Maurice himself and his younger sons. For Priscus, see Patriarch Nicephorus, *Short History*, ed. Cyril Mango (Dumbarton Oaks, 1990), chapter 2 (relations with Phocas and Heraclius) and *The Armenian History Attributed to Sebeos* trans. R.W. Thomson (Liverpool Univ. Press, 1999) chapter 34, 113.
12. See Sebeos, chapters 32–3, and Theophanes, *Chronicle*, ed. C. De Boor (Leipzig, reprint 1972) p. 299.
13. Theophanes *Chronicle*, (ed. Turtledove), pp. 1–8.
14. See Sebeos, chapter 34; *Vie de Theodore de Sykeon*, chapter 153; and Walter Kaegi, *Heraclius, Emperor of Byzantium* (Cambridge U.P., 2003), pp. 58–83. The fact that Chosroes apparently turned down a request for peace on Heraclius' accession shows that he was by then confidant enough to proceed with an outright war of conquest into Syria.
15. Theophanes, *Chronicle* (ed. de Boor), pp. 306–35; Nicephorus, *Short History*, books 12–18 (ed. Mango), pp. 57–67; Sebeos, 126–7; Kaegi, *Heraclius, Emperor of Byzantium* (Cambridge U.P., 2003), pp. 122–92. For the Arab attack on Iraq, see Hugh Kennedy, *The Great Arab Conquests* (Phoenix, 2007) pp. 98–138.
16. It may also have helped that traditionally Abu Sufyan, related to the Prophet and father of the main invasion-commanders of Syria (Yazid and Mu'awiya), owned property in Jordan and the general who attacked invasions of the Byzantine Levant seem to have been a total of around 30,000 at most, provided the oral sources (written down generations later) were accurate. See Hugh Kennedy, *The Great Arab Conquests* (Phoenix, 2007), pp. 66–97, and Walter Kaegi, *Byzantium and the Early Islamic Conquests* (Cambridge, 1992).
17. See Kennedy, *The Great Arab Conquests*, pp. 255–333.

Bibliography

Original sources

Agathias, *History*, trans. Joseph Frendo (Berlin, 1935).

Ammianus Marcellinus, *The Later Roman Empire AD 354–78*, trans. Walter Hamilton (Penguin, London, 1986).

The Anglo-Saxon Chronicle, trans. G. Garmondsway and J. Simpson (London, 1968); trans. Michael Swanton (Phoenix, 2000).

Annales Cambriae (Rolls Series, vol. 20; London, 1860).

The Anti-Pelagian Treatises of St. Augustine, ed. F. Bright (Oxford, 1880).

Appian, *The Civil Wars*, trans. John Carter (Penguin; London, 1996).

The Armenian History Attributed to Sebeos (trans. R..W. Thomson, Liverpool University Press; 1999)

Aurelius Victor, *De Caesaribus*, trans. H.W. Bird (Liverpool University Press; 1994).

Aurelius Victor, *Epitome de Caesaribus*, trans. F. Richlmayer (Leipzig, 1911).

Bede, *The Ecclesiastical History of the English Peoples*, ed. Judith McClure and Roger Collins (Oxford University Press; 1969).

Caesar, *The Civil Wars*, trans. John Carter (Oxford University Press; 1997).

Cassius Dio, *Roman History*, books 51–60, translated by Ian Scott-Kilvert (Penguin; London, 1987); books 61–70 and books 71–80, trans. Earnest Cary (Loeb Classical Library; Cambridge, Mass., 1925 and 1927).

Cicero, *Ad Familiares*, ed. D.R. Shackleton Bailey (Penguin; London, 1978).

Claudian, 'De Bello Getica' , in *Works*, ed. and trans. M. Platnauer (1922).

Anna Comnena, *Alexiad*, trans. E.R.A. Sewter (Penguin; London, 1969).

Emperor Constantine VII, *De Administrando Imperio*, ed. Romilly Jenkins (Dumbarton Oaks,1967).

Constantius, 'Life of St. Germanus', trans. F. Hoare, in The Western Fathers (London, 1954).

Eusebius, *Life of Constantine*, trans. E.C. Richardson (NPNF, 2nd series, vol 1: Grand Rapids, 1986); trans. Alan Cameron and S. Hall (New York, 1999).

Evagrius, *Ecclesiatical History*, ed. J. Bidez and L. Parmentier (London, 1898).

The Gallic Chronicle, ed. Theodore Mommsen (Paris, 1882).

Gildas, *De Excidio Britanniae*, ed. John Morris (Phillimore; 1978)

Gregory of Tours, *The History of the Franks*, trans. Lewis Thorpe (Penguin; London, 1974).

Harleian Mss. 3582 (Bodleian Library, Oxford).

Herodian, *History*, trans. C. R. Whittaker, 2 vols (Cambridge University Press; 1969–70).

Hesiod, 'Theogony', in J. Banks (trans.), *The Works of Hesiod, Callimachus and Theognis* (George Bell and Sons; London, 1909).

John of Ephesus, *Ecclesiastical History*, trans E.W. Brooks (1936).
Jordanes, *De Rebus Getica*, ed. T. Mommsen, trans, C. Mierow (New York, 1960).
Josephus, *The Jewish War*, trans. G. Williamson (Penguin, London, 1981).
Liber Pontificalis, ed. L. Duchesne, 2 vols (Paris, 1886).
Lives of the Later Caesars, trans. Anthony Birley (Penguin, 1979).
John Malalas, *Chronicle*, trans. E. and M. Jeffreys and M. Scott (Melbourne, 1986).
Patriarch Nicephorus, *Short History*, ed. Cyril Mango (Dumbarton Oaks, 1990).
Orosius, *Historia Adversos Paganos*, ed. C. Zangemeister (Vienna, 1882).
Pliny the Elder, *Natural History*, trans. A. Rackman, 2 vols. (Harvard University Press; Cambridge, Mass., 1971).
Plutarch, *Fall of the Roman Republic* (Penguin, London, 1958); *Makers of Rome* (Penguin, 1965).
Priscus, *The Embassy to Attila*, ed. Blockley (1982).
Procopius, *Buildings*, ed. and tr. H.B. Dewing (London/Cambridge, Mass., 1940).
Procopius, *History of the Wars*, trans. H. Dewing (Loeb Classical Library; Cambridge, Mass., 1914–28).
Procopius, *The Secret History*, trans. H. B. Dewing (Cambridge, Mass., 1935).
Michael Psellus, *Chronographia*, translated (as *Fourteen Byzantine Rulers*) by E.R.A. Sewter (Penguin, London, 1966).
Saxo Grammaticus, *History of The Danes*, ed. P. Fisher and Hilda Davidson (D. S. Brewer: Cambridge, 1979).
Life of St. Severinus, translated by G. W.Robinson (Harvard; Cambridge, Mass., 1914).
Sidonius Apollinaris, *Panegyric*, ed. W. Anderson (Cambridge, Massachsetts, 1986).
Socrates, *Historia Ecclesiastica*, trans. A.C. Zenos, (New York, 1891; reprinted Grand Rapids, 1989).
Sozomen, *Historia Ecclesiastica*, trans. C. Hartranft (New York, 1891 reprinted Grand Rapids, 1989).
Suetonius, *The Twelve Caesars*, trans. Robert Graves and revised by Michael Grant (Penguin; London, 1979).
Tacitus, *Annals*, ed. M. Grant (Penguin; London, 1969, revised 1996).
Tacitus, *Agricola and Germania*, trans. H. Mattingley (Penguin; London,1970).
Vie de Theodore de Sykeon, trans. A. de Festiguiere , 2 vols (Brussels, 1970).
Theodoret, *Historia Ecclesiatica*, trans, B. Jackson (New York, 1892; reprinted Grand Rapids, 1969).
Theophanes, *Chronicle*, ed. H.Turtledove (University of Pennsylvania Press, 1982).
Theophylact Simocatta, *History*, ed. M. and M. Whitby (Oxford University Press; 1986).
Victor Vitensis, *De Persecutione Vandalorum*, ed. C. Halm.
Zosimus, *Historia Nova*, trans. R.T. O'Reilly (Melbourne, 1982).

Secondary sources
Abels, Richard, *Alfred the Great: War, Kingship and Culture in Ninth Century England* (Longman, 1993).
Alcock,Leslie, *Arthur's Britain* (Allen Lane; London, 1971).
Arjava, Antti, 'The Mystery Cloud of 536 CE in the Mediterranean Sources', in *Dumbarton Oaks Papers*, no. 59 (2006), pp .73–93.
Ashe, Geoffrey, *From Caesar to Arthur* (Collins, 1960).
Ashe, Geoffrey, *Land to the West; St. Brendan's Voyage to America* (Collins; London, 1962).
Austin, N. J, 'Constantine and Crispus', in *Acta Classica*, vol. 23 (1980), pp. 131–88.

Baillie, M, *Exodus to Arthur: Catatrophic Encounters with Comets* (London, 1991).

Balsdon, J., *The Emperor Gaius* (Oxford, 1934).

Barnes, T., *Constantine and Eusebius* (Cambridge, Mass., 1981).

Barnes, T., *The New Empire of Constantine and Diocletian* (Cambridge, Mass., 1982).

Barrett, Anthony, *Caligula: the Corruption of Power* (Batsford; London 1989).

Bartrum, P.C., *Early Welsh Genealogical Tracts* (Cardiff University Press; 1966).

Bassett, S., *Origins of Anglo-Saxon Kingdoms* (Leicester University Press, 1989)

Baynes, Norman, *Constantine and the Christian Church* (London, 1929).

Birley, Anthony, *Marcus Aurelius: a Biography* (Batsford, 1987)

Bethel, Leslie, *The Cambridge History of Latin America*, vol. 1, (Cambridge, 1980).

Birley, Anthony, *Septimius Severus: the African Emperor* (Batsford, 1999).

Brauer, George, *The Age of the Soldier Emperors: Imperial Rome AD 244–284* (Park Ridge, New Jersey, 1975).

Butler, J., *The Arab Conquest of Egypt* (Oxford, 1978).

Cameron, Alan, *Claudian: Poetry and Propaganda at the Court of Honorius* (Oxford Uinversity Press, 1970).

Cameron, Alan, *Circus Factions: Blues and Greens in Rome and Byzantium* (Oxford, 1976).

Cameron, Averil, 'The Empress Sophia', in *Byzantion*, vol. 45 (1975), pp. 5–21.

Cameron, Averil, *Procopius and the Sixth Century* (Routledge, 1985).

Campbell, J. B., *The Emperor and the Roman Army* (Oxford, 1984).

Cavadin, J. C., (ed.), *Gregory the Great* (Notre Dame, Indiana, 1995).

Chambers, E.K., *Arthur of Britain* (Sidgewick and Jackson, 1927).

Chadwick, H., *The Early Church* (Penguin: London, 1967).

Chadwick, H., *The Church and Ancient Society* (Oxford University Press; 2003).

Collingwood, R.G., and J.N. Myres, *Roman Britain* (Oxford University Press, 1932).

Collins, Andrew, *Gateway to Atlantis: the Search for the Source of a Lost Civilization* (Headline; London, 2000).

Courcelle, P., *Historie litteraire des grandes invasions Germaniques* (Paris, 1964).

Cox, Michael, *The Mayas* (Thames and Hudson; London, 1999 edition).

Cunliffe, Barry, 'Excavations at Portchester Castle: I. Roman' in *Society of Antiquaries Research Report*, no.32 (London, 1975).

Dark, Petra, *The Environment of Britain in the First Millenium* (Duckworth, 2000).

Davies, Nigel, *The Aztecs* (New York, 1973).

Davies, Nigel, *The Toltec Heritage* (Norman, 1980).

Dillon, Myles, and Nora Chadwick, *The Celtic Realms* (Weidenfeld and Nicolson; London, 1967).

Dodgeon, M. H., and S. Lieu, *The Roman Eastern Frontier and the Persian Wars, AD 226–363: a Documentary History* (London, 1991).

Drinkwater, J., and H. Elton (eds.), *Fifth Century Gaul: a Crisis of Identity?* (Cambridge University Press, 1992).

Dumville, David, 'Sub-Roman British History and Legend' in *History*, vol.62 (1974), pp. 173–92.

Elton, H., *Warfare in Roman Europe, AD 350–425* (Oxford University Press, 1996).

Empereur, J., *Alexandria, Jewel of Egypt* (Harry N. Abrams; New York, 2002).

Evans, J.A. S., *The Age of Justinian* (Routledge; London, 1996).

Everitt, Anthony, *Cicero: A Turbulent Life* (John Murray, London, 2001).

Gelzer, M., *Caesar: Politican and Statesman* (Blackwell, Oxford, 1968).

Gibbon, Edmund, *Decline anf Fall of the Roman Empire* (Everyman edition), 6 vols (Dent, London, 1966).

Goffart, W., *Barbarians and Romans AD 418–584: The Techniques of Accomodation* (Princeton University Press, 1980).

Golz Huzar, Eleanor, *Mark Antony* (Croom Helm, London, 1986).

Grant, Michael, *Constanitne the Great: the Man and his Times* (New York, 1994).

Grant, Michael, *The Climax of Rome: the Final Achievments of the Roman World, AD 161–337* (Weidenfeld and Nicolson, London, 1968).

Griffin, Miriam, *Nero: the End of a Dynasty* (Batsford, 1984).

Gruen, E., *The Last Generation of the Romna Republic* (University of California Press, 1974).

Gunn, D., *The Years Without a Summer: Tracing AD 536 and its Aftermath* (British Archaeological Report International Series, Oxford, 2006).

Guthrie, Patrick, 'The Execution of Crispus' in *Phoenix*, vol., 20 (1966).

Hanning, P., *The Vision of History in Early Britain* (Columbia University Press, 1966).

Head, Constance, *The Emperor Justinian II of Byzantium* (University of Wisconsin Press, 1972).

Heather, P., *Goths and Romans AD 332–489* (Oxford, 1991).

Heather, P., *The Fall of the Roman Empire: a New History* (Macmillan, 2005).

Higham, Nicholas, *Rome, Britain and the Anglo-Saxons* (London, 1992).

Higham, Nicholas, *Arthur: Myth-Making and History* (Routledge, 2002).

Hills, Catherine, *The Origins of the English* (Duckworth, 2003).

Hitti, P., *History of the Arabs* (Macmillan, London, 1970 edition).

Howe, Nicholas, *Migration and Myth-Making in Anglo-Saxon England* (Yale University Press; 1989).

James, E., 'Did Medieval History Begin with Catastrophe?', in *Medieval Life*, vol. 12 (2000), pp. 3–6.

Jenkins, Geraint, *The Foundations of Modern Wales 1642–1780* (Oxford University Press; 1987).

Jones, A.H. M., *The Decline of the Ancient World* (Longman, Harlow, 1966).

Jones, A H.M., *The Later Roman Empire: a Social, Economic and Administrative Survey*, 3 vols (Oxford, 1964).

Jones, Brian, *The Emperor Domitian* (Routledge, 1992).

Jones, Gwyn, *A History of the Vikings*, 2nd edition (Clarendon Press; Oxford, 1984).

Kaegi, Walter, *Byzantium and the Early Islamic Conquests* (Cambridge, 1992).

Kaegi, Walter, *Heraclius, Emperor of Byzantium* (Cambridge University Press, 2003)

Keays, David, *Catastrophe: An Investigation into the Origins of the Modern World* (Ballantine Books, London and New York, 1999).

Kennedy, Hugh, *The Great Arab Conquests* (Phoenix, 2007).

Koch, John T., *The Gododdin of Aneirin* (University of Cardiff Press, 1997).

Kulikowsky, M., *Rome's Gothic Wars From the Third Century To Alaric* (Cambridge University Press, 2007)

Lacey, W. K., *Augustus and the Principate: the Evolution of the System* (Francis Cairns; Liverpool, 1996).

Lamb, H., 'Climate From 1000 BC to AD 1000' in M. Jones and G. Dimbleby (eds), *The Environment of Man*, British Archaeological Report 87 (Oxford 1953–65).

Laycock, Stuart, *Britannia – The failed State* (History Press; Stroud, 2008).

Lemerle, Paul, 'Invasions et migrations dans les Balkans depuis le fin de l'epoque romaine jusqu'au VIII siecle', in *Revue Historique* 21 (1994), pp. 261–308.

Levick, Barbara, *Tiberius the Politician*, (Croom Helm; London, 1976).

Levick, Barbara, *Claudius* (Batsford, 1990).

Lindsay, Philip, *Arthur and His Times* (Frederick Muller, London, 1958).

Luttwak, Edward, *The Grand Strategy of the Roman Empire* (Baltimore, 1976).

Maas, Michael, *Cambridge Companion to the Age of Justinian* (Cambridge University Press, 2005).

Macmullen , Ramsey, *Soldier and Civilian in the Late Roman Empire* (Cambridge, Mass., 1963).

Matthew, J.F., *The Roman Empire of Ammianus* (London, 1989).

Matthew, J. F., *Western Aristocracies and Imperial Court 364–425* (Oxford University Press, 1975).

Mattingly, David, *An Imperial Possession: Britain in the Roman Empire* (Allen Lane; London, 2006).

Meier, Christian, *Caesar*, (Fontana, London, 1996).

Millar, Fergus, *The Emperor in the Roman World* (Duckworth, London, 1977).

Millar, Fergus, and E. Segal, *Caesar Augustus: Seven Aspects* (Clarendon press, 1984).

Moorhead, Owen, *Justinian* (Oxford, 1994).

Morris, John, *The Age of Arthur: Britain AD 350–650* (Weidenfeld and Nicolson; London, 1973).

Odahl, Charles, *Constantine and the Christian Empire* (Routledge, 2004).

O'Day, G.P, *Augustine's City of God: a Reader's Guide* (Oxford, 1999).

Oppenheimer, Stephen, *The Origins of the British* (Constable and Robinson; London, 2006).

Padel, Oliver, 'The Nature of Arthur', in *Cambrian Medieval Celtic Studies*, 27 (1994), pp. 1–31.

Pearson, A., 'Construction of the Saxon Shore Forts' in *British Archaeological Report*, no. 49 (Oxford 2003)

Pearson, A., *The Roman Shore Forts: Defences of Coastal Britain* (Tempus; Stroud, 2000).

Peddie, John, *Alfred the Good Soldier: His Life and Campaigns* (Bath, 1989).

Pryor, Francis, *Britain AD* (Harper Collins, London, 2004).

Rice-Holmes, T., *The Architect of the Roman Empire* (Clarendon Press; 1928).

Rice-Holmes, T., *The Architect of the Roman Empire: 27 BC to AD 14* (Clarendon Press; 1931).

Rolfe, J.C., *Ammianus Marcellinus* (London, 1964).

Rosen, William, *Justinian's Flea* (Pimlico, London, 2006).

Rousseau, Philip, *The Early Christian Centuries* (Longman, 2002).

Severin, Tim, *The Brendan Voyage* (Hutchinson, 1978).

Southern, Pat, *Augustus* (Routledge, 1998).

Southern, Pat, *The Roman Empire from Severus to Constantine* (Routledge; 2001).

Stenton, Sir Frank, *Anglo-Saxon England*, 3rd edition (Oxford University Press; 1989).

Syme, Ronald, *The Roman Revolution* (London, 1952).

Syme, Ronald, *The Augustan Aristocracy* (Clarendon Press, 1986).

Talbert, R. J., *The Senate of Imperial Rome* (Princeton University Press, 1984).

Thomas, Hugh, *The Conquest of Mexico* (Hutchinson, 1993).

Treadgold, Warren, *The Byzantine State and Society* (Stanford University Press, 2003).

Treadgold, Warren, *The Byzantine Revival: AD 780–842* (Stanford University Press, 1997).

Vasiliev, A. A., *Justin the First* (Dumbarton Oaks Studies; Cambridge, Mass. 1950).

Wallace-Hadrill, J., *The Barbarian West, AD 400–1000* (Blackwell, 1967).

Ward, J. H., 'The Notitia Dignitatum', in *Latomus*, no. 33 (1974).

Ward-Perkins, Bryan, *The Fall of Rome and the End of Civilization* (Oxford University Press; 2005).

Watson, Alaric, *Aurelian and the Third Century* (Routledge; 1996).

Whitby, M., *The Emperor Maurice and His Historian* (Oxford; 1988).
Williams, Stephen, *Diocletian and the Roman Recovery* (Routledge; 1997)
Williams, Stephen, and G. Friell, *Theodosius: the Empire at Bay* (Batsford 1994).
Wood, Ian, *The Merovingian Kingdoms 451–751* (Longman; 1974).
Yorke, Barbara, *Kings and Kingdoms of Early Anglo-Saxon England* (London, 1990).
Yorke, Barbara, *Wessex in the Early Middle Ages* (Leicester University Press, 1995).

Index